She didn't give *De_____ ___ ___ warm up: she just lunged up thr_____gines that screame_____ing for her in the _____atmosphere. Thirt_____glittering like metal insects __ ___ _____sunlight, waiting. . . .

The instant she saw them she altered her course, skipping sideways like a startled dragonfly; but the whisping fringe of atmosphere and the terrible pull of Earth's gravity clutched at her, blunting the swift precision of her maneuver. Both were forces with which she was largely unfamiliar. The Patrol knew that. They knew the Skyrider just might outfight and outfly even thirty-six Patrol boats in deep space. But not here, not within reach of that killing monster rock called Earth.

And they waited for her first mistake.

PIRATE PRINCE

Look for these Tor books by Melisa C. Michaels

PIRATE PRINCE

MELISA C. MICHAELS

A TOM DOHERTY ASSOCIATES BOOK

PIRATE PRINCE

Copyright © 1987 by Melisa C. Michaels

First printing: February 1987

A TOR Book

Published by Tom Doherty Associates, Inc.
49 West 24 Street
New York, N.Y. 10010

Cover art by Bruce Jensen

ISBN: 0-812-54572-9
CAN. ED.: 0-812-54573-7

Printed in the United States of America

0 9 8 7 6 5 4 3 2 1

To my sister Ardis
and all those others who
with love and hostility
taught me what little I know.

PROLOGUE

The Stanford torus model space colony was designed in the summer of 1975 at NASA's Ames Research Center near Stanford University in California during a "Summer Study on Space Colonization" project sponsored by the American Society for Engineering Education and by NASA. This was many years before space colonization was begun, but the design on which the participants finally agreed was so well conceived that it was not appreciably altered when reality finally caught up with its designers' dreams.

The basic design resembled a bicycle wheel with six spokes. When the first colonies were built, the only known way to create artificial gravity was by giving the colony itself sufficient spin to produce gravity by centrifugal force. That let the colonists in for some difficulty with Coriolis force, but this was in the days before the freefall mutation, and in a colony where Terrans were to live and work for all their lives—transport back to Earth was prohibitively expensive in those days—Coriolis force was considered preferable to freefall.

Diadem was one of the earliest Stanford torus colonies

7

built. It had a diameter of just more than a mile, and a four mile circumference. The outer "tube" of the wheel was about four hundred feet wide, with a spin rate of one rpm producing gravity near that of Earth. Inside the torus there were originally three small cities of just over three thousand residents each; between the cities were the farms that made the colony nearly self-sufficient.

At the center of the torus was a sphere, referred to as "the Hub," with a docking area at the "top" or north pole and a transport tube leading from the "bottom" or south pole to the construction shacks where most of the original colonists had worked, building satellites for Earth. The Hub itself was more than just the physical center of the colony; it housed recreation areas including low-gravity gymnasiums and a swimming pool as well as some low-gravity resort housing and a few offices; and it was the main crossroads of the colony. All people and freight entering the colony passed through the Hub from the docking area at the north pole. The six spokes leading out to the torus converged at the Hub, each containing elevator shafts, power cables, and heat pipes; some offices, shops, and laboratories; and Diadem University.

Light and power were provided to the colony from the sun by means of solar cells and immense angled mirrors that could be adjusted to provide diurnal and seasonal rhythms. The inner one-third of the toroidal rim surface area consisted of permaglass panels mounted on aluminum rims to let in sunlight from the mirrors, so that from inside the colony the familiar day and night rhythms of Earth were duplicated, complete with bright sunshine and starlight, lacking only Earth's moon.

The remaining toroidal surface area was an aluminum hull of solid metal about three centimeters thick, wrapped with cable, forming a great hollow wheel containing cities, terraced agricultural areas, parks, and gardens: a small, bright island in the vast emptiness of space. It was within that toroidal island that pioneers first truly challenged the umbilical ties that bound Humankind to Earth.

When it was first established, Diadem was an ordinary working colony. Huge ore-carriers brought megatons of rock and soil from Luna that were processed at the colony's construction shacks and the resultant aluminum, magnesium, titanium, iron, glass, and oxygen were used primarily in the construction of power satellites for Earth. The remaining slag, which would have been waste in a similar operation on Earth, became an essential part of the space colony, providing fill for the protective outer ring that shielded the inner inhabited one from the various forms of radiation in space that would otherwise have killed the colonists. Later colonies were built large enough to include an atmosphere deep enough to protect the colonists as Earth's atmosphere protects her inhabitants; but in Diadem's day a space colony large enough to hold an atmosphere more than two miles deep was only just imaginable, certainly not yet possible.

In those days Diadem's population was near ten thousand, and the colony was frugally self-sufficient in almost every respect. There was balance as long as the ore-carriers kept carrying tons of Lunar material into orbit to be turned into power satellites for Earth, in return for which Earth provided the ore-carriers and the few highly specialized technological products the colony couldn't produce.

The discovery of malite changed all that. Power satellites became obsolete. Space travel was revolutionized. The new possible speeds (it was theoretically possible even then to travel from Earth to Luna in perhaps fifteen or twenty minutes) and payloads opened up the whole Solar System for colonization. Within the first few years Mars was settled and the asteroid belt had become the new frontier. The great mining concerns shifted from Earth orbit to the Belt, slowly at first, then more rapidly after the Homestead Act of 'Fifty-Nine was passed, culminating in that mad exodus later known as the Rock Rush of 'Sixty-Two.

For some time after that, the ore-carriers still made regular runs between Luna and the orbiting man-made colonies. The major colonies switched their production lines to goods of greater value than the power satellites they had originally been designed to provide. The smaller dependent colonies whose factories, mostly supplied from Earth, were in effect nothing more than freefall extensions of Earth, continued to produce and were actually better off after malite.

The mid-sized colonies like Diadem, too small to be entirely self-sufficient and likewise too small to convert to some of the more ambitious production lines the larger colonies provided, but too large to be entirely supplied from Earth and too valuable to be casually disbanded and discarded, struggled on as best they could while their populations dwindled and their governments and scientists tried to find a place for them in the strange new malite-powered world.

Some were eventually closed down despite the best efforts of their residents, who were understandably reluctant to leave their homes. One closed down voluntarily during the Rock Rush, its inhabitants all opting for a new life and new freedoms in the Belt. A few became exotic suburbs of Earth and Luna, providing outrageously expensive housing for a tiny elite population that could afford status symbols on a truly grand scale. One was converted to a prison. One became the University of Space. One devolved, through legal and financial accidents, into a forgotten slum, minimally housing and feeding a dying population of societal outcasts and failures who, by contriving to be left behind or by "escaping" to that abandoned colony, achieved their own freedom and sealed their children's eventual doom by starvation and/or technological breakdown. And one, tiny ancient Diadem, became a religious colony.

The residents of Diadem liked to call it a sociological experiment. They didn't like to call their philosophy of life a religion, arguing reasonably enough that their society included practitioners of nearly every major religion of Earth, none of whom had any desire or intention to renounce their Earth religion for anything Diademan. Still, most outsiders called Diadem a religious colony, and after a while the residents stopped arguing the point.

They were few enough by then—some four or five thousand where there had once been ten thousand—that their available farmland was easily adequate to support their numbers if they could import enough water and oxygen to maintain it. Most of the workers who once built power satellites had gone, of course, when the power satellite construction closed down. Many of the ore processors had gone when the amount of ore available for processing had diminished. Some people emigrated during the Rock Rush, and some when the Diademan government became solidly "religious" or "sociologically experimental."

By the time Earth started legislating against independent space colonies there were only a few thousand determined Diademans left, none of whom wanted to emigrate just because Earth had begun trying to make things difficult for them. Actually, Earth had no intention of making things difficult for Diademans; Earth had all but forgotten Diadem. Diademans had never entered Earth politics, and they no longer delivered to Earth the once-important power satellites whose production had been the primary purpose of the original colony. Minor Earth agencies in charge of supplying the colony cut their shipments over the years, explaining that supplies were few and that Diadem's return contribution was small. When Diademans pointed out that they would be glad to produce satellites or any other manufactured goods they were equipped to build, if only they had the raw materials Earth was ceasing to supply, no one on Earth was interested.

Interactions between the colony and Earth decreased year by year as the flow of supplies decreased. When Earth began her anticolonial legislations in earnest, it was natural for the few insignificant agencies still dealing with Diadem to let their records get shuffled into oblivion. With the first war between Earth and the colonies impending, Diademans decided to let the matter ride; they didn't want to be involved in any wars. And when the war was over and they attempted renewed communications with Earth, they found they had at last been entirely forgotten. Some Earther individuals still remembered Diadem, or could be convinced of its existence; but officially Diadem did not exist. The ore-carriers brought no more rocks and soil from Luna. Supply ships brought no more Terran goods or passengers. Proffered goods from Diadem to Earth were refused not because they were undesirable but because Earthers could not legally purchase anything from a colony that did not, legally, exist.

In the end, Diademans took to scavenging for their needs. Within a few years they had developed a whole subculture of scavengers whose sleek ships were designed for fast runs hauling heavy cargo, and whose crews were adept at tracking lost ships and all the abandoned technological debris with which generations of pioneers and colonists had littered the Solar System.

Diadem was not the only colony reduced to scavenging for supplies, and all too soon what had at first seemed an endless supply of dead satellites, wrecked shuttles, lost cargoes, and abandoned space weapons was depleted to the point that tracking the things and bringing them home to Diadem was almost more expensive than they were worth. Then came the Brief War, and new wreckage that would have been plentiful if Earth and the recognized colonies had not this time undertaken thorough salvage operations of their own: the colonies because they needed the supplies almost as badly as Diadem did, and Earth because she did not want the colonies to benefit from her losses.

Diademans, wishing again not to be involved in any wars, were reluctant to call attention to themselves by letting their presence be known to either side; but battle sites were a likely place to scavenge even though competition had become fierce. Diademan scavengers hung on the edges of battles, out of scanner range or concealed from the participants behind the natural rocks and debris of space, and waited to claim whatever the two warring factions left behind. Usually they were able to salvage a shuttle or two unnoticed. Shuttles were a valuable source of metals, and on the best of them there were technological goodies still usable as well.

In their first sortie to an active battlefield the Diademans salvaged something more than they intended: they salvaged a man.

The battle was the first one in the Brief War, and it took place in open space out near Mars. The Earth Fighter Fleet had assembled first, their sleek shuttles gleaming like sharp-faceted jewels against the darkness of space as they took up their battle formation and hung there, glittering with the cold fire of reflected sun and distant stars, waiting.

The ragtag Colonial Fleet appeared hours later, gliding out from Mars and Mars Station like battered birds of prey, all shapes and all sizes of shuttles and ships and boats, some few as brightly painted as the Earth Fighters, but most of them badly scarred with old battle damage and hasty repairs. They flew with swift precision equal, almost, to that of the Earth Fighters: and it was obvious from their first assembly in battle formation that they made up in cunning what they lacked in training and equipment.

The battle itself was short. The watching Diademans,

who were colonists but not Colonials and were largely uninformed of world news, did not understand the significance of the single sleek Colonial shuttle that punched a hole through the Earth Fighters' defending lines and fled with astonishing speed toward Earth. That there was some significance to the event was obvious; the battle, afterward, collapsed more from apparent lack of interest than either side's notable success, though the Colonials seemed at least nominally victorious. The Earth Fighters fought on sporadically for a while, then finally turned tail and ran.

Afterward the Diademans watched in mounting frustration while first the Colonials and then returning Earth Fighters searched through the debris of battle and salvaged shuttle after wrecked shuttle till all that was left was floating rubble too small and worthless for even the Diademans to retrieve.

"Space take them!" said the Diademan captain. "They might have left us *some*thing for our trouble!"

"What trouble?" laughed his daughter, who was also his navigator and a very beautiful woman whose unmitigated good humor was remarkable, even among Diademans. "All we've done is exactly what we wanted to do—hide and wait. Even if they'd known we were here, I doubt if either side would have wanted to give us a shuttle. Besides, they did, you know."

"Did what?" asked her father.

"Leave us a shuttle." She was studying her computer screen and making rapid calculations. "Try this course, and I think we'll intersect; it can't have gone far."

Her father frowned, but he punched in the course she recommended before he asked, "What can't have gone far?"

"That Colonial Falcon whose pilot sacrificed himself for the one that got away toward Earth. Didn't you see it? He took a direct laser hit, and it breached the hull all right—made a spectacular explosion—but the shuttle was mostly intact afterward. I saw it. It may not be good for anything but scrap metal even if we find it, but scrap metal's better than none.''

"*If* we find it,'' said her father.

She laughed at him, watching her screen, and pointed. ''There. See it? That's a big chunk of scrap metal.''

He had to admit it was. The outer hull had a hole in it the size of a small asteroid, and the wings were folded back over the engine nacelles like tissue paper, but not even a tail fin was actually missing. As damaged as she was, they couldn't hope to salvage much of any value beyond the metal she was made of; but for scrap metal she was about as big a piece as they could have asked.

When the scavenger shuttle got her shattered Falcon home and the crew discovered the Falcon's pilot still aboard and alive, nobody wanted to space him, and they had gone to too much trouble over the Falcon already to feel happy about spacing her whole and pretending they had never caught her. Somebody suggested taking her pilot back to the Colonials, but nobody wanted that job, so in the end the only option left was to take him into Diadem and see if they could find a doctor who wanted to tend him.

He was very nearly dead by the time they got him to the clinic, and as a result they had trouble finding a doctor who wanted to undertake his care. The first doctor to see him was in her first year of practice and still somewhat unsure of her skills, so she didn't want to take on such a difficult case. The second doctor who saw him didn't want an additional patient of any description; he was already busy with a measly boy, a worker's broken arm, and a goat's impending parturition, and he was trying to get free to begin his annual vacation. The third doctor who saw him didn't want to treat him because in his opinion the head injuries were such that there was already extensive and irreparable brain damage that would impair the quality of his life even if he should survive.

The fourth doctor who saw him had become interested in facial reconstruction when her beloved older brother had committed suicide as a result of irreparable and grotesquely disfiguring facial injuries. She decided she could in good conscience take the not inconsiderable risk that the extensive brain damage would prove mentally and/or physically crippling. "After all," she said with a hint of bitterness, "if he survives and doesn't like it, he can always opt for suicide." In a society in which everyone has an acknowledged right to do exactly what he wants to do, suicide might be a perfectly acceptable option, but there was nothing to guarantee that one's survivors would be any more happy about it than they would be in any other society.

Thus the arduous task was begun to save the unknown Colonial Warrior's life. At the same time, elsewhere on Diadem, the wreckage of his shuttle was hastily broken down, reworked, and its materials pressed into service as needed on the space colony. The Diademan scavengers realized the hazard of keeping any recognizable portion of the injured pilot's ship whole and reclaimable if he recovered. They didn't want to lose their precious scrap metal. And they didn't know that they were destroying the pilot's only link with his past.

CHAPTER ONE

Pain made him as dully obedient as a sick child. When a voice invaded his darkness he listened; when he understood the words, he obeyed. Meaningless instructions: wiggle your toes. Bend your left knee. Bend your right knee. Lift your fingers. Flex your wrists. He obeyed without thinking, but the effort wearied him, and when darkness flowed up over the voice and carried him down into its deep silence he did not struggle against it. The voice had not instructed him against darkness.

He became aware that it was a pattern that had been repeated a great many times, far back into the dim recesses of his earliest memories: wiggle your toes. Bend your left knee. Bend your right knee. Make a fist. Can you feel this? If you can feel this, tap your fingers. . . .

There were degrees of darkness. At first, the one he knew best was the deep, silent dark of unconsciousness, empty even of dreams. It was a restful place, safe and serene and mercifully free of the pervading, all-encompassing pain that was the primary component of all the other states of consciousness he knew.

Sleep, which should have been a refuge, was not. The pain was with him in sleep; and crowded, inexplicably unnerving dreams wearied him, though he could never afterward clearly recall them. Being awake was better than being asleep. He knew the difference between the two states, and could almost always tell which he was enduring at the moment. When he was awake there were fewer dreams. More things to listen to. And the woman's voice, which sometimes sang to him and sometimes instructed him on the movement of his extremities and sometimes either talked or read to him—he wasn't sure which, and hardly heard her words at those times, but relaxed in the comforting and companionable atmosphere her voice conjured for him in the dark.

It did not occur to him to wonder about the dark. The bandages that blocked his vision did not bother him, for he had no memory of vision. He had no concept for anything but dark. Actually he had no exact concept for dark, either. Dark was how the world was, and he had not given the world any thought. He accepted it. Dark, quiet, warm, painful, occasionally unexpectedly frightening, generally quite simple: that was how the world was. For him there was no past to regret, no future to worry about, and only an infant's concept of the present to cope with. Things were done for him; simple movements were required of him, and aside from the pain, that was the extent of his involvement with life.

Since he knew no existence without pain, it did not occur to him to complain of pain in any way except when it was so overwhelming that it forced from him some feeble, wordless protest. Then the woman's voice would soothe him, and a pinprick would sting his arm, and soon the deep silence of unconsciousness would whisk him out of pain's reach. But he didn't know there was any connection between his fitful protest, the soothing voice, the pinprick, or his escape into unconsciousness. For him it was not even a series of events; it was a random collection of isolated incidents without reason or meaning. Things happened. He accepted events as he accepted the world and his own existence, without question. Indeed, almost without thought.

It was a sound that finally knocked him out of this comfortably mindless existence, back into the world of the living: the sound of a child's voice, laughing. He had been dimly aware of new voices somewhere in the range of his hearing, but they were only background noise; a new feature of an environment in which he had no interest. When the child laughed it woke something deep inside him. Something he had not known existed.

He sat up without knowing it, and a sound formed in his throat. A name. A wordless, voiceless cry of pain and loss he did not understand. Hands touched him. The background voices ceased abruptly, cut off in mid-sound, stopped with a metallic click. The familiar woman's voice soothed him and reassured him while the hands pushed him gently back onto the bed and a pinprick stung his arm. Darkness darkened. He slept.

Dr. Linda March carefully disengaged her hand from her patient's unconscious grip and straightened, looking down at his bandaged and battered body with sympathy and concern. "Now, what do you suppose that was all about?" she asked half-aloud, and shook her head. "Surely not the holoplay. I'd swear you never even knew I had the holovision on. Some dream, then? You shouldn't be in that much pain." She was smoothing his bedding as she spoke, and putting in order the various medical accoutrements arrayed by the bed. "Besides, that didn't look like pain. Not physical pain, anyway."

She returned to her chair, moving with easy grace in the greatly reduced gravity of the Hub quarters she had adopted for the two of them as soon as she realized he was a freefall mutant. But instead of turning her holovision back on, she sat quietly before the blank set, looking at her sleeping patient. They had been sharing these Hub quarters for nearly three months, and she knew almost as little about him now as she had when the scavengers first brought him in.

He had been a Colonial pilot: that much was obvious just from the circumstances in which he had been found. He had been engaged in that first battle of the last abortive little war between Earth and the Colonies. He was a freefall mutant and thus probably a native Belter; there were freefall mutants born on space stations and colonies outside the asteroid belt, but the great majority of them were from the Belt, so it was a reasonably safe assumption.

And that was the last safe assumption she could make about him. She could make informed guesses based on his general state of health and physical condition before he was shot down in battle, but few of them really said anything about the man himself except the evidence that he had spent most of the last several years in gravity. That was odd indeed for a freefall mutant, and she could think of no reasonable explanation. As far as she knew, even in the advanced medical science of the world Outside there was no method or medication for making a freefall mutant truly comfortable in gravity.

"Damn it," she said aloud, "your whole metabolism is different. It just wouldn't work. Obviously they've got something to keep you alive—even I could do that, and I suppose I'll have to if you ever leave that bed, since our freefall accommodations are minimal. . . . But I can't make you comfortable, and by the gods I don't believe they could either. So why in the name of all that's balanced would you choose to live like that?"

His still form told her no answers. The long, broken body was as limp as death, only the faintest movement of his scarred chest showing that he still breathed. The visible portions of his bruised and only partially rebuilt face were wholly enigmatic: useful to determine the rate of his healing, but barely recognizable as a face. Any clues it might have held to his past or to his character had been wiped out by laser burns and crushing blows. She hoped she was successfully recreating the original bone structure, but even that wouldn't tell her much about him.

She shook her head and smiled at him ruefully. "You're the original Mystery Man, my friend. I just hope you'll be willing and able to answer my questions someday." And she hoped his answers would be as interesting as some of her better speculations; it would be an awful disappointment if he turned out to be just some kind of data-pusher. But that didn't seem likely, though she couldn't quite have said why.

A worse—and much more likely—possibility was that he might never give her any answers at all. She didn't want to consider how likely that was. She had found the best specialists to put him back together, and had herself done the best work on him that she had ever done, but the initial damage had been severe. She was more confident each day that he would survive; the time he had already survived spoke well for that. But that he had never made any effort to communicate did not speak well for the condition in which he might survive.

Still, his brain was alive and active. His body was healing. In the last month he had emerged from coma and had even occasionally, as this afternoon, initiated movement. The rare sounds he made were increasingly human. He *might* heal.

The Comm Link signaled, startling her, and she reached for it without looking, punched it on, and said, "Yes?"

"How's the Pirate Prince today?"

She glanced at the screen and grimaced at the grinning

freckled face that met her gaze. The "Pirate Prince" had been one of her wilder speculations about her mystery patient, which she had jokingly described to Dr. Simon Hale in an effort to prove a point about the hazards of trying to deduce a man's past life from present physical evidence. She had plausibly explained every scar, every unusual muscular development, every aspect of physical appearance and attire and even his presence in the Brief War, and made it all add up to an exotic Pirate Prince who was implausible in the extreme. Dr. Hale had conceded the point. Unfortunately he had also adopted the nickname for her patient. "I wish you wouldn't call him that," she said.

"What do you call him?" Hale's grin held a challenge.

"When I'm talking to him, or about him?" At Hale's startled look she added quickly, "Oh, I don't mean talking *with* him. He still doesn't respond."

"Has there been any change at all?"

March shook her head. "I don't think so."

"You don't *think* so?" He let both eyebrows creep toward his hairline in an expression that he fondly imagined conveyed mild surprise.

"Well, he sat up, just now." She hesitated. "It might just have been some kind of reflex, but . . ."

"Some kind of reflex!" said Hale. "Linda, I wish you would learn to . . ."

"I know, I know. Sound like a doctor," said March. "I don't want to, Simon." It wasn't the first time they had discussed this.

"It would give your patients more confidence in you."

"Piffle. You psych-tenders always think you can impress people by confusing them."

"I wish you wouldn't call me that."

"What?"

"Psych-tender." Repeating it made his mouth pucker as

if he had bit into something sour. "It sounds like an agricultural implement of some sort."

March grinned at him.

Hale sighed, watching the image of her pixie face on his Comm Link screen. "Okay. Call me whatever you like. As long as you agree to go to dinner with me tonight."

"To a restaurant?"

"Of course to a restaurant, what else would I mean, we should maybe go out to the farms and graze?"

"You're cute when you're mad."

Hale glared at her. "I am not angry." Someone offscreen spoke to him and he looked around impatiently, shook his head, reached for a proffered paper, and turned back to the screen. "More bad news. I get it before the news services, these days; they want me to tell them how to present it so people won't panic—which of course most of them wouldn't, anyway—and nobody cares if I panic."

"Is it that bad?" asked March.

"I'm afraid so." Hale let his eyebrows draw together in the hint of a dignified frown. "Earth's Bureau of Regional Resources has set up a new batch of restrictions on shipment and salvage. Since we don't exist, they won't ship to us, of course; but they'll put our scavengers in jail quickly enough if they catch them in improper salvage procedures." He glanced at the paper he held and sighed. "I could wish that Pirate Prince of yours were real. We're a nation of decent, law-abiding people, trying to abide by Earth laws that are not decent, and it just doesn't work." He paused to savor the sound of that; it hadn't been entirely spontaneous, but it came out sounding even better than he had hoped.

"I hope you're not going to put that in your summary to the news services," said March. "Unless you want us to join the Colonials in another war against Earth."

He shook his head and smiled, touched by her interest in

his affairs. "I just want to take you to dinner. You name the time and place. . . . But make it soon, okay? I'm starving."

"And you have work to do after dinner."

"And I have work to do. How about the Diner? Or would you rather go over to Monterey?"

"Actually, I'd rather not go to Monterey; I don't want to leave JanMikal that long."

"JanMikal?" It had been her brother's name. He wondered whether it was altogether healthy for her to call her mystery patient by her dead brother's name.

She ignored the repetition with its implied question. "The Diner would be great, Simon. In an hour?"

"Make it half an hour. I told you I'm starving."

Hale waited till March agreed, then cut the connection and leaned back in his chair, feeling disproportionately self-satisfied. Like a cat with cream on its whiskers. Dr. Linda March would not be an easy catch, but she was worth as much trouble as it took.

That thought wasn't fully formulated before he reprimanded himself for thinking of her as if she were a fish. He prided himself on his ability to see his own failings and to correct them. It was dehumanizing to think of Linda as a "catch." He was fond of her, he wanted to marry her, and the idea was not to "catch" her but to convince her of the wisdom of marrying him. He could make her happy: he was sure of it. He was a good man and would make a good husband. They shared similar interests. His expertise in the field of psychiatry would be useful to her in her reconstructive surgery. And, most important, they were genetically a perfect match. They would make fine, strong, healthy, intelligent children.

Of course they would both have to alter their lives to some extent to accommodate children. Easier for Linda; most of her work was elective surgery, so it could be put off till the children were older, and if necessary Hale could help counsel her patients toward that end. He was willing to cut back on his own work hours, too, but she would have to admit that his work was more pressing, less amenable to rescheduling at his convenience. He hesitated over the words "more important"; doubtless even Linda would agree they were apt words, but perhaps it would still be prudent to leave them unspoken.

It was logical that his work should not suffer for their children, and that her career could wait till the children were grown. But he was aware of the importance to children of time spent with their father, and he didn't mean to deprive his children of that. Boys in particular needed a good strong male role model, and Hale meant to provide it. There would be two boys, and perhaps one girl, to start. He hadn't consulted Linda, but felt confident that she would agree. After that, they might let nature take its course in the matter of sex selection for further children. He thought they should have at least six; with their genetic heritage they owed Diadem at least that many strong, healthy children. Intelligent children. Beautiful children. Sons a man could be proud of. And at least one daughter to carry on Linda's delicate feminine beauty. . . .

Satisfied with this comfortable view of the future, Hale put aside the paper his assistant had handed him while he was talking with Dr. March, programmed his Link to answer for him in his absence, surveyed his tidy desk with a self-congratulatory smile, and glanced at his watch. Twenty-five minutes till his appointment with March. Ample time to shower first and slip into one of the jumpsuits he had recently learned she found attractive. There was no harm in allowing Linda's preferences to influence his wardrobe to some extent. He did want to convince her to marry him. And a certain amount of willingness to accommodate himself to his woman's tastes in matters of little consequence was an admirable trait in a secure, successful man.

Whistling contentedly to himself, he selected a jumpsuit from his office closet and headed for the shower, his mind already occupied with the question of what to order for their dinner and how much detail about his current work it would be wise to share with his future wife. It did not occur to him to wonder how much detail she would be interested in hearing, any more than it occurred to him to wonder about the details of her work.

CHAPTER TWO

The Brief War was over. Home Base, the giant asteroid whose tunneled interior housed the Company, the Belt branch of the Earth-based government known officially as the World, Incorporated and familiarly as the Corporation, had suffered surprisingly little damage in the war. It had changed hands several times, but always with most of the fighting done inside, with hand weapons. There had been some laser damage on the flight deck, where during the final takeover the Skyrider in her modified Falcon *Defiance* had singlehandedly held off the entire defending forces of the Patrol while a small group of space-suited warriors broke in by means of an airlock on the opposite side to retake Home Base from within. But even a shuttle fight on the flight deck hadn't done much damage, and what there was had all been repaired by now.

Most of the displaced homesteaders and miners of the asteroid belt had already reclaimed their disputed rocks and were determined, regardless of legalities or of any future tempting government promises, not to relinquish them again. Their temporary lodgings on Home Base, thus deserted, had been quickly filled again with returning government workers, replacement workers from Earth, bands of experts and officials to oversee the reconstruction of the Company, and pilots.

Most of the Colonial pilots had returned without hesitation to their homes and jobs on Home Base; the Company was still the only major employer in the Belt. Their ranks were smaller now. A few had found new friends, lovers, and opportunities they were unwilling to leave behind on Mars or Mars Station, and chose not to return to Home Base. But the vast majority of those missing were missing forever. Missing in Action. Dead.

It wasn't something about which those remaining tended to talk very much. They came home a little wiser and a lot wearier, not nearly as gratified by victory as they had expected to be. When they were alone together they often talked and laughed and bragged about battles and dogfights and about the inevitable fistfights they'd had among themselves between battles. The pilots who had not returned were mentioned as frequently in these reminiscences as those who had: but with a difference. When somebody said whatever happened to old so-and-so anyway, did he (or she) stay on Mars? They laughed if he or she had, and made up outrageous stories about the possible consequences in his or her life by now. But if he or she was among those missing, somebody would say shortly that he or she "didn't make it." Sometimes there were details, sometimes not. Always, afterward, there was a brief uncomfortable silence before the talk started up again, usually just a little too defiantly cheerful at first.

It had been a brief war, with a disproportionate number of casualties. Time to die, but not time to adjust to the dying. Those who had fought in the First War seemed more reconciled to the losses than the young ones who had never before witnessed or engaged in such wholesale slaughter of their fellow men; but nobody is ever really reconciled to war. The older veterans simply had more experience at refusing to react, refusing to think, and changing the subject.

Melacha Rendell, better known to friends and enemies alike as the Skyrider because she was the best (some said the craziest) pilot most of them would ever know, had experience at refusing to react, refusing to think, and changing the subject. She had, for reasons that were clear to no one including herself, avoided the First War; but between that and the Brief War she had fallen in love and by her own account killed her lover. It had been an accident. Nobody but the Skyrider would even have made a case for negligence. She had not checked the air filter coils before their last flight, but nobody checked the air filter coils before every flight.

When the air filter exploded, Melacha had very nearly been killed with Django, her Gypsy lover. She survived because she was too stubborn to die. And because even grievously, almost fatally wounded, she was the best (and perhaps the craziest) pilot in the Belt. She had brought her broken shuttle home and tried to steal another to go back out after the Gypsy she had left behind her floating dead in space.

The med-techs had been obliged to replace a part of her damaged skull with a metal plate, and to heal a number of lesser fractures, abrasions, and contusions, all of which had taken time and patience. Melacha had time; but patience, as she herself said, had never been one of her "better tricks."

During that time she had become expert at refusing to react, refusing to think, and changing the subject. And now she needed all those skills again. Always egocentric, she had eventually learned not to blame herself too harshly for Django's death, but still tended to feel personally responsible for anything bad that happened around her. At the beginning of the Brief War, her best friend had given his life to protect her and to send her safely on a mission that had been instrumental in shortening the war; afterward, she had killed any number of enemy warriors who got in her way and had watched a great many Colonial Warriors' ships explode in a brief glory of silent sheeting flame under enemy fire. With the reckless ferocity of the not wholly sane, she had subsequently taken chances no one could reasonably have expected to survive. And she had survived.

Jamin was gone, his son Collis sent to Mars to live with Melacha's cousin Michael and his family, and Melacha survived. It had in consequence become second nature for her to refuse to react, refuse to think, and change the subject.

Before the war, she had been accustomed to taking chances no one else would take, reveling in the thrill of cheating death. Now she took those chances one step further. The thrill was gone. Death didn't matter anymore. She was introspective enough to know that something had changed, but not quite honest enough with herself to know what it was. She still thought of herself as the Outlaw Queen, and still imagined she had every intention to live forever, and didn't know why she no longer got the shakes after a bad run, or why she nonetheless got into more fistfights than ever. Before, fistfights had been a reaction to the stress and excitement of danger. Now they seemed to be a reaction to life.

On a conscious level, she had acknowledged Jamin's death, grieved deeply for him, and carried on. On a deeper level she never quite believed he was dead. And on a still deeper level, she never quite understood that *she* was *not* dead. At least, so the psych-tenders told her. They told her a lot of things that she pretended not to understand or pretended to understand exactly and in detail, according to her mood. None of it changed her behavior. She would have gone on pretending to be the Outlaw Queen in Hell or in Heaven. Put very simply, she didn't know what else to do.

All of which was why she was now facing down a Patrolman across the rock-strewn space at the edge of New England; a region so hazardous that even smugglers hesitated to cross its shifting boundaries. But not the Skyrider. Rat Johnson lived on a rock in New England, and she had been supplying him for years; he could seldom pay, but she said she considered him an investment. If he ever struck the rich vein of malite he claimed his rock was hiding, he would pay her back with interest. Meantime, she could afford it.

Ian Spencer had seen the Skyrider go into New England and had stationed his bright red-and-black Patrol boat to intercept her when she came out. Before the war a Patrolman who saw her go in would have stationed himself to kill her in a surprise attack when she came out; but now the Patrol was encouraged not to notice smugglers, at least until the question of legal ownership of all the disputed rocks was settled. Ian Spencer wasn't an ordinary Patrolman. He had no official reason even to wait for her. His business with her wasn't official.

While she was in New England, presumably off-loading Rat Johnson's supplies, Spencer had ample time to go over his plan and rehearse possible scripts, but he had been too nervous to make good use of the time. He had never been so nervous prior to a job before, not since he was a six-year-old gutter rat on Earth out to pick his first pocket. He had been studying the Skyrider since before the war. Her legend was formidable; but the reality, particularly since her friend Jamin had been killed by a laser bolt meant for her, was even more daunting than the legend.

When she saw him and automatically jockeyed into battle readiness in one swift motion so smooth it looked like she always came to a full stop with her weapons bristling on the way out of New England, he had to clear his throat three times before he turned on the Comm Link to hail her. She had not hailed him. That calm, patient silence was the most alarming thing she could have done, and she probably knew it.

He didn't activate the visual. He told himself it was because she might not go along with the gag if she saw what he thought of as "my damn babyface," but the truth was he wasn't sure he could pull it off if he had to look at her beautiful, cold, impassive face on the screen while he talked. He said, "Skyrider?" and was surprised by the sound of his own voice; it came out flat, unfamiliar, and too loud.

"That's my name." Her tone was balanced on the hostile edge of boredom. "So what, I owe you money?"

That line, spoken in Company English but with the singsong cadence of Belter pidgin, was a direct challenge to battle if he wanted it. Spencer knew it, though at the moment the ancient joke in which it had originated escaped him; that phrase, punch line of the joke, had survived as a useful challenge in situations where no grievance existed, only the aimless Belter urge to fight. He had read it before, and on a few occasions had heard it spoken to someone else; the asteroid belt was still a frontier and its native residents were not altogether civilized. They found frequent use for a phrase that would start a fight where there was no reason to fight.

Had Spencer been a native Belter, he would have responded with lasers instead of with words. He had been in the Belt long enough that, much to his own surprise, he had to push down an almost blinding surge of responding hostility. *Once a gutter rat, always a gutter rat,* he thought disgustedly. Aloud he said in his most innocent voice, "Not yet."

It took her a moment, as he had known it would, to figure out what he meant. Belters had been using that phrase for so long that most of them were no longer

consciously aware of its literal meaning. Link static cracked
between them while she thought about it. Spencer stared
out his viewport, past her shuttle, at the stars. She said
finally, in wry astonishment, ''You go loan me some?''

He smiled, but his voice was carefully not amused.
''Can't you speak Company English?'' Even when the
words in pidgin were basic English, the pronunciation
combined with the irritatingly repetitive singsong rendered
them almost incomprehensible to the English speaker. Spencer had grown up in a very cosmopolitan gutter, where he
had learned to speak six languages fluently, three only
adequately, and another three quite poorly though he understood them well. With that background it had taken him
only three months in the Belt to speak pidgin like a native;
but he often found it to his advantage to admit to under-
standing only one language at a time. ''I think you asked if
I meant to loan you money. If so, the answer is no. The
way I hear it, you've got more than you need already.''

''Suddenly you're my financial advisor?'' Her shuttle
nose came up, preparing to jump over him. ''How 'bout
you get the hell out of my space before I shove that pretty
Patrol boat down your throat?'' She didn't sound angry.
Oddly, that intensified the threat.

He ignored it. ''The way I hear it, the President of the
World, Incorporated gave you a fortune for stopping that
assassination attempt; and an almost unlimited, no pay-
back, coded credit account after you took her the news of
how the Company was using the Redistribution Act before
the Brief War.'' He tried to make the Skyrider's act sound
like high treason. In fact, it had been heroism, and he
admired her for it.

After the Corporation had passed the Redistribution Act,
granting Colonials—including freefall mutants—the right
to own real estate on Mars and in the Belt, the Company
had found a way to turn the Act into a very effective
means of getting homesteaders and miners permanently off

rocks that had been in their families for generations. The Skyrider, because she was the best pilot for the job and the only Colonial pilot personally acquainted with the President, had carried the news to Earth. The whole Colonial Fleet had backed that run, and it was in the battle to get through a Patrol cordon and on her way that her friend Jamin had died. A lesser hero than the Skyrider would have been provoked by that loss to stay and do battle with the Patrol, but the Skyrider had resolutely punched her way through the cordon and carried her message to Earth, thereby cutting the war short and so saving thousands of lives.

Spencer had hoped his tone would make her angry, but it didn't seem to work. He would have liked to be able to see her face. But that would mean she could see his face, and women always felt maternal toward him when they first saw his face. Maybe the Skyrider would be different. The legend implied she would. But he knew better than to put his trust in legends.

She jockeyed her shuttle sideways needlessly, dodging a rock that would have missed her anyway, and he mirrored the move so smoothly that they never cleared each other's laser screens. She said in a flat, bored voice, "If you're looking for a loan, try a bank."

"I'm not looking for a loan." His fingers were cramping on the controls. He clenched his fists hard and released them, stretched his fingers, and waited.

"Then get out of my space." She had lost patience suddenly and completely. There was still no anger in her voice, but there was a hard edge to it, close to anger. "Or I'll go through you."

Time to take the plunge. "Bet you can't." He was expert at that line. He knew how to make it a challenge without any confusing undertones. No anger, no fear, no uncertainty, not even pride: just confidence.

"Can't what? Go through you? Just try me." She didn't

sound as though she really cared one way or the other. It made her threat more menacing.

He didn't move. "I'm serious, Skyrider. I'm willing to bet that you can't kill me. Hell, I'll bet you can't even hit me."

"Honey, I bet I can," she said sweetly. "But why should I?"

"I'll wager anything you like, against your no-payback account, and I won't even return fire. I will run, of course. But I'll stay in range." He wouldn't have much choice about that; *Defiance* was at least twice as fast on the straight as his little Patrol boat. "I'll just dodge, and work my way back to Home Base. If you can't kill me by the time we get there, I win. What do you say?" He held his breath.

"It's a sucker's bet. I could kill you three times before breakfast." She sounded impatient. "Don't involve me in your suicide plans, Earther." She jockeyed again, trying to edge past him.

He matched the movement easily. "It's no good trying to get past me without killing me. And it's not a suicide plan. Come on, what do you say, hotshot?"

"How're you planning to pay if you're dead?" She spoke only to distract him while she jockeyed, but he wasn't distracted. She sighed audibly. "Damn it, I don't *want* to kill you, but I sure as space will if you don't back off."

"I've left a will, in case I lose." He had, too; an empty gesture that he pretended was fair. "I own a little piece of Manhattan that won't be quite as easy to spend, but should be worth just about as much as your credit code number." *And don't ask how a gutter rat happened to acquire ownership of a piece of Manhattan!* But she didn't know he was a gutter rat.

"What in space is Manhattan?" She didn't really want to know; she asked only to cover another jockey maneuver, which he mirrored perfectly.

"It's on Earth." The jockeying was the easy part. He was almost as good as she. For a mad instant he wished the wager were an honest one, his skill against hers.

"You own a piece of *Earth*?"

"A very expensive piece. So is it a wager, or what?"

"What." She leapfrogged past him, ignoring the very real possibility that in his effort to mirror her move he would meet her head-on and crash them both.

He didn't. At the last moment he saw what she was doing and dodged sideways, at the same time jockeying backward so swiftly that he was in her path again before she could hit her thrusters and run. "That's not very sporting, is it?" He was suddenly very glad after all that it wouldn't be a fair competition.

"This isn't a sporting event." She pitched over and hit the thrusters, bouncing his little boat out of the way on the trail of her exhaust.

He flipped and went after her instantly, but his boat couldn't match her *Defiance* for running speed. He had lost her interest, and very nearly lost her. *Damn!* She was sailing away free and clear, and his only hope of getting her back was to use one of the dirty tricks his research had suggested. He hadn't wanted it that way. He hated that part of the job: it stank of the gutter. But he had too much invested in this already to let her go now.

He closed his eyes, opened them, swallowed hard, watched her sleek shuttle receding in the viewport, and told himself that sometimes gutter tactics were the only way out of the gutter. He would not go back.

He cleared his throat soundlessly. "Whatsamattah you?" His voice was steady and mild. "You only kill your lovers?"

She flipped the *Defiance* over and fired almost before he had finished speaking. One thing about gutter tactics: they worked.

CHAPTER THREE

She chased him all the way back to Home Base. At first he could tell she was getting more furious with every missed shot; then her fascination with the problem overcame her anger, and her maneuvers got trickier and harder to second-guess. He was a damned good pilot, but she was better, and she proved it more than once, out-jumping and out-thinking and out-maneuvering him. By all rights he should have been dead a dozen times over, and they both knew it. But when the laser glare faded, he was always safely clear, the little black-and-red boat glistening, unmarked, as often as not waggling his wings at her in cheerful mockery.

She could see that her lasers were working just fine, but he knew she would run a computer check anyway. He had prepared for that. The check would show nothing wrong with the lasers or with their sighting screens. The only real danger he had faced had been the possibility that she would try out her photar weapons, but he never seriously thought she would. They would seem like overkill for his little boat. If he had been threatening her, she would have used any weapons at her disposal. But he wasn't a threat to anything but her pride. And if he had judged her character accurately, once she was past the first rage of frustration she wouldn't need to destroy just for the sake of her pride. It wouldn't have looked good to attack a mere Patrol boat with photars. Never mind that nobody had been there to see except the two of them, and he would have been in no condition afterward to carry tales. From what he knew of her, he thought it would be the principle of the thing that mattered.

He was riding inertia now, ahead of her and just enough to starboard to be off her screens. When she kicked in the thrusters to fly alongside he didn't even twitch: Home Base was in sight and he knew he had won. "How in space did you *do* that?" she asked.

This time he switched on the visual straightaway, giving her a disarming grin calculated to defuse any residual anger. "That would be telling." He couldn't quite keep the triumph out of his voice, so he tried all the harder to look modest. "You're good, Skyrider, but I guess I'm just a little bit better."

"No." She shook her head, her expression serious, her eyes unreadable. "No, you're not better. That's just the trouble."

This was dangerous ground. "But I won," he said innocently. "You couldn't kill me. You couldn't even hit me." With the ease of long practice he let his eyes narrow in sudden distrust. "Or are you trying to welsh on our bet?"

She shook her head again, looking impatient and tired. She was as beautiful as her holograms, but there was a haunted look in her eyes that he hadn't expected. She seemed alarmingly capable, yet curiously undefended: as though a laser couldn't kill her, but a harsh word from someone she cared about just might. "I never agreed to that bet with you in the first place," she said.

The shock of it stunned him. And he had been feeling sorry for her!

She smiled faintly, acknowledging his momentary panic, and said in a hard, flat voice, "But I accepted the challenge, and I lost. I accept your terms."

Home Base loomed before them, dark and tumbling, the glow of the flight deck spilling out of its apparently open tunnel and lighting nothing, swallowed by the long night outside. The outlaw and the Patrolman lined up side by side for landing clearance, automatically matching the asteroid's orbital and rotational velocities while they waited.

Spencer forced himself to return to the usual script. "You didn't expect this. You're not prepared." It wasn't easy to look deliberately and calmly thoughtful; she had shaken him badly. "It was part of the deal, or I meant it to be, but I never got a chance to say that you'd have a month to make any necessary last purchases before you turn over your account to me."

"Don't do me any favors." The words were angry, but her tone was indifferent.

He shrugged. "I don't care whether you use it or not, but you've got a month." He didn't have to pay his investors before then, so it was all the same to him.

Flight Control cut into the conversation to grant her clearance. She gave Spencer one last expressionless glance, switched off the visual Link between them, and went in. He watched the graceful ease with which *Defiance* slid forward, popped the invisible screen that protected the flight deck from the vacuum of space, and glided lightly down onto the panels.

Well, he had won, and that was the main thing. She was better than he, but he won. If the last step of the plan went well, by the time she shipped out again there would be nothing wrong with her weapons systems and no way anybody could prove there ever had been. He signaled her again and said with careful mockery, "Don't worry, Skyrider. I won't tell anybody how easy it was."

She flipped on the visual to look at him, steadily and without expression. "I'll take that month you offered. You're right, I do have a few necessary purchases to make."

"Maybe you ought to buy yourself a new shuttle. One you can fly." Flight Control granted him clearance and he came in fast, showing off, and had to waste power to slide to a neat halt next to *Defiance*. The Skyrider was out of her shuttle by then and waiting for him when he popped the Patrol boat's hatch.

He had known it would give her a lot of satisfaction to break his face, and even if it hadn't been part of his plan, he would have owed her the chance. He hadn't known how effectively she could use such an opportunity. He had expected to win. The gutter had taught him more than languages. But twenty years in the Belt was apparently a better education. He didn't win.

Afterward she was patient with the med-techs who patched them both up. She even walked with him to Sick Bay before she turned her full attention to the problem of spending money.

The first thing she bought was a rock of her own. It wasn't hard to choose one. There were three she had been keeping her eye on for years, and one of them was vacant since the war. It belonged to a smuggler who had decided to stay behind at Mars Station when the Colonial Fleet disbanded; the woman he had married out there hadn't liked the idea of living on an isolated rock in the wilds of the Belt.

He was delighted to sell to the Skyrider. He even told her how to get into the secret storeroom and included the contents in the deal. (That turned out to be a freezer full of genuine beef, a case of dark French roast coffee, three cases of fruit juice, and several kegs of beer: not a badly supplied larder, in Melacha's opinion.)

There were two shuttle docks on the rock, complete with synch systems. Besides the secret storeroom's contents there were less exotic supplies in additional storerooms, plus the accumulated debris of bachelor living in the three furnished rooms of the living quarters. It was a relatively large rock. There were storerooms, workrooms, utility rooms, living quarters, and plenty of solid rock in which to expand if she decided to. She signed on the dotted line; watched the seller's signature and ID code reproduced by Comm Link and computer; and waited while the legal programs investigated, adjusted, cogitated, filed, and finally spit out a piece of paper that established her ownership.

The clerk who had operated the computer through all this was a Belter born and bred; it showed in her accent and in her appearance. She had straight black hair cut short, framing her face with gamine wisps and emphasizing the size of her startlingly dark, expressive eyes. She wore the standard Belter costume of tunic and tights with a very nonstandard aura of unconscious elegance. There were silver and gold rings on every one of her small, quick fingers, but the effect was ruined by nails so fiercely bitten that they tended to bleed if her fingers struck her computer keyboard too hard. She put one finger in her mouth now, to keep it from bleeding on Melacha's document, and used the other hand to push the paper across the counter. With her finger in her mouth she looked very young. She took it out, looked at it, looked at Melacha, and said, "Well? How does it feel to own real estate?" Her voice was as expressive as her eyes, and as pleasant.

"Expensive," said Melacha. But she grinned and shrugged, studying her deed with satisfaction. "But it ain't my money, so what the hell?"

The clerk managed to look sympathetic, amused, and

curious all at once. "I heard," she said. "Did you really bet your whole no-payback credit account?"

"Not exactly," said Melacha. "But it doesn't matter; that's what he won."

"I heard he's an Earther."

" 'Fraid so."

"Jeez." The clerk shook her head. "How did he do it?"

"If I could tell you that, he wouldn't've done it." Melacha looked up from her deed. "But it's not that bad, you know. He gave me a month to use it before he takes over. It's pretty much unlimited, so I don't suppose I can clean it out, but I intend to get my month's worth."

"Couldn't you just draw it out in cash?"

Melacha looked faintly shocked. "That wouldn't be right. He said I could make necessary purchases."

"I hadn't heard the terms."

Melacha grinned again. "It's about the same, since there's nobody but me to say what's necessary. Cash is about the only thing I can't fairly take."

The clerk's dark eyes sparkled. "Gold? Jewels? Coffee? Spices? Malite?"

"I find I've developed a really pitiful need for all those things," said Melacha. "And a few more, besides. It'll be a fun month, yeah?"

She didn't take time to visit her new rock. She had seen it before. She knew roughly what was on it and what she wanted to put on it; and most of what she wanted was on Earth. She wanted luxury items: things valued both on Earth and in the colonies, and therefore costly in both places, but native to or manufactured only on Earth and seldom transported because they were not necessities, and so even more costly in the colonies than on Earth. It would be in the colonies that she would be hoarding them, selling them as needed, using them as a sort of durable bank account.

It only made sense to stop at Mars on the way to Earth, to visit her cousin Michael and his family. And Collis, Jamin's son. A seven-year-old, blue-eyed, Buddha-faced boy whose blinding smile would one day break some pretty girls' hearts. The last time she had seen him he hadn't been smiling much. Neither had she.

Spencer had just completed his task when Melacha arrived on the flight deck. Since his meddling had all been done externally, by linking his boat's powerful computer with that onboard *Defiance*, there was no physical evidence to give him away. His newly healed hands weren't even greasy. Still, he would have preferred not to be caught on the flight deck at all. His original plan had called for the reprogramming of her computers the moment she left the flight deck after their chase and subsequent fistfight. That was back when he still assumed he would win the fistfight.

She stopped when she saw him, and grinned irrepressibly. "Spencer."

"Skyrider." He felt unaccountably shy under the force of her grin. What minor damage he had done to her face the med-techs had already healed. She hadn't even broken her hands. He knew he still looked battered despite the med-techs' attentions, but she looked completely unruffled.

"Checking for damage?" She looked seriously at his bright Patrol boat. "I never touched her, did I?"

He shook his head. "No damage. At least, not to my boat." He touched his forehead carefully, where a newly healed scar cut a pink line across one eyebrow. "You sure did a job on me."

She shrugged. "You outweigh me. A little practice and you could beat me easy. Where'd you learn to fight, anyway? You're damn good, you know."

Guileless was an expression he did very well. He sometimes wished he could just look daft and babble nonsense:

failing that, he looked guileless and ignored the question. "Not good enough; I lost, didn't I?"

"That you did." She studied him unblinkingly. "You know, for an Earther you're pretty okay."

It was quite a compliment. To his confusion and disgust he blushed, feeling like a complete fraud under her friendly gaze. The mark wasn't supposed to be so friendly. And of course he was a fraud. He had always been a fraud. What else would he be? "Thanks." He managed not to scuffle his feet and duck his head in a display of total idiocy. "You're not so bad too, you know. For a Belter." As he said it he realized with surprise and dismay that it was true. *Don't get involved with the mark.* He scowled in sudden self-loathing and turned away. "Well. I, um. Have things to do. See you around."

"Sure." She sounded only moderately surprised; and, he thought, not even moderately interested.

Well, the job was done; that was the important thing. Now he had a month in which to relax before she paid up and he, after paying off his investors, could start the next job.

And she had a month in which to do her best to clean out a nearly limitless account. He hoped she used it wisely. That way in a sense they could both win.

It wasn't like him to worry so much about the mark. What did it matter to him whether she salvaged anything out of their deal? Maybe he was going soft.

In an effort to prove to himself that he wasn't, he went to the ready room and picked a fight. He won, too. But it didn't prove anything at all.

CHAPTER FOUR

The first time Linda March let JanMikal look in a mirror he was prepared for a shock. She had told him the extent of his injuries and described some of the rebuilding process she had done; and although she had also told him that he now had a quite acceptable face, even a handsome face, he was subconsciously prepared for horror. What he experienced instead was disorientation.

"It's not my face." He looked at March in surprise and confusion. "It's not my face. I know that." He looked back at the mirror, a frown of bewilderment and something like fear darkening his eyes. "But I don't know why I know it. Or what my face should look like."

She said quickly, "It's all right, JanMikal. That's a normal reaction. It's okay." She saw at once that even that wasn't altogether the right thing to say; she could see him make a deliberate effort not to point out that his new name, like his new face, seemed wrong even though he didn't know what would seem right. "Don't worry about it," she said. "Don't *try* so hard. If your memory returns at all, it will surprise you; it won't be as a result of concerted effort." She hesitated, but his face had a pinched white look that tore at her heart, and she had to say something. Anything. "It may come back, JanMikal. That you know that your face and your name are wrong is a good sign. Really. Now come on, you've admired yourself long enough. Let's let the rest of the world have a look."

He turned away from the mirror, but not toward her. "You're sure it'll be all right? What if I don't know how to act in public?" His voice was strained, reaching for indifference he didn't feel.

"You'll know how," she said. "Don't borrow trouble."

He shook his head, still not looking at her. "I know you say that sort of thing will be as automatic for me as it ever was. But you don't know that it ever was." He looked at her then, and his blue eyes were cold and distant and oddly arrogant. "You don't know *who* I was."

"JanMikal." She made her voice deliberately impatient. "I know that whatever else you were, you were a Colonial Warrior. I think that has to mean you had—have—some redeeming qualities, don't you?"

He stared, and she saw him consider being hurt or angry that his fears weren't being taken seriously. But reason got the better of him, and he grinned. "I don't suppose they took on hopeless criminals or barbarians, even for the Brief War." He was wrong about that, but it was as well that he didn't know it.

"That's better. Now are you ready to go?" She was briskly cheerful: her Dr. March voice, her "you aren't going to let a little thing like permanent total paralysis get you down are you?" attitude. She didn't like the voice or the attitude, but they served a purpose that she wanted served. Even hypocrisy has its place in the natural scheme of things.

"I guess I'm as ready as I can get." But he didn't move. And he didn't look again in the mirror. She had expected him to show either shock or considerable curiosity, but when he did neither, she had realized that an entirely new face was of no particular moment to him; the whole world was new in his eyes.

He was studying the buttons on his jacket again. They seemed to fascinate him. Perhaps buttons were uncommon wherever he came from. Were they uncommon in the asteroid belt? She didn't know. "At least you weren't grotesquely ugly," she said. "I suppose it's something to know even that much."

He glanced at her. "How do you know?"

She hesitated. "Well, I suppose you could have been grotesque, and just extremely well adjusted to it. But no, I think even so you'd be pleased to have acquired a handsome face. You might not have known why, not consciously anyway, but that sort of thing runs deep. If you'd been even moderately unattractive you might react now. But you take good looks in your stride. That much you did expect, on some level." She smiled. "Of course I knew that from your bone structure. I couldn't have created such a handsome Prince without a very good frog as a basis."

He didn't return her smile. He was in an odd mood, sullen and unexpected. "Do I look much like him?"

"Like who?"

"JanMikal." He didn't look at her. "Who was he?"

The question caught her by surprise. "He was my brother. No, you don't really look like him at all. I suppose I gave you his name because . . . it was because of what happened to him that I went into facial reconstruction. Otherwise I wouldn't have been able to . . ." She cleared her throat. "I'll tell you about him sometime. Not now." She moved toward the front door. "We'll be late meeting Simon." Without looking at him, she asked, "How did you know JanMikal was anybody?"

He followed her, looking more arrogant as they approached the door. Terrified; it was his first trip outside. "Just the way you say the name sometimes, I guess." He hesitated at the door, but she opened it and half led, half pulled him through before he could object.

Their apartment was in the Hub where gravity was at a minimum: one-sixteenth Earth normal was the maximum anywhere in the Hub, and nearer the core it decreased considerably until, in the very center, it was as near freefall as one could find on a rotating space colony. As a result, the Hub contained few of the parks and gardens found in the torus beyond. There were some experimental patches of greenery in a few areas, but mostly the Hub was like a small, very odd and oddly compact city, comprised of five- and six-story buildings vaguely reminiscent of pyramids, their vertical axes all pointing toward a central area where the open-ended cylinder containing the colony's low-gravity swimming pool seemed to hang suspended at the core of the Hub.

JanMikal had been ambulatory for some time now, and he had spent hours staring out of their apartment's large living room window. But it was a different matter entirely to step outside the door, onto the open walkway, and look at that same view with no pane of glass to insulate him from it. Through the glass it had been a fantasy. Out here was reality.

She had seldom seen him make any concessions to his own fear, and he made none now. He squared his shoulders and looked straight out over the railing, taking his time, studying the whole scene before him. "That's the swimming pool?" He gestured with his head. She nodded, and he pursued his panoramic study. "Some things seem familiar," he said slowly. "But most of it seems . . . strange. Alien. A little scary."

"The unknown is often scary, and you're having to face a lot of it lately." She tried not to look like she was watching him. "How do you feel?"

"Physically?" He was still looking at the view, a small boy determined to complete a difficult task.

"Any way."

He grinned at her fleetingly. "Like I'm facing a whole squadron of Patrol boats. How do I look? Will I pass for human?"

"You'll do." He didn't seem to notice that he had used an analogy out of his forgotten past, and she didn't want to point it out just then; it hadn't exactly been an auspicious analogy. Maybe it was from his time as a Colonial Warrior; the Patrol had been major defenders of the government's oppressive policies in the Belt. But if it was not from the war . . . who but a criminal would worry about facing a squadron of Patrol boats? "The tube to Monterey is this way. You're sure you feel ready for gravity? I mean full Earth-normal gravity?"

"How would I know? I've never experienced it."

"Now you're being difficult."

"I know. You're right. I'm sorry."

"Oh, JanMikal." She wanted to hug him, but was afraid it would embarrass him and he wouldn't know what to do. It wasn't always easy, interacting with someone who hadn't grown up knowing he had the right to do whatever he wanted to do. It made many otherwise simple situations seem complicated and fraught with unexpected peril. "Don't take everything so *hard*," she said helplessly.

He looked at her. "Do I?"

"Yes, you do, and there's no reason to," she said. "Unless you *want* to, but I don't see why you would. It makes everything so difficult."

"I don't think I know how *not* to take things hard, if that's what I'm doing. I just take things how they feel."

"I suppose you do. I'm sorry. It must be so hard for you. I guess I forget that. Or I don't give it enough importance. I guess I want you to be more comfortable and I forget it's not something you can necessarily get just by choosing to have it. So many emotions are, you know."

"Are what?"

"Something you can get just by choosing to have it."

"Are they?"

"Oh, I don't know. Maybe not, for you. Not because you have amnesia, I don't mean, but because you weren't raised here."

"What's so different about being raised here?"

"Just our philosophy. We've talked about it, a little. *The Way of Life According to Bill.* Here's our elevator. If you want to talk about the *Way of Life*, Simon will jump at the chance. Just ask him. Now get ready: the gravity will increase as we go down."

Since he had no idea what increased gravity would feel like, it was difficult for him to get ready. But he looked ready for almost anything, braced against unimaginable shocks, his eyes like expressionless blue mirrors that showed, by the thoroughness with which they concealed it, how very near panic he felt.

She had painkillers with her, and she had given him the best medication the Diademan medical community had been able to devise for a freefall mutant faced with gravity. There was nothing more she could do for him. She knew he had spent the last several years in gravity; that surely meant it wouldn't kill him to visit it for an evening. The knowledge was not reassuring. She felt as if she were condemning him to death.

His expression never changed, but she knew the moment the gravity became a problem for him, and they weren't even at half Earth-normal yet. If there had been any way to back out of the project at that moment, she would have; but the elevator they had taken was an express, which would take them relentlessly nonstop all the way out to the torus.

Neither of them said anything. By the time the elevator stopped to let them out, March was so tense she almost had to pry her fingers off the handrail. JanMikal didn't move. March stepped forward to hold the door and looked back at him. "You okay?"

"I don't know." He turned his head carefully, as if the weight of it were too much for his neck muscles to bear. As perhaps it was. "I don't know what I expected." He tried to smile at her, but it wasn't a big success. "Whatever it was, this isn't it."

"Can you walk?"

"I don't know."

"I can call a med-team. Get you a wheelchair. You could ride to the restaurant."

He blinked. "No."

"We could take this elevator right back into the Hub."

Just perceptibly, he shook his head. "No." With an obvious effort, he let go his grip of the handrail, put one foot in front of him, and shifted his weight. She could see the shock of the movement travel through his body. But he balanced, as carefully as if he were made of spun glass, and did it again. "I've done this before." His surprise almost concealed the stress in his voice. "I've done this a lot."

She nodded. "Your muscular development indicated that you had. I don't know why you would. I mean, if you're from the Belt, where *anything* is available in freefall. And you must be from the Belt. It only makes sense."

He was still moving carefully, but beginning to give a greater appearance of ease. "I think I could be from anywhere except Earth or Mars, couldn't I? They're the only places a freefall mutant can't leave, and my parents might have been Floaters. Floaters can live anywhere."

"This way." She guided him with a hand on his arm; he was concentrating so completely on simple movement—and on making it *look* simple—that he had no attention to spare for his surroundings. He followed her docilely, his face expressionless, his eyes shadowed with pain. "I brought painkillers," she said.

He shook his head again, fractionally. "No. Or . . . not yet. I think . . . I don't know. It gets easier, or . . . I feel like I don't use painkillers."

"That choice might have been dictated more by pride than reason."

"Or it might have been dictated by reason. Maybe painkillers confuse me. Or dull what needs *not* to be dulled. Maybe I need the pain, to keep from making mistakes. To keep from getting careless."

She shook her head. "It's not as if you were a normal person trying to move in multiple gravities. You're not as fragile as you feel. You won't break your ankle if you put your foot down wrong, any more than I would."

He gave her a very tight smile. "You're not *normal*. You're a *Grounder*."

"Sorry. You're right. I've never . . ." She shook her head again. "Don't change the subject, JanMikal. Why do you want to suffer needless pain?"

"I don't want to. I feel like I should. I feel like it's safer." He was moving more easily now, and managed a fairly creditable smile. "Besides, it doesn't hurt as much now. I'm getting used to it."

"Fortunately we're almost there. I won't argue with you. See the building just past those trees? That's—" She broke off when she saw his face. He had looked where she pointed, and it was the first time he had really looked at anything around them since they left the elevator. His face went dead white, and he stumbled and had to catch her arm for support. "What's wrong?" She looked wildly around, uncertain what to expect. "What is it, JanMikal?"

He was staring up at the tops of buildings and trees. Slowly he lowered his gaze to the horizon, where the torus curved "up" and out of sight some half a mile away. He stood absolutely still, his hand on her arm, staring, hardly breathing, for a full minute before he said in a hushed, awed voice, "It's too big."

"What is? What's too big?" She looked foolishly ahead for something oversized in their path before she realized what he meant. "Oh, you mean the colony? The torus?"

"I've never even imagined a chamber this big. That part, where our apartment is, that was big enough to make me nervous, but it was real. It was possible. But *this* . . . !"

They were on a path between apartment buildings, their feet crushing a minty ground cover that sent up clouds of sweet sharp scent around them. Most of the buildings were no more than six stories tall, but the more distant ones on either side looked taller because the ground beneath them sloped upward to meet the down-sloping "sky." Their sharp angles were softened by trees and bushes crowded around them. Herbs and flowers cascaded over the railings of colorful translucent balconies. Light spilled in bright pastels through stained glass windows, and from a nearby apartment came the soft, mournful notes of a solitary guitar, haunting in the rainbowed darkness.

Overhead, the inside curve of the torus that served the colony as "sky" was dark, the complex system of mirrors and shields letting in the cold pinpoint lights of distant stars so that it looked almost like a real sky open to space. Before and behind them the horizon stretched out till the curve of the torus blocked further view; in the distance just before the curve they could see the dark patches of agricultural fields and the lonely white headlight of a tractor rolling along the narrow road between them.

To March, the scene was so familiar that she had not really looked at it in years. Now she saw it for the first time through JanMikal's eyes, and could have kicked herself for not realizing it would be yet another shock for which she should prepare him in advance. She gave him a wry smile. "Well, now we know you aren't from any of the major artificial colonies like this one. Come on; you'll feel better when we get inside." She put her free hand over his on her arm and gently tugged him forward. He came stiffly, still staring at the horizon. "I'm sorry I didn't think to warn you about this," she said. He probably wasn't capable of listening, but perhaps the sound of her voice would be reassuring. "I have to admit I just didn't think of it. It never occurred to me. There are so many differences between us, and I was busy looking for all the little unexpected ones that might trip us up; I never thought about such a big one."

They made it safely into the restaurant, and he seemed to relax somewhat once they were inside a room he considered more normal in size. His face was still white, his eyes glazed with shock, but his grip on her arm lightened and she could almost see him trying to force himself to let go entirely.

The area inside was more like what he must be accustomed to. It was certainly smaller, anyway. A large room, perhaps twice the size of the living room of their apartment, it was crowded with tables and chairs in shining plasteel and stained glass so that it seemed even smaller than it was. There were diners seated at nearly every table, their conversations overlapping and their laughter occasionally drowning the soft chamber music playing on the owner's stereo system. March and JanMikal had both known he had to prepare himself for crowds, and after the first panicky glance around he seemed to accept being surrounded by people. But he hadn't known about the size of the torus and she hadn't thought of it.

She gestured toward a table on the far wall, next to a window. "There's Simon," she said, privately thinking uncharitably that things like agoraphobia were Simon's field and he might have warned her how likely JanMikal was to suffer it. But while phobias were his field, JanMikal wasn't. He had less reason to think of it than she had. He was barely aware JanMikal existed.

By the time they reached Simon's table, JanMikal had managed to release her arm and she had forgotten her momentary irritation with Simon. Anxiety over JanMikal's handling of this first social encounter pushed everything else from her mind. She wanted to protect him, to help him over this potentially difficult hurdle that she knew he must take alone.

She needn't have worried. He handled it so well that Simon, always glad to overlook anyone else's problems in favor of his own, obviously forgot the momentous nature of the occasion. "JanMikal," he said, "glad to meet you. I've heard a lot about you, the last few months. Linda, I'm sorry, but we'll have to cut the evening pretty short; I've got to prepare another news release. They're blockading abandoned stations now."

JanMikal shook Simon's hand, accepted the brusque greeting with equanimity, and seated himself at the table with his back to the window so he wouldn't have to look out on the vast open area of the colony. "Glad to meet you, Dr. Hale," he said. "Who's 'they'? And why are they blockading abandoned stations?"

"The Terrans," Simon said, needlessly adjusting March's chair before he seated himself. "They don't want us to get the materials; it's one of our primary sources of supply." He looked curiously at JanMikal, and March smiled privately as she saw him remember who this was, and watched the sequence of reactions cross his face, culminating in lively paternal sympathy. Hale was good at paternal sympathy. "But you don't know any of this, do you?" he said. "We can supply most of our own needs, you see; we're almost self-sufficient. But some things always had to be brought out from Earth, and in the last twenty years Earth has systematically denied our existence in every legal way. Which inevitably resulted in practical denials as well. Put simply, they began by saying we don't exist, and then they had to pretend that they couldn't see us." He looked at March. "But that doesn't stop them from firing on our scavenger shuttles when they approach abandoned stations."

March told JanMikal, "That's abandoned space stations. There were a lot of them, and other technological rubble, left in Earth orbit during the early days of space exploration. The orbits of some of them decayed or will decay till they collide with the atmosphere and fall to Earth, but some of them are up here to stay, and they're no good to anybody now. When Earth stopped supplying us or trading with us, we turned to scavenging, and the abandoned stations have been a rich source of materials we badly need."

"I knew you scavenged; that's how you got me," said JanMikal.

"We thought battles would be a good source during the war," said Hale. "But the Colonials needed materials as badly as we do. They cleaned up the battle sites so well, there was seldom anything left for us. So we went back to stripping stations."

"But why would they try to stop us, if they're so determined to believe we don't exist?" asked March. "They keep making all these new rulings—no more lost liners, no more space stations—why? We were doing a job that benefitted everyone. Nobody else wanted the materials badly enough to salvage them, but everybody's glad to see space cleared of the litter. Why are they doing this to us?"

"Probably they're really trying to do it to the Colonials, wouldn't you think?" asked JanMikal. "I doubt if Terrans care all that much about Diadem one way or the other, but they care about Mars and the asteroid belt. There's money out there, and supplies Earth needs. And any way they can increase the colonies' dependence on Earth is a way they can keep the colonies obedient to Earth government."

"My thought exactly," said Hale; but he had the grace to look sheepish immediately afterward, since that hadn't been his thought at all. "Well, anyway," he said, "I have to prepare a news release for later tonight, so I can't spend as much time over dinner as we had planned."

"If we can't trade and we can't salvage, what will we do?" asked March.

"I don't know," said Hale. "I begin to wish your Pirate Prince were a reality. Short of that, I don't know what we *can* do."

CHAPTER FIVE

JanMikal's lunch with Robert Matlock, overseer of the colony's farms and JanMikal's prospective employer, was a disaster. JanMikal didn't *do* anything wrong. He *was* wrong. Linda March, who brought JanMikal to the restaurant and was to meet him again afterward, thought when she saw the two of them sit down together that it was altogether too like watching a lion sit down to lunch with a lamb. JanMikal didn't mean to be a lion. Indeed, he was doing his very best to masquerade as a lamb. But it was a masquerade. He was a warrior alone in a land of tranquility. He did not remember any life beyond Diadem, but he had been shaped by forces Diadem had never known. He was not and perhaps could not be Diademan.

Matlock tried to like JanMikal, but like a lamb at lunch with a lion he couldn't quite get comfortable. Under ordinary circumstances Matlock did not in any way resemble a lamb: he was a big man with fierce eyes shadowed by bushy silver eyebrows, a jutting chin, and a beaked nose that reinforced the ferocity of his dark eyes; he looked more like a bird of prey than like a lamb. But in JanMikal's presence the piercing eyes seemed wild and alarmed, and the jutting chin gave an appearance of false bravado instead of its usual impression of fiery self-assurance. He felt suspicious and uneasy, and it showed. It was a very unusual and confusing state for any Diademan, and not one he would want to prolong. Matlock cut his lunch time short, told JanMikal the truth—that Matlock didn't want to let loose such a disturbing element among his other workers and he was sorry but he wanted to leave now—and rose to go.

Puzzled and feeling vaguely guilty without knowing why, JanMikal thanked Matlock for his time and watched him leave, finished his own lunch, and sat back to wait for Linda March, who had agreed to meet him after lunch. This time he was facing the restaurant's windows: gravity hadn't got any easier for him, but the colony's vast open spaces were less alarming once he was really convinced it was meant to be that way and that although it was very large, it was nonetheless adequately enclosed to retain its atmosphere.

March knew what to expect when she saw he was alone. "He didn't want to hire you?"

"He said I would be a disturbing element." He was as tense as a coiled spring, watching her. "What d'you s'pose I did wrong?"

She shook her head and hailed a waiter to order coffee. "Nothing, I think, except be who you are."

His eyes darkened with hurt or anger, she couldn't tell which. "But who am I?"

"I don't know." She touched his hand. "But I know you were a warrior. It shows, JanMikal. It's in everything you do, how you think and speak, how you look. . . . You're a fox in the henhouse, I'm afraid."

He looked puzzled. "Fox?"

She smiled. "It's an image from a children's story. You know what hens are. Chickens. Foxes are predators of some kind. They look rather like small dogs. Never mind. I only meant you can't help being a disturbing element. Sometimes you even disturb me. You tend to look dangerous, without meaning to. And we're a very peaceable society.''

"I feel very peaceable," said JanMikal.

"I know you do. I'm sorry, JanMikal. I don't know what we'll do about it; a warrior, even at peace, is simply too . . . *untamed* for Diadem. But *The Way* says 'There is no one from whom one can't learn something of value.' We just have to figure out what it is that Diadem might be willing to learn from you.''

"What can a warrior teach a peaceable colony?" he asked bitterly. "I'm not even allowed to farm.''

"We'll think of something. Or, if you'll pardon another quote from *The Way*, 'Something will happen.' ''

When they returned to the Hub, JanMikal decided to go swimming. He was still feeling despondent, so March went with him to see if she could help cheer him up. But the low-grav pool supplied all the cheering he needed, at least on a temporary basis. The pool was in a way like a miniature version of the colony itself: a cylinder of glasteel with the water inside it, held against the "walls" of the cylinder in the same way water is held against the bottom of a spinning bucket. The gravity generated by centrifugal force here at the center of the Hub was very low, about one-fiftieth Earth-normal, which was adequate to keep undisturbed water in place. Since the density of the human body is very near that of water, underwater swimming was much the same as it would be on Earth. In few other ways did the Diadem pool resemble one on Earth.

If one stood on the tile at the edge of the pool and looked around, everything seemed normal, but at a distance the pool curved upward to meet itself overhead. Waves and ripples in the water were much higher than they would have been on Earth, and traveled more slowly. When anyone jumped into the water, it made a noticeable hole in the water which took a second or more to fill. A double handful of water lifted out of the pool was held more or less together by surface tension, so one could throw it like a snowball—though there were rules against doing that to excess, since it would fill the atmosphere with droplets of water which would settle only slowly and could be a hazard to unwary swimmers or divers.

Diving in low gravity was a graceful exercise, the simplest dive becoming an elegant slow-motion arc as the diver rose dozens of feet above the water, slowly turned, and glided back down. It was like flying, like dancing on air, breathtaking to watch and exhilarating to perform. JanMikal sometimes judged the jump exactly right from the diving board to enter the region near the pool's center at slow enough speed that, with a few careful waves of his arms against the resistance of air, he could bring himself to a stop and rest there in freefall, watching the pool and the colony rotate around him. Eventually the rotating air against his body started him moving again with the colony, and centrifugal force brought him back out to the water in the delayed completion of a beautiful dive.

That afternoon, JanMikal played in and around the pool with the happy abandon of a child, diving and floating both in and out of the water—and walking on water, slapping the surface with the soles of his feet to stay on top. From the first time she had introduced him to the pool he had loved it, inventing new games and acrobatics even more enthusiastically than the colony's children did. They were all Grounders; so far, Diadem had produced no freefall mutants, and as they were a closed community living almost entirely in gravity it was considered unlikely that they ever would. Although most Diademans spent a lot of time during their formative years playing in the low-grav pool, no Grounder could be as comfortably inventive in near-freefall as a mutant Faller.

JanMikal was having such a good time that March was momentarily dismayed when a group of seven-year-old boys, accompanied by two cheerfully harried instructors, arrived to crowd into the pool. She thought JanMikal would, like most childless adults, retreat in nervous distaste at such an invasion. Instead, he incorporated the children into his games, and, perhaps more surprising, they reacted exactly as if he were a new pool toy. No shyness, no hesitation, no hanging back. In minutes they were all clustered around him, imitating his acrobatics and clamoring for his attention.

The instructors, seeing their charges so satisfactorily occupied, joined March at the side of the pool. "Is that your patient?" one asked. "The freefall mutant? What do you call him?"

"JanMikal," said March. "But you make it sound like he's a pet."

"Sorry, I didn't mean to. Look how well he gets along with the children!"

"Look what they're *do*ing!" said the other teacher, pointing in amazement at a particularly complex acrobatic maneuver performed by boys who had never before shown much talent for anything at all. Then he looked at March and said, "Oh, sorry, I guess I should introduce myself. Tom Karnak, from Adair. You must be Dr. March, if that's the freefall mutant? And I guess you know my associate Dr. Sarah Brady."

"I wish you wouldn't call him 'the freefall mutant.' He's a person, and he has a name," said March.

Brady looked at her with evident sympathy. "Look, I don't want to intrude in your business, but you know, you've been living with him for months; you've had time to adjust. To the rest of us he's that mysterious Colonial Warrior March is mending, who turned out to be a freefall mutant on top of everything. You know?"

"I know," said March. "I guess I'll have to get used to it. I'm sorry I snapped at you."

"He sure does get along with the children," said Karnak. "Just look at that, he's got little Mikey laughing and shouting like anybody else." To March he added, "Mikey has problems at home. We haven't wanted to take any drastic steps yet, but he's not a happy child. I've never seen him play like that with the other boys."

"And look what JanMikal has them doing," said Brady. "I didn't even know you *could* do that without swim fins."

"Say, have you found him a job yet?" asked Karnak.

"No, why?"

"Because he just might be exactly what we've been looking for." He looked at Brady. "What do you think?"

"What, low-grav phys. ed.?" Brady looked blank for a moment, looked at the excited tumble of children around JanMikal, and said thoughtfully, "Maybe so."

"What?" asked March. "You need an instructor? And you'd accept JanMikal? But he has no credentials. . . . You know almost nothing about him. . . ."

"And we can see just about everything we need to know, right out there," said Karnak, nodding his head toward the pool where the children had begun to collect a huge blob of freefalling water in the center of the pool. JanMikal was overseeing their efforts, and nobody was throwing his bucketful too hard or losing interest and deciding to have a waterfight instead. "He's good with them, they like him, and he has them playing with the physics of the place more comfortably than we've ever managed. It doesn't matter whether he can explain to them what they're doing; if he can't, someone else can, and the important thing is to get them to *play*. Directed group activities, that is." He looked at March. "You know we don't let a little matter of credentials get in the way when we want somebody."

"I think he'd be interested," said March. "But . . . d'you really think the parents would accept him? You haven't seen him with adults. You don't know what he's like.''

Brady looked interested. "Why, does he pick his nose in public? Even if he's disgusting, surely he'll want to clean up his act when he sees what manners are, and meantime we could put up with a little uncivilized behavior outside the class situation if he's always this good in it.''

"It's not that he's uncivilized, at least not the way you mean," said March. She hesitated. "He just had lunch with Robert Matlock. We were asking for a job on the farms; I thought it would be a good place for unskilled labor, where he wouldn't have to deal with a lot of people at a time, and there are a lot of farm jobs that don't require more strength than he has in gravity.''

"What happened?'' asked Brady.

"Matlock didn't want him. Didn't even want to finish lunch with him; he was really unnerved. He said he thought JanMikal would be a disturbing element among his other workers.''

"Disturbing?'' said Karnak. "How, disturbing?'' He looked suspiciously at JanMikal, but the boys were still playing happily with him and JanMikal hadn't suddenly developed horns or overt perversions.

"If you'd seen him at lunch, you'd know,'' said March. "I don't blame Matlock. I don't think I would have wanted to hire him, either.''

"Well, for goodness sake, why?'' asked Brady. "What did he do?''

"Nothing, exactly,'' said March. "It's just that he was a warrior.''

Brady looked encouraging. "Well? We knew that. He won't suddenly pull out a gun and start shooting everybody, will he?''

"No, of course not,'' said March. "But . . .''

"Well?'' said Brady.

"I don't think he'd really hurt anybody," said March.

"But?" said Karnak.

"But sometimes . . . sometimes he makes people . . . well, he makes people nervous. He even makes me nervous, sometimes. Not really because of anything he does. More because of who he is." She looked away from them, at JanMikal. "He looks so happy, so relaxed, doesn't he? But with grownups, and especially in gravity, I don't know. It's a little like being in the same room with an armed bomb, sometimes. You know there's no reason for it to go off, but you're very aware that it could if a reason came up, so to speak."

"Reasons for bombs to go off don't just come up at random," said Karnak.

"And I don't suppose one would come up at random for JanMikal, either," said March. "Still, we're a very peaceful society. In the time JanMikal has been up and about, I've become aware exactly *how* peaceful we are. We don't know anything about the world outside, not really. Those people don't know what they want, much less know they can have what they want, or do what they want, or whatever. Oh, even *The Way* becomes confusing when I'm talking about JanMikal. I don't know how to explain. It isn't that he's really dangerous. It's just that one becomes so very aware of the potential."

"What does he think of us?" asked Karnak.

March looked at him in surprise; it was a very perceptive question. "I'm not just sure," she said. "Except I think he finds our lifestyle . . . disquieting."

"Look, they're diving," said Brady.

JanMikal had begun it with a vertical dive; because the pool was on the inside of a huge cylinder, there was water overhead as well as beneath the boards. If one could get sufficient thrust off the board, one could dive into the water overhead, though most beginners ended up in the air somewhere in between, and had to wait for gravity and air currents to bring them back down. JanMikal made it to the water overhead, swam quickly around to where the boys were getting up their courage to imitate him, and guided them instead in less ambitious dives into the water beneath the board. They were clamoring for their turn, and he patiently showed each of them how to get off the board gracefully and to land where he wanted.

"That does it," said Karnak. "Look, there goes Mikey. Look at that!" He shook his head. "If he'll take the job, it's his. We can put up with him making us nervous if he can put up with our disquieting lifestyle. For somebody that good with the kids, we'll put up with a lot of flaws when he's away from the kids."

"You don't want to check with anyone about it before you commit yourself?" asked March.

"No need to," said Brady. "We're all on the lookout for somebody, since Turk Remington retired. We'll just tell the others what we've seen here today, and they'll be as pleased as we are."

A boy went off the board, bumped into a huge waterball that another boy had thrown, panicked, and began flailing helplessly. He would have been in no danger at all, except that another boy came up out of the water just then in an old trick they all taught themselves, swimming so rapidly upward that they emerged from the water like dolphins, letting their momentum carry them right out of the water and, if they were practiced at it, well above the water. This boy was practiced at it; and he wasn't looking where he was going. Neither was the diving boy who had panicked. The two collided in midair and tumbled, screaming more in rage than in pain, back toward the water.

They still weren't in any real danger if they kept their heads. But enraged as they were, they might have hit the water still screaming, and not had enough breath left to fight their way back to the surface before they had to inhale. Both instructors and Linda March stood up, watching, the instructors ready to dive to the aid of the boys if need be.

There was no need. JanMikal moved so swiftly they hardly knew, afterward, what he had done. He was already on the diving board when the two boys collided. He went off it in a spectacular flying leap that took him neatly under both boys, where he managed somehow to give both of them a shove back into the air before he entered the water. The boys, startled by this new turn of events and frightened by their own screams, fell abruptly silent, tumbling helplessly toward the water again, staring with huge eyes at the three adults beside the pool. Then JanMikal came back out of the water dolphin-style, ready to keep the boys in the air if necessary. They seemed to be all right now, so he grinned at them and let his dolphin-leap curve up over them as they went into the water. When he came up the second time, he was between them, ready if anything further went wrong.

The boys grinned and attached themselves to his body like limpets. In seconds all the other boys had joined them in the water again, and they had begun a new game, the brief crisis apparently forgotten.

"Wow," said Brady.

"There wasn't really any danger, was there?" said March.

"You don't know boys," said Karnak. "Those two could easily have drowned themselves for no reason at all."

"It would seem that JanMikal guessed that," said March.

"Understatement," said Brady. "Maybe he has kids of his own, or something."

"I don't know," said March. "He doesn't know."

"He doesn't remember anything?" asked Karnak.

"Not about himself," said March. "He may never remember. It's almost a miracle that memory is all he lost."

"Well, anyway, he's got a job if he wants it," said Karnak.

When he was told of it, JanMikal wanted it.

CHAPTER SIX

Melacha had never before visited her cousin Michael's farm on Mars. It was in one of the deep valleys near Marstown, where the Terraforming of the early settlers had been most effective: the soil was good, the atmosphere was rich enough to breathe without a respirator, and the climate was mild. She had landed *Defiance* at Marstown and rented a surface vehicle to drive out to the farm, arriving just as the planet was rotating the farm onto the down-sun or night side, so that her first view of it was in the warm golden glow of evening. The sky was already a deep purple, almost black. Rays of the setting sun cast golden streamers across the valley from mountain passes on one side to mountain tops on the other. Between the mountains lay the vast expanse of Michael's farm, lit like a faerie garden in the fading sun.

She had not told them she was coming. Now, as she paused on the last hill and stared down into the peaceful, alien valley, she wondered whether she should have. Maybe Collis wouldn't even be there. She stared at the mountains, dusty purple against the darker sky, their jagged peaks shadowing the valley below. This was a beautiful place in its own strange way, but the open space was too big and there was no barrier between it and the starred evening sky. How could Collis be happy here? He was a Belter child born and bred. Could any Belter ever really adjust to a planet?

For a fraction of a second she thought she should discuss it with Jamin; then she remembered and immediately blanked her mind of anything but the scene before her. The last rays of the sun had swung skyward and died. Lights had blinked on in the valley below, spreading a tattered pattern of stars beneath the thickening blanket overhead. The wind, so disquieting to one from the Belt where any really noticeable breeze meant a breached chamber, turned suddenly chilly and she shivered. The dark peaks beyond the valley were no longer beautiful: they were obscurely threatening; a somber row of broken teeth in the gaping maw of a hostile planetary night.

Now you're deliberately being morbid, she thought, and put the groundcar in gear. When she switched on her headlights, the world was abruptly compressed to contain only what fit within the two yellow beams. She steered down the hill, and bushes leapt into existence at the side of the road; boulders and sudden cliff faces appeared and rushed into darkness behind her; the dusty, battered concrete of the roadbed blurred under her wheels; a rabbit froze red-eyed and staring in the opposite lane, and was passed before it could decide which way to run. Everything beyond the headlights was plunged into vast darkness, out of sight but somehow horribly looming. . . . Or perhaps it was the too-vast darkness itself that seemed to loom.

Space from a shuttlecraft looked vaster and possibly darker, but it never loomed. One was separated from it by more than an intangible bubble of light. One was enclosed, protected, safe within the artificial world of plasteel and technology that was a Belter's proper home. Melacha had been born on Earth, but she had spent more of her life in the asteroid belt than on planets, and she felt uncomfortable and unwelcome on rocks this big.

"Stop it." She said it aloud and the sound of her own voice in the rushing darkness startled her. Then she was at a gate and the action of sliding the car to a halt, jumping out into the resultant billows of dust, and viciously slamming the gate open with all her strength relieved some of her nervous tension, so that she was able to drive through almost calmly and pull the gate closed behind her with considerably less force. When it was slow to latch, though, she kicked it so fiercely that she warped the plasteel frame.

What she needed was a good fistfight. But she couldn't expect to find one on Mars; the residents were so annoyingly civilized. Not as bad as the residents of Earth, but not as comfortably rowdy as residents of the asteroid belt, where a nice fight could almost always be had on the smallest of excuses.

When she pulled up in the center of the housing compound she realized she hadn't any idea how to find Michael or Collis, or what would be the polite way to go about it. The compound, built on a low hill near the center of the valley, consisted of a number of low brick houses more or less identical and all facing the planted area surrounding the small gravel lot in which she had parked. They had different-colored curtains at the windows, and different plantings in window boxes and in strip flower gardens on either side of the front walks, but there was no way to tell which one housed whom. Presumably these were the homes of Michael's various spouses and children; some Martians liked to clump everybody together in one big mansion, but groups of smaller houses like this were more common.

Well, there was nothing for it but to knock on a door and see what happened. At least she could be confident

that any one of them would know who Michael was. She
shouldered her traveling bag and climbed out of the car,
slamming the door and staring in frustration at the profusion
of entryways to choose from.

A door opened behind her and a broad band of yellow
light spilled out across the lot. Melacha turned, a small
graceful figure alone in the wide darkness, and stepped
aggressively toward the open door. The light silhouetted a
tall man standing within who gazed silently out at her,
unmoving. In sudden nervous fury she told him, "This is a
hell of a way to greet a guest. It's polite at least to speak,
you know. You could say 'hello,' or 'who the hell are
you,' or 'get off this property,' or damn near anything you
please really, but it's foully rude to just stand there and
stare." She hesitated, and when he still didn't speak she
said crossly, "It provokes anger. Would you like me to
kick your teeth in, whoever you are?" Her tone almost
made it a polite invitation.

He didn't have a chance to respond. A small figure
pushed past him out the doorway, shouting, "Skyrider!
Skyrider!" and she was nearly bowled over by Collis's
delighted hug.

"Collis." She sounded relieved. Hugging him hard, she
glared over his shoulder at the silhouetted man still standing in the doorway, as if to challenge him to comment on
this overt display of affection.

Collis had hurled himself into her arms so forcefully that
he was lifted off his feet: now, recalling his dignity, he
squirmed in the way of small boys finished with hugs, and
she let him down gently. Taking her hand, he turned to
face the man in the doorway. "Thank you for dinner,
Peter," he said. "I'll go with the Skyrider to Michael and
Jenna's house now."

The tall silhouette nodded without speaking.

"Nice to've met you, Peter," said the Skyrider.

He nodded again and turned away. His door closed, shutting off the light.

"What's with him?" asked Melacha.

"He's one of our fathers," Collis said indifferently.

"Why didn't he say anything?"

"Oh, he can't talk. This is Michael and Jenna's house over here. Really it's Jenna's house but Michael's staying with her while Brad and Mary use his house because Rachel and Ruth are in Mary's." He paused before they started up the walk to the indicated house. "Skyrider? Have you . . ." His voice broke and he swallowed hard, then rushed on before she could speak: "I know prob'ly not but I have to ask: have you heard anything about Papa?"

She shook her head. "No. I'm sorry, Collis."

He looked away, then looked back at her with his big blue eyes as unreadable as ever Jamin's had been. "I know. It's all right. Come and meet Jenna; she's one of my favorite mothers." He led her toward the house, his face obscured by darkness. She knew it would be expressionless. Perhaps even arrogant, like his adoptive father's. He was more like Jamin now, she thought, than he had been when Jamin was alive.

When Jamin was alive. . . . She had never put it that bluntly before. And she didn't really believe it now. Somehow Jamin *was* alive. She knew it: she felt it. But *where*?

Then Collis was opening the door and pulling her into a warm firelit room, and in a moment she was exchanging greetings with a boyishly delighted Michael and the big beautiful elegant wife named Jenna in whose house Michael was staying.

"I'm glad to meet you at last," said Jenna. "Collis has told us so much about you."

"Oh." Melacha looked at Collis, who returned her look with a genuinely innocent grin.

"Don't worry," said Michael. "He has the whole fam-

ily convinced you're a hero. Sit here; can we get you
something to drink?''

"Caffeine, if you have it." Melacha obediently sat
where she was told, in a huge soft chair by the glowing
fire, her back to the window through which the lights of
the farm and distant stars were visible in the black of
night. Collis leaned against her and she helped him climb
into her lap. To her relief neither Michael nor Jenna
seemed even to notice the activity, much less find anything
odd in the notion that the Skyrider, risk taker, lawbreaker,
and outlaw queen that she was, would be fond enough of a
child to want him in her lap.

"My dear," said Jenna, tossing her thick mane of red
hair in a truly regal gesture which she then spoiled with an
impish smile, "we have genuine coffee. Would you like
it hot or cold?''

"Hot, please.'' She gave Collis a furtive one-armed
hug. "How do you get coffee? Do you grow it?''

"We do,'' said Michael, "but we don't get a very good
yield. We're working on it. Meantime what Jenna's brew-
ing is contraband from Earth. We have a friend staying
here from one of the space colonies that Earth legislated
out of existence. Newkansas. I don't suppose you've heard
of it; nobody has, much. Anyway, Cam went down to
Earth to see if he could get a drug Newkansas needs. He
couldn't, because it's government-controlled and they
wouldn't sell to a representative of a colony they don't
admit exists. But he was able to pick up some good coffee
that he thought maybe he could trade on Mars for what he
needed.''

"And could he?''

Michael shook his head. He had been standing; now he
folded his long body into a chair opposite the Skyrider and
looked past her, out the window at the stars. "We don't
have it, and we can't legally get it. It's *very* controlled.

What they've got on Newkansas is an outbreak of Bronson's disease.''

"Oh." There wasn't anything else to say. Bronson's had been one of the new diseases that developed along with space colonization, got carried back to Earth, and ravaged the population until a cure was finally found in the form of a new drug called oxyaminocilinase. Since the control of Bronson's disease was the only legitimate use for oxyaminocilinase, and since it was also, in combination with a common nonprescription cold medication, the most effective—and frequently fatal—means of getting intoxicated that the criminal community had ever discovered, the government had confiscated all supplies and managed with unprecedented and inexplicable success to keep its manufacture and distribution entirely in government hands.

Michael smiled distantly, still staring at the stars. "In this case, 'oh' seems like a fairly well educated response. You see what we're up against."

"Nobody ever managed to synthesize oxyaminoetcetera, or to duplicate it, or whatever you say about drugs?"

"No. I've talked to a couple of chemists since Cam came here, and they told me why not, but I didn't understand a word of it. Apparently it can't be done; that's the bottom line." He looked up as Jenna returned bearing a tray with coffee, cups, and an assortment of cookies.

"You'll have to get your own milk," she told Collis. "There wasn't room for it on the tray."

Michael cleared a space on a low table and she put the tray down and began pouring out coffee. Collis said, "Excuse me," very politely and squirmed out of Melacha's lap.

Melacha stared after him in astonishment and said, half-aloud, *"Milk?"*

He heard her and hesitated, looking back at her with a peculiar expression she didn't quite understand. "Cow's milk," he said. "It's pretty good." His tone was oddly diffident.

"Oh." She realized Michael and Jenna were watching her apprehensively. She stared at them helplessly, totally at a loss as to what was expected of her, and looked back at Collis. He was looking at his feet. His shoulders were just perceptibly hunched in a defensive posture that had the curiously opposite effect of making him look terribly vulnerable. She said again, with dawning awareness, "Oh. Oh, Collis. There's nothing wrong with learning to like new things when you live in a new place. I was just startled; you *know* we don't have milk, except that powdered junk people use for cooking, nobody drinks it, it tastes like chemicals. . . . It was a strange concept, that's all. I didn't mean there was anything *wrong* with it."

Michael and Jenna seemed to relax. Collis hesitated a moment longer, flashed Melacha a brief worried smile, and went on to get his milk. Melacha accepted a cup of coffee from Jenna in silence.

"He's been adjusting pretty well." Jenna's voice was hesitant, her smile sympathetic.

Melacha shook her head, staring at her coffee. "This isn't easy for either of us. Just seeing him like this, without Jamin . . ." She couldn't finish the sentence.

"He needs you," said Jenna.

"Hell. He needs his father." She shook her head. "I shouldn't have come."

"Jamin's dead. You both have to face that," said Michael.

"We don't have to wallow in it. We don't need our damn noses rubbed in it for chrissake. But that's what's happening. We remind each other. Just by existing. By seeing each other."

"You can help each other, too." Michael's voice was as sympathetic as Jenna's smile had been. It unnerved her.

He saw her distress, misunderstood its cause, and said gently, "We can talk about it later."

She didn't want to talk about it, ever. She looked at him, unaware that her expression was as arrogantly bland as Jamin's had ever been, and was saved from having to make any response by the return of Collis carrying a brimming glass of milk. He seemed to have forgotten the awkwardness that had accompanied his departure; he arrived grinning, put his milk down on the table very near the cookies, and asked with cheerful impishness if he could have one of each variety.

"There are too many kinds," said Jenna. "Have three, okay?"

"Only *three*?" Clearly he might starve to death on the spot if he were limited to only three.

"Three for now," said Jenna. "We'll discuss more when you've had three."

He looked at Melacha. "We'll discuss it means no," he explained seriously.

"Life's like that," she said. He took the largest cookie on the platter and settled contentedly to eat it. She looked at Jenna. "This is good coffee. Too bad you guys didn't have what your friend from Newkansas needed; this should've bought plenty of just about anything."

"Well, now he's rich; we paid well for it." Michael looked at her speculatively. "I don't suppose you're still in the smuggling business?"

She shrugged. "Maybe. Why?"

"Cam could pay for the drug."

"*If* I could get it. I do smuggle sometimes, but I seldom perform armed raids."

"Would you consider a little space piracy, if your 'victim' were willing?"

"What, you'd fake an outbreak of Bronson's disease on Mars? But then what would you need me for? You could just get the drug and hand it over to this Cam person without a middleman.''

"There are problems with that plan," said Michael. "One is that the Earthers will send armed guards and doctors with the drug. They really want to contain the disease as well as its cure, you know. And the other is that when we discover we were mistaken about the Bronson's, how do we explain that we misplaced the drug in the meantime?''

"They wouldn't like that." She met his gaze. "I don't think the armed guards and doctors would like being involved in the misplacing, either. Like I said, I don't do armed raids.''

"I was thinking of an inside job. Your temporary partner could take care of the armed guards, and all you'd have to do is convincingly threaten the doctors and crew, and transfer the cargo. The crew would go along with it.''

"And the doctors?''

He shrugged. "They're doctors.''

"What, you think all doctors are by their nature nonviolent? I could introduce you to a couple I met in the war.''

"What would *you* do about them?''

"Whatever you're doing about the guards, I suppose.''

"Good, that's settled, then.''

"What's settled?''

He wasn't as good as Ian Spencer at looking innocent, but he got the idea across. "You'll do it, won't you?''

"No.''

He stared. "Why not?''

"Do I look like the Red Cross or somebody?''

"You'll be *paid*!'' His voice was pained.

"For the job you describe, there isn't enough pay. It's too risky, inside man or no inside man. Besides, if we did pull it off, I'd have to share." She shook her head. "Nope. It's not my kind of work. Sorry.''

He sighed. "What do you want?"

"I'm not bargaining."

He put his coffee cup down too hard on the table, his wolfish warrior face dangerous. "I don't be*lieve* this!"

"Michael," said Jenna.

Collis looked confidently at the Skyrider and smiled. She winked at him. To Michael she said impatiently, "Let me think about it. You worry too much. Something will happen." She made a wry face. "Something always does."

CHAPTER SEVEN

Gustov Haioshi prided himself on being able to provide a wide range of products, legal, illegal, or quasilegal, that his customers might require. He could supply workers in any quantity for farms or factories; slaves of either sex for the pleasure domes of Earth or for the pleasure stations in space; exotic foodstuffs from pickled newts' toes to Spam, strawberries to starberries; drugs from penicillin to comet dust; jewels, silks, precious metals, and malite; real estate on Earth or in the colonies; fresh or salt water for Mars, and Martian sand for the riverbanks and seacoasts of Earth: in short, he could supply nearly anything to nearly anyone, and usually with very little lead time required. Nonetheless, the Skyrider's request momentarily baffled him.

She had come into his office unannounced, looking harried by what she would call the "rigors of Earth." He knew how she felt; when he had first moved to Earth, he had been as unnerved as anyone by all the little differences between the enclosed environments of the asteroid belt and the huge open spaces of Earth. Wind had felt like a breached chamber; rain made no sense at all and so was both alarming and oddly exciting; constant inescapable gravity had seemed exhausting; the sky had been a bottomless eternity into which the unwary might fall and go on falling forever. It had taken him months to adjust to those and all the other little things that felt so terminally *wrong* about Earth to one accustomed to the asteroid belt. It had taken him years to stop being constantly aware of the adjustment.

He had been a wild and reckless boy then, and quite possibly he had looked as much like a sullen young animal as the Skyrider did now. But now he was old and fat and sourly content with the illegal empire he had built for himself in a world that had never done him any favors.

It amused him to do occasional favors for others when he could. Not on a regular basis, and certainly not often enough that there was any danger of anyone coming to expect it of him. But the occasional favor pleased him, and he would have liked to do one for the Skyrider; she was one of his most valued customers. She wasn't, of course, asking for a favor. She was only asking for the impossible. He decided it would please him to provide it.

"The jewels and so forth," he told her, "will be no problem." He waved a pudgy arm negligently, dismissing jewels and so forth. "We can work out the details later, but I suppose you'll find we have everything you need of that kind in stock. Now, this oxyaminocilinase, though. That's not so simple." He scowled at her in an effort to express concern. "I suppose someone has Bronson's in the Belt?"

"Not in the Belt. One of the old space colonies: Newkansas." She had pushed a stack of papers off a battered leather chair to make a space for herself in his tiny cluttered office, and now she leaned back and put her feet on a crate of cheap porcelain figurines that supported one end of a dusty shelf crowded with computer terminals. "Earth says Newkansas doesn't exist, so of course they can't have any oxyaminoetcetera. And if they don't get it, after a while they *won't* exist. I said I'd see what I could do; they'll pay plenty.''

He nodded pensively, turning a pencil over and over between stubby perfumed fingers. ''I say the same: I'll see what I can do. In a way, you ask at an excellent time. I suppose you're aware of the President's illness; that's why you're cashing in your account?''

''I'm cashing it in because I lost it.'' She made a wry face. ''Another damnfool gamble by the overconfident Skyrider. Lost to an Earther, no less!''

''You bet an Earther your entire no-payback account?'' He patted his perspiring face with a perfumed handkerchief and brushed limp curls off his forehead. ''On what? And why didn't you just kill him? I suppose you thought it wouldn't be sporting?''

''Actually, that was the bet: that I couldn't kill him. In a firefight. My *Defiance* against an aging Patrol boat.'' She shook her head, looking sheepish. ''I don't know how in space he did it, but the lousy groundhog won.''

''I suppose you're sure it was a fair bet? I mean, he didn't trick you in any way?'' He tapped his pencil eraser on his desk top, watching her sternly.

''How could he? I was in the *Defiance*. I know her weapons system's okay, and I could see the lasers flare okay, *and* I ran a computer check to be sure, because every time the lasers faded he had dodged them just fine, and waggled his wings at me to show off.''

''I suppose he's a pretty good pilot,'' said Haioshi. ''But it's hard to imagine he could be that much better than you are.''

''He isn't. That's what bothers me. He was too damn slow.'' She shrugged. ''But I ran a check, and nothing showed. If he was slow, I must've been slower. I was cross and tired, I know that. Anyway, he did win. That's the important part. So he gave me a month to make any necessary last purchases, and that's what I'm doing. I bought a rock, first thing.''

Haioshi nodded abstractedly. "Who was he? What's his name?"

"Ian Spencer. Why?"

Haioshi scowled again, this time to indicate deep thought. "The name is not wholly unfamiliar. Ian Spencer." He turned his pencil over and tapped the lead on his desk top. "I'm sure I've heard of him somewhere."

"Doesn't matter. Listen, what's this about the President, though. She's ill? How bad is it?"

"Bad." Haioshi riffled through a stack of papers on his desk, didn't find what he wanted, and shoved them onto the floor. "I suppose somebody should clean this office," he said vaguely. Turning his chair, he punched a query into his computer, looked at the response, nodded, and turned back to the Skyrider. "She may not make it. We've got a political mess here; you know the Vice President isn't worth rockdust." He flipped his pencil between his fingers impatiently.

"I know. He seems to be all show, no tell. I guess they elected him for show. And he does make a good impression on state occasions where he doesn't have to do anything but smile and shake hands. In fact I understand he's under strict instructions never to open his mouth in case something ridiculous comes out. Given that, who'll succeed the President if she doesn't make it?"

The computer beeped at Haioshi and he glanced at the screen. "Nope. I thought I had your Spencer tagged, but that's not him. Give me time to think about it, though; I'll remember. Nobody knows who'll succeed the President. Not for sure. The Board is planning a special election."

"Any favorites?"

Haioshi's florid face took on a lugubrious expression. "One. Stephen B. Newcomb. I suppose you've heard of him."

She stared. "You're joking!" Every colonist who ever saw a newsfax was familiar with Stephen B. Newcomb: he was probably the most rabid antiColonial Earth politics had yet turned out. His general idea seemed to be that Earth should cut off all commerce with the colonies and, where possible, exterminate all colonists. He had been publicly and loudly at odds with the President for allowing the Brief War to conclude without at least attempting to destroy a few of the major inhabited asteroids, and perhaps Mars and Luna as well. His most famous statement was: "Colonies? I say nuke 'em."

Haioshi nodded. "Old Nuke 'em B. Newcomb. Looks like he'll get it, too." He tapped the pencil against his teeth, studying a chart on the wall above his desk.

"Are they insane?"

"Quite possibly." He nodded at the chart for a moment, suddenly looked alert, turned his chair, and punched a query into the computer. It beeped. He punched in a command. It beeped. He turned away. "I think I've got it." Looking smug, he turned the pencil over and over in one hand.

"Got what?" She didn't know whether to be pleased or alarmed. Haioshi's quick mind could work on half a dozen projects at once, and as often as not he would arrive at a brilliant solution to one problem while he seemed completely absorbed by another. When he made an ambiguous statement one had to ask what the topic was; there was no way of guessing.

"Your oxyaminocilinase. The thing about political turmoil is that it gets a lot easier to break the law when nobody is sure who's in charge, or what exactly the law *is* right now. I think I've found the woman who can get it for us."

The computer beeped again, signaling a Comm Link connection, and he swiveled his chair to answer it. The screen remained dark and he pulled out a sound baffle so Melacha couldn't hear what was said at either end, so she relaxed in her chair and closed her eyes.

Michael and Jenna had probably been right; she and Collis needed each other. But it wasn't easy. Apart, they had each achieved a reasonable adjustment to Jamin's death. Together they hadn't. They inadvertently reminded each other at every turn, because he wasn't with them. Where he had always been. Where he should be. There was an empty place between them, and try as they might, they had not been able to ignore it. Even time couldn't fill it. The best they could hope for was to learn not to mind.

But not yet. It was too soon. Right now they both needed to return to their solitary adjustments; neither felt his absence as deeply when not with the other. Perhaps later, when their adjustments were sturdier. . . . Now they were made of rubber bands and sealing wax, and couldn't stand up to any strain at all.

"That's it," said Haioshi. "She'll do it."

Melacha opened her eyes. He had put the sound baffle away and turned away from the computer. His little eyes danced with pleasure, and he grinned as he patted perspiration from his face again. "I suppose you wonder what I'm doing."

She smiled. "I suppose you won't tell me."

That pleased him. "You always ruin my fun; here I am being deliberately secretive, and you're not even curious." He smiled at her delightedly.

"My curiosity was shot off in the war."

"Don't talk like that." He shook his head, scowling again, though whether in sympathy or in disapproval she couldn't tell. "I suppose it was a joke?"

"So what, I'm not supposed to joke about the war?"

The scowl disappeared as he examined a chart on the wall, then suddenly lifted a book off a shelf and riffled its pages. "It's all right with me to joke about the war. It's not all right with me to sound embittered, by the war or by anything else. You are too young to be embittered, my child." He made a note of something with his much-handled pencil and put the book away. "But I suppose my kindly grandfather act doesn't carry much weight with you."

She shrugged. "So did you get a line on the oxya-minoetcetera, or what?"

"A line! A line!" He rolled his eyes in mock disgust and pinched his lips together, tossing his pencil aside. Then, catching sight of an invoice still pasted to the side of a crate, he leaned forward to pull it off and examine it. "Not just a line, my child, I got the drug. I suppose I shouldn't say that till it's actually in one of my warehouses, but it's as good as there. I can't tell you who did what to whom to get it, but I can tell you that with a modicum of luck and skill we will, my silent partner in this venture and I, manage to bury the transfer so effectively that no one will ever know it left the government's warehouse. In fact, no one will know it ever existed."

He picked up the pencil, made a note on the side of the invoice, folded it up again, and tried to stick it back on the box, but the glue was no longer tacky and he had to settle for stuffing it into a cubbyhole on his desk. "Ian Spencer," he muttered. "Ian Spencer." He looked up at the Skyrider and smiled, suddenly and with evident delight. "Now, about those jewels. Diamonds, I think you said, but those are junk, worthless; what you want is rubies, opals, emeralds, sapphires, and I suppose you should have some, oh, a little of everything, yes? I have a good stock of everything. Precious metals, too. I suppose you wouldn't want some nice silks? I have some silks coming in later. They do well in the asteroid belt. And will you want any foodstuffs, or only durable goods? Oh, my, this *is* fun, isn't it?"

CHAPTER EIGHT

The passenger liner *Westlake* lunged up out of Earth's atmosphere with a shattering moan and thunder that shook the land below. She trailed a raging flame bright as a miniature sun that reflected orange and gold and brilliant yellow on her dazzling white hull. When she was clear of the last thin veil of atmosphere the flame dimmed, then blinked out. Two pinpricks of fire glowed for a fraction of a second as the first fuel pod was jettisoned. It tumbled away from her, caught in a low Earth orbit that wouldn't decay enough to drag it back down into the atmosphere for years. *Westlake* floated serenely on out toward Luna. She wouldn't fire her next fuel pod till she was halfway there.

The Diademan scavenger ship *Jewel* caught sight of the jettisoned fuel pod in her scanners and swooped down on it like a bird of prey; it would contain not only metals but traces of malite and possibly even some undamaged electronics that would prove useful. With abandoned space stations blockaded, not even fuel pods were beneath Diademan attention.

Nor were they beneath the attention of the Patrol. Unnoticed by the Diademans, a squadron of Earth Patrol boats had followed *Westlake* up out of atmosphere in time to see *Jewel* match speed with her discarded fuel pod. They changed course with one motion and circled *Jewel* like a school of hungry sharks.

Abraham Melville, *Jewel*'s captain, was a man in his middle forties who had never in his adult life encountered any situation that he felt could be improved by violence, and this was no exception. He was a short, broad man with a normally cheerful round face made cheerier still by the affectation of a long bushy carrot-colored moustache. Clothing styles were very much a matter of personal taste on Diadem, and Captain Melville had unique tastes: he wore the basic jumpsuit popular for leisure and labor both, but his was an unusual color—very like a carrot, matching his hair—and it was adorned with decorative patches in bright colors and odd locations, as well as mint-green piping that matched his mint-green jacket-length cape.

Now, looking into the scanner screen at the circling Patrol boats, he threw back the cape in a consciously theatrical gesture and straightened abruptly to face his crew. "We'll surrender, of course," he said calmly. His voice was deep and rasping, a surprising contrast to his almost comical appearance.

The crew, consisting of a navigator, a pilot, and two cargo experts, were considerably less comical-seeming than their captain. The navigator was a young man who looked like Central Casting's idea of a criminal mastermind: dark and sinister with a scar near one eye (the result of a childhood accident with a tricycle in low gravity). He frowned at Captain Melville and said nothing.

The pilot was an old man with a bushy white beard and thick white eyebrows who did his best to dress like a Wild West cowboy, complete with ten-gallon hat and awkwardly high-heeled, hand-tooled, fake-leather boots. He frowned at the scanner screens and said nothing.

The cargo experts were identical twins: tall, sturdy women with patrician faces and well-tended, muscular bodies. They wore standard jumpsuits without frills, and sensible hair styles. They frowned at each other and said nothing.

"Even if we were armed for battle," said Captain Melville, "I wouldn't want to fight a whole squadron of Patrol boats."

"I wouldn't want to fight *one*," said the navigator. His voice was as sinister as his face.

"Nor I," said the twins.

Everyone looked at the pilot, who turned reluctantly from the scanner screen to face them. "There's no telling what they'll do with prisoners." His voice was reedy and thin. "Maybe we should try to get a message home before we surrender."

"Do it," said Captain Melville.

Simon Hale was at lunch with Linda March when the message reached him. One of his assistants brought it to him in person; he had told her where he would be and that it would be fine to interrupt him with any news the services wanted him to write up for public consumption. It would, he had thought, be too bad to have his lunch with Linda interrupted; but it would be impressive to her if it happened. He didn't consciously think that it would make him look important, but that was what he felt.

It had even occurred to him as a positive factor that the assistant who would deliver such a message was a young woman possibly even more beautiful than Linda. Not that he seriously hoped Linda would be jealous; in fact, jealousy was a childish emotion that he would be very sorry to think Linda insecure enough to experience. Still it could do no harm to let her see, to in a sense remind her, that competition for his attentions did exist.

The assistant could be relied upon to make the point clear. It had recently come to Hale's attention that she was seriously interested in him as a potential mate. His other assistants had noticed long before he had; she wasn't shy about letting it show. She wanted him, and everyone else, to know that she wanted him. A healthy attitude. He approved entirely. In fact he approved of nearly everything about Celia Graham. She was beautiful, healthy, reasonably intelligent, well-adjusted, and had an excellent genetic background. Healthy teeth, too. Teeth were important; one wanted one's children to have sound teeth. He dismissed that thought with such guilty haste that he was hardly aware of it.

Celia Graham displayed many of her healthy teeth in her greeting smile as she approached their table. She was dressed very tastefully in a light brown jumpsuit with darker brown piping and a dark wide-collared shirt underneath, the full sleeves and open collar showing. Her hair was pulled back in a French twist, very dignified for the office, with wisps of soft curls framing her face and keeping the style from looking too severe. She wore tastefully expensive pearl earrings and a single pearl on a chain around her neck, visible through the open collar.

"Dr. Hale," she said, still smiling a broad but enchanting smile. "I'm glad I caught you; this just came in." She looked at Linda March as she handed Hale a sheet of printout. "Sorry to interrupt your lunch, Dr. March, but this really is terribly important." Hale didn't notice the predatory gleam in Graham's eyes when she looked from March to him; he was busy reading the printout.

"Oh, damn." Conscious that his tone sounded just faintly contrived, and aware that the message he held was more worthy of sincere curses than he had expected when he accepted it from Graham, he looked up at March and cleared his throat. "I'm afraid I'll have to leave you," he said, and was pleased to hear a more satisfactory note of concern in his voice. "This really is serious." He suddenly realized that it really *was* serious; and, staring down at the printout in his hands, felt his expression stiffen. "Oh, Lord."

"What is it?" asked March, looking from his stricken face to Graham's vicious smile and back again. "What's happened?"

Hale looked at her and absentmindedly pushed his tousled red hair back from a forehead on which the freckles stood out like paint splatters against suddenly pale, almost translucent skin. "*Jewel* was caught salvaging a liner's fuel pod. She'd been confiscated, her crew imprisoned. On Earth."

"But . . . won't they just have to pay a fine, or something? Surely we can come up with the fine, whatever it is. Everyone will want to help."

Graham's smile became condescending. "If we existed, Dr. March, I'm sure that's what we would be expected to do. But as you'll remember, Earth doesn't recognize our existence."

"But surely, in a matter like this . . . ?" She stared from Graham's hypnotic smile to Hale's harried frown. "Simon?"

He shook his head. His color was coming back, but his frown was deepening. "I'm afraid the situation doesn't make any difference to Terrans, Linda. Legally, we don't exist, and as far as they are concerned, that's final. We'll try to get *Jewel*'s crew back, of course, but . . . it's not going to be a simple matter of paying a fine."

"The Terrans may not even admit they have *Jewel*'s crew," said Graham, "if they know *Jewel* is our ship." She relinquished the smile at last, exchanging it for a look of extreme seriousness and sympathy, which she directed at Simon Hale with the force and precision of a laser beam. "I knew you'd want to know who the crewmembers were, Dr. Hale. I have the list here." She referred to a paper taken from a tastefully disguised pocket in her jumpsuit. "Captain Abraham Melville commanding. Navigator Bill Hardy. Pilot Gus Kerstan. Two cargo experts:

the Sjdwrdjenski twins Najda and Talia.'' Looking up from her paper, she flashed her smile briefly and looked serious again. ''You'll want to put that in your news report. I've put a copy on your desk.''

''Thank you, Celia,'' said Hale. He looked distrait. ''Perhaps I'd better volunteer to be in charge of negotiations. I may be best qualified for the job.''

Graham exhibited concern. ''Are you sure you want to, Dr. Hale? If the negotiations fail . . .''

He nodded. ''It could have serious repercussions for my career, I know. But I think I'll have to take the chance. I want those people safely returned to Diadem.''

''We all want that, Dr. Hale.'' Graham neither looked nor sounded as though her desire for their safe return were any stronger than her desire for a good cup of coffee with dinner. Hale didn't notice; he was reading his printout again. ''You'll want to come back to your office now, of course,'' said Graham.

He nodded abstractedly. ''Yes, of course.'' He looked at March, and there was real worry in his eyes. He had forgotten how important he wanted to look in her eyes; the stress of actually being important had wiped it from his mind. ''I'll have to go, Linda. I'm sorry.'' He rose, absently folding the printout into a small square which he put in the back pocket of the dignified blue jeans he always wore to the office. ''I'll call you.''

March nodded, watching him. ''You'll let me know what happens?''

''Of course.'' He looked without seeing it at the half-eaten lunch he was deserting. ''If anything does happen.''

'' 'Something will happen,' '' Graham quoted encouragingly.

March looked at her in disbelief. Hale, however, looked grateful. ''Thank you, Celia. However, we must also remember: 'Things happen; people act.' ''

" 'What happens to us may be God's choice,' " Graham quoted piously. " 'But what we do about it is our choice.' "

March was tempted to join the quoting session with her personal favorite from *The Way of Life According to Bill*: "Some people get too intent on movement because they mistake it for positive action," but she decided they were doing just fine without her.

Hale produced yet another confident smile for yet another face on the Comm Link screen. "Inspector Dobzhansky, please."

The face looked back at him without interest. It belonged to a woman who had never been beautiful and who was, in her declining years, no longer even remotely attractive. Her eyes looked like the bulging black eyes of a fish. "Who shall I say is calling, please." Her voice was nasal and bored.

"Dr. Simon Hale, of Diadem, calling in regard to the Diademan ship *Jewel* which was recently confisca—"

"I'm sorry, sir." She didn't sound sorry. "I have no record of any city, country, or colony named Diadem. Please clarify."

"We're a space colony," Hale said wearily. "A manmade space colony. Built in the early—"

"I'm sorry, sir." She sounded smug. "I have no record of a space colony named Diadem. Please clarify."

Hale drew in his breath and let it out again slowly. "Could you please tell Inspector Dobzhansky that Dr. Simon Hale wishes to speak with him regarding the matter of the space cruiser *Jewel*, which was—"

"What was that name again?" She was flipping through a stack of computer printouts just visible in the lower right corner of the screen. "*Jewel*?"

"That's right," said Hale.

She nodded and turned her fish eyes back to his face. Her lank hair fell across one eye and she made no move to push it away. It was dark, streaked with coarse gray. "Fine. Continue."

"We received a message that—"

"Who is 'we,' please, sir?"

Hale drew in his breath again and closed his eyes briefly. "I," he said with infinite patience. "*I* received a message stating the *Jewel* had been apprehended during a salvage operation—"

"Salvaging what, sir?" Her tone this time was primly disapproving, but still not very interested.

"A fuel pod. They were salvaging a fuel pod. From a passenger liner."

"Pursuant to section ten, subchapter B—"

"We're aware that the salvage operation was illegal."

"Who is 'we,' please, sir?"

"I," said Hale. "I am aware—"

"Then you know that any ship apprehended in such an operation will have been confiscated, its crew incarcerated pending trial," she said. "Please check with the court clerk for the date of the trial. If you have any further questions—"

"There *is* no scheduled trial!" Hale's voice was less than patient, and the woman lifted her fishy gaze to him in distaste. He forced himself to continue on a more even note. "That's why I'd like to speak with Inspector Dobzhansky, please. I was told he might be able to help us—me."

"What is the nature of your request, please, sir?"

"May I speak with Inspector Dobzhansky?"

"On what subject, please, sir?" she asked with exaggerated patience.

"On the subject of the cruiser *Jewel* and her crew."

"I'm sorry, sir, but I'm checking my records right now, and I find no reference to any cruiser *Jewel* or crew. Are you quite certain she was apprehended in the commission of a crime? Perhaps you should check with Registration."

"She was apprehended in the commission of a crime," Hale said firmly. "I've already spoken with Registration. They can't help me. Nor can the Department of Space Vehicles, nor the Colony Court system, nor the Court of Space-Related Crimes. I've even talked with Import-Export and the Treasury Department. Treasury directed me to Inspector Dobzhansky."

"If this cruiser *Jewel* had been apprehended during the commission of a crime," she said, "I would have a record of it."

"Do you have a record of *any* cruisers apprehended during the last twenty-four hours?"

"During the commission of a crime?"

"*Yes*, during the commission of a crime!"

"There's no need to take that tone with me, sir."

"I'm sorry." He shook his head. "I am sorry. I didn't mean to raise my voice. This has been a very trying afternoon for me. Look . . . *do* you have a record of any cruisers apprehended, during the commission of a crime, in the last twenty-four hours?"

She studied him for a long moment, her fishy eyes gleaming with malice. "I'm sorry, sir, I have no record of any such apprehension, at this time."

"Not within the last twenty-four hours. Not *any* cruiser."

"Not at this time, sir."

He allowed himself a shallow, almost inaudible sigh. "Then may I just speak to Inspector Dobzhansky, please?"

"Who shall I say is calling, sir?"

"Dr. Simon Hale. I'm still Dr. Simon Hale." He was unable to keep the irritation from his voice; he had been through this conversation, with minor variations, more times during the last few hours than he wanted to think about, and it was obvious that this one wasn't going to reach any better conclusion than any of the others had. But he had to try. Somehow he had to get through to somebody.

"Dr. Simon Hale," said Fish-Eyes, making a note on

the corner of her computer printout sheets. "And your place of residence, Dr. Hale?"

"Is that necessary?"

"It's essential, sir. Inspector Dobzhansky will need to know the area of jurisdiction."

"Diadem," Hale said wearily.

"I beg your pardon, sir?"

"Diadem. My place of residence is the space colony Diadem."

"I'm sorry, sir, but I have no record of such a colony."

"Do I have to specify the colony? Couldn't you just tell him I'm a colonist?"

"Hardly, sir." She gazed at him suspiciously.

He had a sudden inspiration. "Tell him I'm from Vermont." It was the name of the Diademan city in which he lived.

Fish-Eyes made another note on her computer printouts. "Vermont is not a colony, sir."

Hale kept his gaze steady on hers. "It is my place of residence," he said firmly.

"Very well, sir. You did say you were a colonist. However. Vermont." She appeared to give the matter consideration. "And what was the subject of your call, sir?"

"An apprehended, I mean a missing space cruiser."

"From what port of call?"

"From a colony."

She eyed him suspiciously. "I will have to know from which colony, sir."

"Vermont."

She blinked. "Vermont is not a colony. Also, it has no space ports." She looked pleased. "There are no ships registered out of Vermont."

Hale sighed. The other two Diademan cities were named Monterey and Adair; also not spaceports. "She's registered out of Diadem," he said, defeated.

There wasn't even a note of triumph in her voice as she repeated nasally, "I have no record of any city, country, or colony named Diadem." She gazed at him, her fish eyes implacably bored. "Do you wish anything further, sir?"

"No," said Hale. "No, thank you. Nothing further." He cut the connection and slumped back in his chair.

CHAPTER NINE

"*Damn* them!" JanMikal didn't raise his voice, and he didn't throw or hit anything. In a way, that made his rage all the more unnerving. He stood quite still in the center of the room with his back to March, and although he was as tense as she had ever seen him, he didn't even clench his fists. Simon Hale in the same situation would have been pacing the floor, shouting, waving clenched fists, and quite possibly throwing things, she thought. He said he regarded it a healthy practice to express one's anger.

"They're frightened, JanMikal." Her own voice was not as steady as his. "They don't want to hurt you, but they do want to protect their children."

"Have I done their children harm?" His voice was as taut as his body.

"I don't think so."

"Then what are they protecting them *from*?" He turned pain-blinded eyes to her. "I was happy with them; I was doing something useful; I'd found a place where I fit, where I could belong."

In the window behind JanMikal a hang glider was visible in the near distance, sailing peacefully across the Hub on magenta wings. "I am sorry," she said gently. "I'm so sorry, JanMikal. I thought so, too."

He turned away. "If I have a right to do whatever I want to do, why can't I go on teaching those kids, regardless of what their parents want?"

"You have that right," said March. "But they have the right to withdraw their children from your class. You can't teach children who aren't there."

"They won't stop them from going to the pool at all, will they?"

"They might, until *you* stop going to the pool. They won't resort to violence, if that's what you're thinking. That's their biggest complaint against you; that the boys are becoming violently competitive. Competition and violence are both traits we avoid as much as we can. They do happen. But we find that cooperation usually works better."

"Is it my fault if the boys become competitive? It's natural for them to compete. Isn't it?"

"Perhaps." She had been standing as still as he, several feet behind him, in the position in which she had stopped when they came in the door from the PTA meeting and JanMikal had begun his rebellious cursing; now she moved to one side, watching him, and sat on the edge of a chair facing him. "But nobody cares whose fault a thing is, JanMikal. The fact is, it's happening, and they want to stop it."

"Yeah. By blaming me."

" 'Blame is something many people do when they could be solving a problem.' They don't *blame* you; they just feel they can solve the problem by removing you from the boys' lives."

"But I don't *want* to be removed from their lives. Damn it, I was *good* for them."

She nodded. "In many ways, I think you were. But you know how nervous you make Diademan adults, and you know that people are much more defensive for their children than for themselves. The adults will tolerate you with adults; but they simply will not trust you with their children.''

"It's not fair.''

"Now you're being childish. Life isn't fair.''

"I know. Damn it, I just don't want to lose those boys.''

"But you're in conflict with their parents. To stay with the boys, you must continue and increase the conflict. And because the boys *do* like you, you'll be creating a conflict in *their* lives. In effect, you'll be asking them to choose between you and their parents. Never mind which way they would choose; the choice itself would be a terrible stress. Is that what you want?''

He was silent for a long moment. "I feel like I'd be deserting them if I quit.''

" 'Change is the only constant.' One thing Diademan children are used to is change. They can manage.''

"I wish you wouldn't quote that space-damned book at me.'' He sat down suddenly and buried his face in his hands. "I'm sorry, Linda. I didn't mean that.''

"I expect you did,'' she said mildly. "We all tend to quote *The Way* a little too often. It annoys me, too, when I hear others doing it.''

"I don't know why it *matters* so much!'' His voice was anguished.

"What, quoting *The Way*?''

"No, losing those boys. They aren't mine. I hadn't been with them all that long. I enjoyed the class, but there must be something else I can do. So why do I feel like if I lose them I'll be losing an essential part of myself?''

She hesitated. "Maybe you had children in your life before. Outside.''

He stared: the thought had obviously not occurred to him. "A boy.'' His eyes went blind again, deep brilliant blind blue like the beautiful cold heart of an iceberg. "My son . . ." His voice trailed away. He was banging up against the blank wall of his past again, battering himself against it like a trapped animal against the bars of its cage. "*Collis!*" It was barely more than a whisper, but it had the quality of a shout. The face he lifted to her was translucent, the eyes wide and staring, with dark smudges like bruises beneath them and a sheen of sweat or tears on his cheeks. "That's his name. Collis. I remembered."

March was silent, watching him.

"My son." He tasted the words in wonder, trying them out, listening to the sound of his past. "My son Collis." And then the wonder died. He stood up so suddenly that in the low gravity his feet left the floor for an unexpected moment, for which he compensated without even noticing in his sudden rage. "And he may be six or sixteen. For all I know he may be *dead*. I don't know a damn thing about him, where he is, who he is, whether we even knew each other. Nothing."

March rose instinctively but forced herself not to touch him and not to speak.

"What if we lived together? My God, what if I'm married? If I have a son . . . he must have a mother. . . . And I don't even remember her." He looked at March, new horrors clouding his startled eyes. "They must think I'm dead. They must . . ."

He blinked. His face twisted. "Maybe they're right. That me is dead. I don't remember, I don't remember anything."

"You remember his name." She kept her voice steady with an effort. "More may come back to you. Give yourself time. It's a breakthrough, JanMikal, that you remembered his name."

But he shook his head in sudden irritation and the light of memory was gone from his eyes. "No. I thought I did, but . . . No. It's just a name. Collis." He was trying it again, and this time it meant nothing at all. "It doesn't even sound familiar." He walked abruptly away from her to stare out the window. "I could have made it up because I wanted to remember. I don't know. It doesn't mean anything."

She followed him, wanting to comfort him and not knowing how. "I don't think you made it up."

"It doesn't matter." Another hang glider floated past on iridescent wings. "Thank you, Linda. I know you're trying to help." The hang glider sailed out of sight and he sighed. "Well." He squared his shoulders. "Now what? Looks like I'm unemployed again. Any ideas?" When she didn't respond, he managed a broken laugh. "There's not much demand for a warrior anywhere in a time of peace. I checked, by the way: the Patrol won't accept me, and neither will any other branch of military service. They're Earth-based. Freefall mutants need not apply."

"We'll think of something, JanMikal."

He sighed again. "I don't even know if I'm a good pilot. I believe I am, but I don't know why I believe it. I don't *know*. . . . I guess I could try it anyway, though. It's one thing I haven't asked about—working as a salvage pilot. You think I'm well enough?"

"Physically you're as healthy as you ever were. But salvage is illegal now. You heard Simon—and the newsfax—about *Jewel*. We can't even find out where she is or whether her crew is still alive. You don't have a ship of your own anymore, and I don't expect any of ours will be going out again anytime soon; nobody wants to take the chance of losing another." At his look of resignation she added dubiously, "But if you want to ask . . . It couldn't hurt, could it?"

Davitz looked out his office window at the peaceful Diademan farmland beyond. He was disconcertingly aware of JanMikal's presence like a half-tamed animal in the

chair by his desk. The boy was clearly not comfortable in
Diadem's gravity. Worse, he was not comfortable in Diadem's society. Davitz had heard much about JanMikal
since he came to Diadem, but this was the first time he had
met him, and he was disturbed to see how evident it was to
the casual observer that the boy was out of place. However
one tried to ignore his unnerving explosive potential and
treat him like any Diademan boy his age, he *wasn't* any
Diademan boy his age. He was an alien. A warrior. In all
probability a killer of men. He seemed mild enough, but
there was something in the abruptness of his occasional
gestures that reminded one of violence, of violent energy
barely contained.

Watching him, Davitz felt suddenly old. "I'd like to
help you, JanMikal." It was true; he wanted to help this
unfortunate boy whose only real crime was that he had
been born Outside and raised ignorant of *The Way*. "Lord
knows we need the materials you might scavenge. But you
must see I can't risk another ship now." He looked at
JanMikal, trying to communicate some of his own hard-
won patience in the look. "Earth will tire of this new law.
Even they don't have unlimited resources. Eventually they
will realize they cannot afford to waste the malite and the
man-hours they are spending now to enforce it. They will
rescind it, or at least stop enforcing it. That will be the
time for us to go out again. Not now."

"And now?" JanMikal's voice was as gentle as his
smile. Strange that a killer of men could look so essentially innocent. "How do we get along without the supplies we need now?"

"We will manage," said Davitz. A shaft of sunlight
that had been glistening on the edge of the windowsill
spilled over onto the carpet, dappled by leaf shadows from
the trees that grew in a neat row beside the building. "We
do not actually need anything right now except carbon wastes,
which we would not get in much quantity from fuel pods

anyway, and surely you are not suggesting going after space stations. They are much too heavily guarded."

JanMikal shifted uneasily in his chair. His physical pain was an almost palpable presence in the room. "You'd get carbon wastes from a Lunar garbage drone, wouldn't you?"

"Probably." Davitz sighed heavily. He was only sixty-two years old and in excellent health, but something about JanMikal's fierce impatience, unexpressed but impossible to ignore, wore him down like an old man tired by children's games. There was a ferocious exuberance in everything the boy did; even in the fire and ice of his arrogant blue eyes.

"A Lunar garbage drone was sighted a few hours ago on its way to the sun," said JanMikal. "One of the scout pilots told Dr. March I could go after it. All I'd need is a one-man tug shuttle, sir. I could bring that drone back."

"You could get yourself on the list of people Dr. Hale is trying to recover," said Davitz. "And my tug shuttle on the list of lost resources we cannot recover."

" 'Gambling is a suicidal impulse. But so is refusing to take any risks.' " It was a quote from *The Way*.

Davitz eyed him with a new respect. "You have been doing your homework."

JanMikal shrugged. His eyes were frosted blue mirrors. "It's a good book. Do I get the shuttle?"

Davitz lifted an eyebrow. "I am impressed that you can quote from *The Way*, but I do not quite see why that should change my mind about the shuttle."

JanMikal smiled, more with his changeable eyes than with his mouth. "It wasn't the fact that I could quote from *The Way* that I hoped might convince you; it was the quote itself."

"Bill did not mean that it was suicidal not to take every risk that came along."

"This isn't every risk that comes along." JanMikal

leaned forward, compelling in his urgency. "Davitz, I can get that drone."

"Maybe."

He shook his head abruptly, impatiently. "Not maybe. I can get it. I know it. I feel it. I'm good at what I do, Davitz. And somehow . . ." The blue eyes clouded briefly, blinked, and looked back at Davitz with the same startling intensity as before. "Somehow, that is what I do. Not scavenging, exactly, but . . . something like it. I know that. I'm sure of it." He hesitated, those fierce eyes searching the older man's face. "I'm a good pilot. It's the only piece of my past I have left. And . . . I need to do something. For Diadem. For my life. I owe. I'd like a chance to repay."

Davitz nodded slowly. "I can understand that." It wasn't that JanMikal wasn't sensitive enough to see the risk. It was that he honestly felt unquestionably able to bring the tug shuttle back with a garbage drone in tow. He knew he would be going essentially unarmed against an unknown number of Patrol boats, in a slow tug never meant for firefights. It wasn't ignorance. It might be overconfidence, but was that such a bad thing? And was a tug shuttle so much to risk, against a man's self-respect? Even an alien had a right to self-respect. Davitz nodded again. "You shall have your shuttle, boy. Bring her back safely."

CHAPTER TEN

Defiance was fully loaded. Legal luxury items filled the standard hold compartments; and illegal items, including a good supply of oxyaminocilinase, filled the concealed hold. Melacha felt more like a merchant than like an outlaw queen. Jamin would have laughed at her for hauling such a load.

Change the subject.

Good old Haioshi had certainly come through for her this time. He seemed to enjoy her spending spree as much as she did. Of course he was making a tidy profit. But his enjoyment was more than that. He had got as caught up in the game as she was, choosing her cargo with as much excitement as if it were to be his own hoard. She was going to have to make another Earth run to collect the rest of the things he thought she couldn't do without. Those silks, for instance. They had been his idea originally, but now she was determined to have them.

He still had not been able to find any information on Ian Spencer. She smiled absently to herself, remembering Spencer's absurdly boyish face grinning at her in triumph. Haioshi was suspicious of him, but although Melacha couldn't quite see how he had managed to win their one-sided firefight, she also couldn't see how there could have been any trickery involved. It wasn't as if she had been in an unfamiliar shuttle. There had been a little of the feel of a hustle in the whole interaction, but it must have been only because he was a better pilot than he seemed, or indeed than seemed possible. If she had been in any other shuttle she would have suspected the weapons system. Even in *Defiance* she had checked it twice. There had been nothing wrong with it. She just hadn't been able to hit him.

Okay, but how had he known she wouldn't be able to hit him? How could he have been sure enough to bet his life on it? —The scanner signaled and she looked at the screen: Patrol boats. Looked like a whole squadron of them. But they weren't after her. They hadn't even noticed her. They were closing in on a little scavenger tug that was grappling with a huge garbage drone bearing Lunar registration marks. The tug's registration marks were meaningless to her: not Luna, not Mars, not anywhere she recognized.

The tug's pilot had been so involved in his salvage operation that he must not have noticed the Patrol till after she did. She wondered whether he had any weapons. Or would he just politely surrender? If he was an Earther, he would surrender. Maybe if he was an Earther he wasn't doing anything illegal; Earthers were probably permitted to salvage whatever they wanted to. Then again, why would an Earther want to salvage anything? They *had* everything.

He wasn't going to politely surrender, whoever he was. He had released his drone and turned his tail to it, like a cornered animal, sizing up his adversaries. Curious, she switched on the Comm Link to see what they would say.

The Patrol made the usual bossy admonishments. The stranger didn't respond on the Link. He was keeping his tail to the big garbage drone with expert little jockey maneuvers, and one of his grappling arms was working again. It reached surreptitiously behind him and hooked huge clawed fingers onto the drone, stabilizing the little tug against it. He probably needed a better grip than that to tow it, but that was enough to provide a very satisfactory aft shield. Interested, Melacha let *Defiance* drift nearer the scene. The Patrol boats hadn't noticed her yet.

The tug couldn't maneuver anymore, hooked to the big drone. If he was going to resist arrest, how was he going to fight off six Patrol boats with only an aft shield and no weapons that she could see? The Patrol warnings on the Comm Link were getting serious. Melacha edged closer.

Another of the tug's grappling arms began to move. The Patrol were neatly arrayed in a circle around him, and they could see the arms as well as she could. One of them told him not to deploy it. Nothing happened. The arm didn't even hesitate. And suddenly she realized what he was trying to do: the drone had fuel pods it hadn't yet fired. If he could detach them without disturbing the firing mechanisms, he could conceivably make some sort of weapon out of them. But what was he going to do, *throw* them at the Patrol?

Well, it wasn't her problem. Whoever the little guy was, he wasn't a Belter. Even if he had been, it wasn't her job to rescue every Belter who resisted arrest when he was caught breaking Earth's absurd laws. It was none of her business if that little tug's pilot wanted to suicide over a garbage drone.

He *was* going to throw the fuel pods at the Patrol! He had one loose, and it had fired while the grappling arm still held it. He couldn't draw it back and throw it like a man with a ball in his hand, but somehow he was holding against its thrust while he used the tug's powerful little engines to edge around till the pod was aimed at one of the Patrol boats. The Patrol was, predictably, still issuing instructions. Either they didn't see what he was doing, or they were waiting till the last moment to destroy him.

They hadn't realized what he was doing. They saw it when he released the pod, but that was too late to prevent its collision with the target boat. By then they were all firing on the tug. *Defiance* swooped forward almost without instructions from Melacha. She expected to find herself defending a charred wreck. But the tug's pilot wasn't quite as suicidal as he looked: in the instant that he released the pod, he must have hit his jockey thrusters for all they were worth, and even with the garbage drone in tow it had been enough to pull him out of the line of fire. The drone had taken the lasers instead of the tug.

He was already working on a second pod. But that trick wouldn't work again. He was crazy if he thought it would. It hadn't really worked the first time; the Patrol boat was hit, but it wasn't disabled, and the Patrolman inside was obviously angry. He was crowding down the tug's throat; so close he was in the way so the other boats couldn't fire. But there was no way he was going to miss the tug, even without the others' help.

Unless the Skyrider hit him first. Which she did. Maybe it wasn't any of her business, but she admired that tug pilot's nerve. And his skill. It would be a shame to see the Patrol wipe him out after he'd made such an ingenious effort to stop them.

If the Patrol were startled to find themselves fighting more than a defenseless tug, they didn't show it. The remaining five swung smoothly around to fire on the Skyrider so promptly that one of them caught her and burned out her starboard shield. She skimmed on past them, playing tag, and caught the one who had burned her. Her aim was better than his had been. She didn't kill him, but she disabled the boat, and that was two out of the running. Four to go.

The Patrol had apparently decided the tug could wait till they had taken care of the Skyrider. She wouldn't have blamed the tug if he had taken the opportunity to run, but he didn't. He took careful aim and hurled another of the drone's fuel pods. It hit the nearest Patrol boat full force and tried to go right through it. Three to go.

That made them nervous. Two of them kept after the Skyrider while the third turned back for the tug. The Skyrider leapfrogged back to the tug and flipped end for end when she got there, riding inertia while she kept that Patrol boat on her laser screens. It took two shots, and while she was at it one of the others got in a shot that damaged her port shield. When she had taken care of the one that was after the tug, she jockeyed after the one that had damaged her shield.

But the Patrol had suddenly had enough. There were only two left who weren't in trouble, and they would be needed to help the crippled ones limp back down to a Patrol station where the pilots could get safely out of their damaged boats and pick up new ones. The two undamaged ones backed off and, when they were sure she wasn't going to chase them, collected their damaged fellows.

Defiance was still riding inertia tail-first away from the tug and drone, but her engines had begun to slow the ride. After a moment Melacha cut the thrusters and floated, watching the tug. It had turned away from the Patrol the moment they pulled out, and its pilot was calmly grappling with the drone again as if nothing had happened.

"Hey, hotshot." Melacha flipped on the visual, so the tug's pilot could see who was calling. "No need to go overboard with your thanks. Try to calm yourself."

He flipped on his visual without speaking, and she watched him concentrate on his grappling controls. There was something vaguely familiar about that face, or about the intensity of his concentration, or . . .

Or the mocking arrogance of his ice-blue eyes. When he found time to meet her gaze in the Link screen, those eyes shocked her into a pale, waiting stillness. *Those were Jamin's eyes!*

CHAPTER ELEVEN

"Thank you," the tug pilot said pleasantly. "After all that trouble, I wanted to make sure of the drone." A very small frown pulled at his brows as he studied her image. "Haven't I met you somewhere before?"

"Not impossible; I've *been* somewhere." The eyes were Jamin's, but the face was not. It was similar, but not the same. Impossible to tell about the voice over the Link, but the idea was pure fantasy. This wasn't the first time she had thought she saw him when he wasn't there.

He shook his head slightly and the frown disappeared. "I haven't." At her look of puzzlement he grinned ruefully. "Been anywhere, I mean. It's a long story. Anyway, thanks a lot for your help back there. I couldn't have handled a whole squadron by myself."

"You were an idiot to try. They'll be back, you know."

"Not before I get this drone home."

"They'll follow you."

"I don't think so; to do that, they'd have to admit Diadem exists, and I think they'd rather let us have a Lunar garbage drone."

"You better hope they think so, too. What's Diadem, anyway? I never heard of it."

"Can't be very important, then, can it?" Those eyes challenged her, but his mouth quirked in the hint of a grin.

She shrugged. "Space colony?"

"Man-built. Or imaginary, if you listen to Terrans. My name's JanMikal, by the way." He looked expectant.

"Hello, JanMikal-by-the-way. My name's Melacha Rendell." That produced another momentary frown that dragged his eyebrows together; probably because he had heard of the Skyrider. She didn't give him a chance to comment if he intended to. "Diadem must be pretty hard up, if you'd go to as much trouble as this for a garbage drone. But if you need it so badly, why didn't they send out more ships? Or at least an armed tug?"

"I don't think we have any armed tugs."

"You don't think? Don't you know?"

"Actually, I don't. I'm a new resident. But I do know Diademans avoid violence at all costs, so I don't think they'd have any armed ships."

She looked at him speculatively. "You must fit right in."

Another rueful grin. "Not exactly. But I'm working on it. Listen, you know, I don't think the Patrol will follow me, but they sure will follow you. Don't you think you should get out of here before they come back?"

"It'll take them a little while to gather reinforcements. They've learned not to underestimate the Skyrider."

"Must be nice to feel so confident. What's a skyrider, when it's at home?"

She stared. "Are you serious?" Then she grinned as ruefully as he had. "Of course you are. I should watch my ego. I guess there might be one or two people left in the Solar System who haven't heard of me."

He had fired his engines, and the powerful little tug was slowly overcoming the inertia of the massive garbage drone.

"I'm going to get this thing home, in case they do come back. They might try to catch me before I get there. And Diadem does need this load. Besides, I promised I'd bring the tug back safely."

She jockeyed after him. "Earth really pretends your whole space colony just doesn't exist?"

"They sure do. In fact, they arrested some of our scavengers recently, and now they won't let us bail them out because they can't negotiate with a colony that doesn't exist. Naturally none of the regular scavengers want to go out anymore, after that. And we need materials; Earth won't trade with us, either, so scavenging is our only Outside resource."

"You could get in touch with some Belter smugglers. They'd supply you. We supply the freelancers and home-steaders in the Belt."

If he noticed the change in pronouns, he didn't comment on it. "I think the price would be too high. We don't have much for legal trading, and I assume illegal traders get a higher markup?"

"Well, sure. That's the whole point."

Those blue eyes studied her with icy interest. "Is it?"

"What else?" Jamin would have asked just that, and in just that way, right down to the glacier stare. *Change the subject.* "I have a run to make for another space colony, but afterward I could drop by yours and talk to somebody about it, see if we could work something out."

He blinked, and she realized that piercing stare wasn't even directed at her; it was directed at something beyond her that wasn't really there. "I don't think you need to." His voice was distant, too. As if he were thinking of something so far from the present reality, or so fascinating, that he could barely drag his attention back enough to speak to her. "I've just thought of something."

"I can see you have."

He blinked again, and the full force of his attention turned back to her. "What?"

"I said I could see that you had. Thought of something. Don't ever play poker: your face is no good for it."

He frowned, and one hand went up involuntarily to touch his face in a curiously testing way, as if he were unfamiliar with the shape of it. "It's not?" He realized he was touching his face, took his hand away, looked at it rather blankly, and looked at her again. "Why, what's the matter with it?"

"Nothing. Nothing at all." She looked at him oddly. "I suppose they don't have mirrors on Diadem?"

"Of course they do."

" 'They.' Not 'we'?"

"Okay, we." Something beeped in his background and he turned away from the screen to manipulate a set of controls behind him. He was strapped into his seat, so it took a motion that broad to make it noticeable to her that he didn't have the gravity on in his tug. Even then she didn't think anything about it; a lot of people ran without gravity, especially when they needed all their power elsewhere.

"I've got to go," she said abruptly. "I'll try to stop by Diadem after this run, to see if they can use my services."

"I told you, you'll be wasting your time. We can't afford a smuggler." He put a noticeable emphasis on the word *we*. "And I don't think we'll need one, anyway."

"Why, you go do it yourself?" She didn't notice that she said it in pidgin, so it didn't surprise her in the least that he responded without hesitation, as if she had said it in clear Company English. Or as if he were a native Belter pidgin-speaker. . . .

"Not exactly."

"What *are* you going to do?" She wasn't really interested. Her attention span, lately, was barely longer than a child's; a fact that annoyed her only when she noticed it, which she seldom did. Now she was not really even aware that she had forgotten him already. His face was still on the Link screen, but she was studying the navigation screen, setting a course for Newkansas.

His brief laugh caught her wholly by surprise. *Jamin!* Heart in her throat, she stared wildly at the Link screen; but a stranger's face gazed back at her with Jamin's ice-blue eyes. A narrow, unfamiliar face, registering private amusement and no sign of recognition, watching her with Jamin's eyes. *This is crazy.*

"That would be telling, wouldn't it?" he said without interest.

She had forgotten the question. After a brief, frozen moment she looked away from him and said in a bland, flat voice, "Well, good luck. See you around." She didn't wait to hear his answer, if any. She flipped off the Comm Link and invoked the navigation program, closed her eyes, hit the thrusters, and ran.

CHAPTER TWELVE

She couldn't pick a fight with anyone on Newkansas. The colony was in self-imposed quarantine to prevent the spread of Bronson's disease. She could and did drive a hard bargain for the oxyaminocilinase. It was turned over to Newkansas—carefully, by remote control—only when Newkansas had agreed to give her in return a modified Falcon space shuttle exactly like her *Defiance* in every important respect. She didn't need a second *Defiance*; but then she didn't exactly need any of the material goods she was amassing. The acquisition amused her. It was something to do.

She gave Newkansas the coordinates of her rock, received their assurance that her new shuttle would be delivered within the week, and went there herself to off-load all the cargo she had brought back from Earth. By the time she was finished, the concealed storeroom was getting crowded and one of the other storerooms was downright full. It looked like a pirate's hoard. She closed the doors and walked away, feeling inexplicably cross and dissatisfied.

This was her first visit to her rock since she had bought

it, and she wandered through the rooms for a while, poking into cupboards and examining the spartan furnishings, but she couldn't summon any real interest. She had run from that haunting echo of Jamin's laughter, but the mocking arrogance of his eyes was caught in her mind.

Change the subject.

Her new rock was a nice enough place. She liked it. She could learn to feel at home here. Must be getting old, looking for a place to settle down. Jamin would—

Change the subject.

It was too small and too slow to have natural gravity, but there were big sturdy generators to supply artificial gravity, and controls in every room to turn it down or off. Visiting freefall mutants could be made comfortable. *Careful.* That tug pilot—JanMikal—had the gravity off in his tug; but mutants weren't common on the old man-built colonies. Probably he just enjoyed freefall, or was diverting all his power to tow the drone. It was positively eerie, though, how very like Jamin's his eyes and his laughter were. *Careful!*

More likely it was her imagination that was eerie in its disturbing ability to recreate the sound of Jamin's laughter or the look of his eyes. More than once since he died she had seen him—across a room, or in a crowd—and when she got to him he was always a stranger, often not a bit like Jamin in any way. The psych-tenders called it wish fulfillment or something. Whatever else they called it, they called it guilt. Survivor guilt. That seemed to be one of her better tricks.

She could accept Jamin's death intellectually; she had seen the laser strike his shuttle. Emotionally, though, she could not believe he had died.

"Space *damn* it," she said aloud. "Jamin is dead." Her voice echoed hollowly in the bare rock corridor. It didn't convince her. She had seen the laser strike Jamin's shuttle, but she hadn't had time to see more than that. She hadn't actually seen his shuttle destroyed. Yet he couldn't have survived that blast . . . could he? He must be dead.

JanMikal had his coloring, his eyes, his voice . . . but not his face. JanMikal was a stranger, like all the others she had briefly mistaken for Jamin. Of course he was a stranger. Jamin was dead.

Even if she imagined he was alive, and if she chose to believe that for some unknowable reason he had had his face surgically rebuilt . . . he would recognize her if he saw her. He wouldn't be able to conceal that even if he wanted to. He had never been good at poker. Surgery wouldn't change that.

JanMikal hadn't recognized her. He wasn't Jamin. Of course he wasn't Jamin. Jamin wouldn't leave Collis. *You're losing your grip, Skyrider.*

Change the subject.

With a muttered curse she stalked back to the shuttle dock where she had left *Defiance*, boarded her, and roughly disengaged from her new rock. She wasn't thinking of Jamin. By a massive effort of will, she concentrated on keeping her mind completely blank of anything at all except the complex calculations involved in hurling *Defiance* back down to Earth.

She couldn't pick a fight with Haioshi, either; she knew that from past experience. He didn't fight. And no Patrol boats got in her way on the trip to Earth, so she decided to tackle the problem of the salvage laws. Fighting government agencies wasn't nearly as satisfying as a rousing good fistfight, but it would be better than no fight at all.

She left *Defiance* for Haioshi to load. There were any number of things Earth government didn't want transported into space, for any number of reasons. Complex trade agreements made one product permissible and another brand of the same thing forbidden. Complex legal tangles made some drugs nonprescription on Earth but forbidden to the colonies. Complex political maneuvers made it legal to possess certain products in space, but illegal to transport them into space. Melacha had no interest at all in any of these matters. "If it's illegal to own or to carry," she told Haioshi, "just put it in a separate stack and I'll stow it in the concealed hold when I get back."

"Tell me where that hold is and I'll stow it for you," he suggested with a wide grin.

"No, thanks." She made an effort to return the grin, but it wasn't successful. "Still no information about Ian Spencer?"

He shook his head regretfully, making the bright curls around his face dance. "I know it's just on the tip of my mind. It's one of those things you know, and you can't remember it, and then when you do you feel ridiculous for not having thought of it sooner. I've been on the CommNet, checking every logical reference—*every*body's on the CommNet, even Ian Spencer, but what I come up with is junk. An uneventful boyhood on a midwestern farm, the usual colleges and universities, recently a couple of years in the Patrol. . . . I suppose I may have been mistaken, but I was *sure* his name was familiar."

"You could check illogical references."

"In my copious spare time. Some of us have work to do, you know."

She spread her arms, wide-eyed with injured innocence. "I'm working!"

He looked dubious. "Yes. Well. I suppose cleaning out a bank account *could* be called work. . . ."

"I didn't mean that. I'm working as Ombudsman. It's the job the President made up for me, and I thought I'd surprise her by doing it. It's my next project."

"Indeed. I suppose you wouldn't like to elucidate? What exactly does an ombudsman do?"

She shrugged. "Something about investigating whether

government agencies are infringing on the rights of citizens. Have you heard about the new salvage laws?''

"Ah, yes. The Bureau of Regional Resources. I wouldn't recommend tackling them all by your lonely, Skyrider. Not even you. Their power is formidable.''

She grinned. "So's mine. Listen, Haioshi, do me a favor, will you?''

He lifted his eyebrows. "I supposed that was what I had been doing.''

"I mean another favor, then. Don't let anybody confiscate *Defiance* while she's here.''

"I suppose there's a reason to think someone may try?'' He glanced at his computer screen to check the location of *Defiance*, nodded, and looked back at Melacha. "It's as well she's inside the loading dock. They'll know she's here, of course, but they can't see her, and I can keep them out unless they show probable cause.'' He frowned. "If you're going to fight your way out of here . . .''

"I don't think I'll have to, but I promise if I do I won't damage your loading dock.''

"You can't promise the Patrol won't.'' He shrugged massively. "Ah, well. I suppose life would be bland without these little challenges. What brought you to whose attention?''

"I helped a tug out of someplace called Diadem salvage a garbage drone out of Luna. By accident a squadron of the Patrol got in our way.''

He shook his head. "I suppose it didn't occur to you simply to kill them?''

"I did my best. There were six of them, and only one of me.''

"The tug was of no assistance? Ah, yes, Diadem, you said. Very well, I'll do what I can. Now run along and let a working man get back to his trade.''

"I didn't notice you had stopped. You've been interacting with that damn computer the whole time I've been here. If this is what it looks like when you're *not* working, I don't know whether I want to see what it looks like when you *are*."

He nodded soberly. "It is not a sight for the fainthearted."

"Or the weak-stomached."

"I suppose you will go, eventually?"

She took the skytrain to the capital and an automated taxi to the Bureau of Regional Resources. The taxi was surly. If it had been human she'd have broken its face. Since it wasn't, even an exchange of invectives seemed like too much trouble.

The Bureau of Regional Resources was housed in an imposing modern structure that looked very like a supermarket. The land around it, narrowly hemmed in by neighboring buildings and by the taxi paths between them, was tediously landscaped in a fussy imitation micro-Japan style that would have made an honest Japanese gardener cry. A large plasteel structure near the front entrance proved on close inspection to be giant cutout letters that proclaimed the name of the agency in nearly illegible script. There was no other indication of the intended function of the building.

A vast covered entryway led to four separate front doors, each bearing a discreet identifying sign in the same nearly illegible script as that which identified the building. Melacha tried to read the first she came to, and couldn't make any sense of it. It seemed to say *Europeasterny*, but perhaps she misunderstood. The glass in the door was opaque even when she pressed her nose against it.

The second door said *Southinterests*, or perhaps *Fort Hinterland*. Its glass was also opaque. The third said *Calamitief*, and had opaque glass, and she opened it anyway.

All four doors led to one central waiting room. A receptionist perched in a high glass cage cleverly designed to look like a desk—or a desk cleverly designed to look like a cage, Melacha wasn't sure which—looked up as Melacha entered, and frowned at her with startling severity.

"Oh, did I choose the wrong door?" asked Melacha.

The receptionist scowled even more severely and looked away. She was dressed like a woman, but he had a thick dark moustache and needed a shave. The neat plasteel plaque on the front of his/her desk said *Pneceiiu Anhudz*. That wasn't much help.

The waiting room was empty except for Melacha and the receptionist. Melacha waited by the desk/cage for fully five minutes before the man/woman within looked at her again. The wait would probably have been longer if Melacha hadn't begun to kick the impervious glass of the desk/cage with patient viciousness. The receptionist scowled at her silently and went back to staring at the far wall. Melacha kicked the furniture again. The receptionist, without looking, said in a low-pitched female or high-pitched male voice, "What is it?"

Melacha stopped kicking and clasped her hands behind her back. "Are you free to talk to me now? I don't want to interrupt your more important staring. Or aren't you the receptionist, anyway? Maybe I misunderstood; I can't read these signs very well; they seem to have been designed by a congenital lunatic. Are you a prisoner?"

The receptionist turned pale watery eyes to her. "I beg your pardon?"

"Quite all right," said Melacha, "I'm not offended."

The receptionist looked away.

"Can you please direct me to someone who knows something about the new salvage laws?" asked Melacha.

The receptionist picked up a pencil, licked the lead, and poised the eraser over his/her computer keyboard. "Please state the nature of your interest."

"I'm interested in talking to someone who knows about the new salvage laws."

The receptionist sighed ostentatiously and licked the

pencil lead again before poising the eraser back over the keyboard. "Please state the nature of your interest in the salvage laws."

"I will, to someone who knows something about them. Can you tell me where to find such a person?"

The receptionist turned its head slowly, giving her ample opportunity to study its greasy hairstyle and its pasty complexion before the watery eyes of no particular color were fully in position to stare with total idiocy at Melacha. It sighed again, noisily. "I cannot direct you to one of our executives," it said, enunciating carefully, "until you give me enough information to choose which of our executives is best equipped to solve your problem." It blinked again. "Please state the nature of your interest in the salvage laws to which you relude."

Unaware that she had "reluded" to anything, and unsure how one would go about "reluding" if one wanted to, Melacha said with patience almost equal to the receptionist's, "I'm interested in getting rid of them."

It blinked again. This seemed to be its preferred method of expressing any number of vague emotions. "I beg your pardon."

"Quite all right, I'm still not offended." Melacha blinked amiably. "Please direct me to someone with whom I can discuss the eradication of the new salvage laws."

It licked its pencil lead and turned back to its computer. "Laws are not eradicated on whim. If you still wish to speak with an official of the B.R.R., please state the nature of your interest," it said severely.

"I'm becoming very interested in shoving that stupid pencil down your throat, and possibly the computer with it." The Skyrider was not an altogether patient person.

"As you may have noticed," the receptionist said calmly, "my desk is made of shatterproof glass; glasteel, in fact; and I very much doubt that you can get through it to do anything to my throat. Or to my computer." It looked smug, stared into the distance, and added as an after-thought, "It bounces lasers."

The Skyrider was wearing a holstered stun gun; Belters seldom went anywhere unarmed. A Martian of the Skyrider's acquaintance had once accused her of going to bed with her handgun. She didn't draw it now. She didn't even put her hand on it. She did say, pensively, "I've never heard of anything transparent that could bounce a stun. It won't go through some opaque stuff, but your desk isn't opaque."

The receptionist blinked at the far wall. "What did you say your interest was in the salvage laws?"

"I want to talk to someone about them."

"Ah, yes," It poised its pencil again, hesitated, licked the lead, and used the eraser to punch several keys. "I could call Ground Patrol," it said conversationally.

"And I could stun you," said the Skyrider. "Neither act would get me in to see anyone about the salvage laws."

"Whom did you wish to see?"

"Shouldn't that be who?"

"I don't think so."

The Skyrider blinked again. Maybe it had a sense of humor. "My name is Melacha Rendell. The President appointed me Ombudsman. That means I'm to investigate government agencies that may be infringing on the rights of citizens. I think the salvage laws do that. I want to talk to somebody who can do something about it. Okay?"

The receptionist punched some more buttons, widened its watery eyes, turned its pasty face to the Skyrider, said, "Oh, my," punched a few more buttons, and sighed. "The Skyrider, is it?"

"What, I owe you money?"

"I didn't quite catch that. Oh dear. Never mind, don't bother repeating it; you don't have time. I'm very sorry about the runaround I've given you; it's just my job, you know. But now you'd best be leaving. I did call Ground

Patrol." It blinked. "There was no way around it; I'd already given the computer your name, and it told me there's an APB out on you. They'd have tracked you anyway." It achieved a sheepish smile. "You've always been one of my heroes. Please do hurry; they'll be here quite soon. It was very nice of you, I'm sure, to assist someone in salvaging a Lunar garbage drone, but you must know the Patrol doesn't like to have its boats damaged." It shook its head sadly. "That really is a very severe no-no, Ms. Rendell."

CHAPTER THIRTEEN

Even ordinary miscreants were almost routinely buried alive in the Corporation's ponderous and cumbersome legal system. The Skyrider might get misplaced on purpose. She didn't intend to wait around to find out. If the damned receptionist felt it had to report her to Ground Patrol, it was singularly sporting of it, especially after the bizarre but entirely hostile conversation they had just had, to warn her that it had reported her. She should have asked its name. Maybe even its sex. Then again, she wasn't sure she wanted to know.

She was sure she didn't have time for idle chatter. Ground Patrol were notoriously hasty bastards. Quick to the scene and quick to arrest—or stun—anybody handy, according to some reports. Melacha caught the first taxi she saw and told it to start driving.

"Where to?" Its voice was metallic and grating.

"I don't care. Just get us out of here."

"In which direction?" If a computer can sound impatient, it sounded impatient.

Melacha kicked the dashboard. "I don't *care*. Just *go*!"

She lurched forward in her seat as if the motion of her body might push the taxi forward.

"Lady, you'll have to give me a destination."

"Straight ahead. And don't call me lady."

The taxi moved, though not quickly. "Yes, *sir!*" In what it may have considered an undertone, it added peevishly, "Jeez, this town's full of 'em."

Melacha didn't respond. She was staring out the back window.

"Look, lady, you're gonna have to give me *some*thing. I can't keep going straight ahead forever."

She saw the first Ground Patrol cars pull up in front of the B.R.R. building. The Patrolmen leapt out and raced inside. "Turn a corner," she said. "The next one you can."

"Which way?"

"Either way. I don't care."

"I am not programmed to make decisions of that nature." It sounded prim, but perhaps that was her imagination.

"Then right. Turn right."

"There will not be a right turn for several blocks."

"The next left, then. Turn left."

The taxi instantly turned left onto a side path and they were out of sight of the B.R.R. building. Melacha sat back in the seat and looked ahead. "Take the next right," she said.

"If you have a specific destination in mind, I am programmed to find the shortest route."

"I'm sure you are." She thought about it. "Okay, you mechanical bastard. Take me to the President."

"Would that be the President of the World, Incorporated?"

"That's who."

"Okay, lady. It's your funeral."

"What's that supposed to mean?"

The taxi didn't respond, and Melacha forgot the question. The paths of the capital were fascinating. A planet was by its very nature alien to her, and cities were at least as unsettling as open countryside; but the capital in its infinite variety was downright stunning. Towering plasteel rectilinear buildings shared space with crouched little historical brick structures; micro-Japan gardens blended into chaotic pseudo-rainforest jungles. Passing taxis and walkways were crowded with Earthers in every size and description, and it seemed to Melacha that they all stared at her. Quite possibly none of them really even noticed her. She felt paranoid. She was out of place, and she knew it. *Where can you run on a planet?*

The taxi stopped in front of a serene white clapboard farmhouse menaced by jungle on one side and by a towering glasteel building on the other. "Credit card, please."

Melacha fed it her credit card and realized Ground Patrol would have a report of the transaction before she could get into the building. "Take enough for a drive to the nearest park," she said quickly, "and don't pick up another fare till you get there."

"You want me to go on to the park?"

"That's right. No, open the damn door; I want you to leave me here, *then* go on to the park."

The taxi might have shrugged if it had been capable of it. "Okay, lady." It spat her credit card onto the floor and waited while she retrieved it.

"And don't pick up another fare, damn you. Not till you're in the park."

"Sure, lady. Whatever you say."

She stepped out onto green growing stuff that crushed underfoot and sent up clouds of rich summery scent that made the Skyrider nervous. "What is this stuff?" she asked, looking at her feet, but the taxi was already gone. She shrugged and walked toward the building. It wasn't grass. It wasn't anything she had walked on before. In the asteroid belt one didn't walk on growing things.

This building didn't have an illegible sign to identify it, but the odor that wafted out of the corridor when she opened the door was identification enough. Hospital. Nothing else smelled quite like that. She found a reception desk and asked for the President, fully expecting to be laughed at. Instead she was looked at with real sympathy by the small, straight-backed woman behind the counter.

"I'm *very* sorry," said the woman, "but no one is allowed in to see the President."

Melacha glanced around for the guards or Ground Patrol who would enforce that edict. "No one? Not even her advisors?" There were no guards or Ground Patrol in evidence.

The woman behind the desk shook her head. "No. Not even her advisors. Her condition is critical, Ms. Rendell. All I can suggest is that you go to the President's office; the Vice President and the Board of Directors are taking care of all her business now."

Melacha shook her head. "Where is she?"

"She can't see you now," the woman repeated. Glancing at her computer screen, she looked startled and punched the code button. The Skyrider caught her hand before she could go further.

"I can't let you report me," she said. "Back off from the computer or I'll have to stun you."

The woman stared at her, wild-eyed. "There are guards," she said anxiously. "And Ground Patrol." It was meant as a warning, but it sounded more like a plea. "They'll hear if you . . . *do* anything."

"I won't hurt you if you do as I say. Back off." The Skyrider released her hand and let her back away from the desk. "Stop right there. For all I know there's an alarm button on that wall. Don't go near it."

The woman stood in the center of her small reception area and tried not to cry. "What will you do?"

"I don't know." The Skyrider looked at her, exasperated. "I *said* I won't hurt you."

"But . . ." The woman's voice trailed off and her eyes widened, staring at something behind the Skyrider.

"Good try," said the Skyrider, impressed. "But it's an old trick."

"No trick," said a familiar voice at the Skyrider's back. "What's going on here, Skyrider? Are you terrorizing the staff?"

"Board Advisor Brown!" The Skyrider turned to her with genuine relief. "What in space are you doing here?"

"Probably the same thing you're doing: trying to see the President."

"They wouldn't let you in?"

Board Advisor Brown shook her head and looked past the Skyrider. "I wouldn't," she said softly.

The woman behind the desk, who had taken two trembling steps toward her computer, backed away again. "But . . ."

Board Advisor Brown looked back at the Skyrider. "What is it this time? Have you got Ground Patrol after you, or what?"

"Right the first time." The Skyrider looked past her friend at the front door and drew her stun gun. "And not far enough behind. *Damn!*"

As quickly as Ground Patrol and the Skyrider moved, Board Advisor Brown moved more quickly. She whipped out an identity badge, held it up for the Patrolmen to see, and practically hurled herself into the Skyrider's arms, thus getting her body between the Skyrider and the Patrol. She shouted something the Skyrider didn't understand, which had the startling effect of causing the six Ground Patrolmen in the doorway to freeze where they stood, staring inside with their weapons drawn but fortunately not yet fired.

The Skyrider would have taken advantage of that, but Board Advisor Brown was hanging onto her gun arm with all her strength, destroying her aim. "Don't shoot, damn you!" said Brown. The command could have been directed at the Patrol or at the Skyrider. They all obeyed it.

For a long moment nobody moved. Then the woman behind the desk came out of her trance and scrambled frantically out from behind the desk in a mad charge on the Patrolmen. It wasn't clear to anyone whether she meant to attack them or ask for their protection, but under ordinary circumstances they wouldn't have waited to find out. They would have stunned her first and asked questions later. Board Advisor Brown's shouted command, whatever it had been, must have been a powerful one. The Patrolmen shuffled, and one of them raised her weapon, but nobody fired.

"It's the Skyrider, I tried to call you but she attacked me, she threatened me, she was going to kill me, shoot her, for God's sake, shoot her!" The woman's hysterical outburst ended in a muffled "Mmmph!" as she collided with the frontmost Patrolman, a formidable woman of such stature that the collision didn't even seem to jar her.

"If anybody moves, you're all dead," said the Skyrider, fighting to aim her weapon at the Patrolmen from behind Brown's body and hoping nobody would notice it was only a stun gun, not a laser.

Brown laughed. Everybody stared at her. She retained her firm grip on the Skyrider's gun arm with one hand and folded the other arm across her own ribs, fighting off an attack of belly laughs that threatened to double her over. "Well said, Skyrider," she gasped between chortles. "But unnecessary. As well as impossible." To the Patrolmen she said more calmly as she regained control of herself, "Notify your superiors that I have taken the Skyrider into my custody. I will get in touch with them within the hour as to her future, if any."

To the Skyrider's surprise, the Patrolmen nodded in unison and the back three, who had never quite got into the corridor, turned away and let the door close behind them. The one who had the hysterical receptionist on her hands lifted the little woman bodily and set her down again two paces away, scowled at her, and turned to leave. She and the other two remaining Patrolmen walked calmly out of the building while the little receptionist stared after them in horror.

When the door was closed behind them the receptionist seemed to realize all at once that she was alone in a deserted corridor with the dastardly Skyrider, with only one Board Advisor's body between her own person and certain doom. She threw one startled glance at Brown and the Skyrider and abruptly followed the Patrolmen out the door.

This time Brown succumbed totally to laughter. After a moment the Skyrider, with less abandon but equal amusement, joined her. "Damn," she said eventually. "I've had a lot of trouble with receptionists today. . . . What in space did you say to make those Patrolmen stop like that? I wouldn't have believed it if I hadn't seen it."

The receptionist opened the door a crack, peered cautiously inside, saw Brown release the Skyrider's gun arm, and let the door slide closed again.

"And I wouldn't have believed *you* if I hadn't heard it with my own ears," said Brown. "If anybody moves, you're all dead! That's rich! You couldn't have killed a mosquito right then, even if you'd had a laser, which you haven't."

"What's a mosquito?"

"Never mind." Brown looked up as the receptionist timidly pushed the door open again. "We'd better get out of here before that woman has kittens. Come on. You can't get in to see the President. What did you want with her, anyway? Or were you just running?"

"Mostly just running, I suppose." Melacha holstered her weapon and followed Board Advisor Brown out the door past the quaking receptionist, the sight of whom set them both giggling again. "I had to go somewhere, and I couldn't get back to the *Defiance*; they'd expect me to do that, and besides it would have given them probable cause. . . . It would have got a friend of mine in trouble. I guess I thought running for the President would be about the most unexpected thing I could do just then. Besides, I need to see somebody in authority, and she was in authority last time I was down here."

"In theory, she still is." Brown hailed a taxi and climbed in after Melacha. "My office," she told it, feeding it her credit card so it would know who she was. "What did you need someone in authority for?"

Melacha wouldn't have been surprised if the taxi had responded to that; apparently, however, taxis were less pushy with Board Advisors than with mere ordinary citizens. It didn't utter a sound. "I'm looking into these new salvage laws. You know the President made me Ombudsman?"

"I knew. I even looked up what it meant." Brown looked pensive. "Those salvage laws are ridiculous, I know, but the B.R.R. has a lot of power now. Their top executive is first cousin to Nuke 'em B. Newcomb, and I imagine even out in the colonies you know what that means."

"I hear he's likely to get the President's job."

"I'm afraid so. This town is a shambles right now. Nobody knows who's in charge of what. Or of whom. By the way, my first cousin is a muckymuck in Ground Patrol, in case you wondered how I pulled that one off."

"I did wonder."

Brown nodded. "It's down to that here now. Who's related to whom, who's sleeping with whom, who can prove what about whom. . . . What got you onto the salvage laws? It doesn't seem like your usual field of interest. Too plebeian, somehow."

"Have you ever heard of a man-built colony named Diadem?"

Brown shook her head. "I don't think I have."

"Well, I hadn't either, but I met this guy." She grinned at Brown's look. "Not that way. He was salvaging a Lunar garbage drone. The Patrol didn't like it. And I didn't like that."

"So you stopped the Patrol from stopping him. Is that why Ground Patrol is after you? I'm surprised you didn't kill them."

"That's what Haioshi said. I'm good, but I'm not that good; there were six of them and there is only one of me."

"Excuses, excuses." Brown gave her a curious look. "Why no help from this guy from Diadem? Where was he?"

"Diademans are nonviolent, so his tug wasn't armed. He threw the drone's fuel pods at them, though."

"That doesn't sound exactly nonviolent."

"No. He's a transplant there. Sounded like he didn't even really know that much about them; he just lives there."

"Odd. People don't often emigrate to the man-builts anymore. Oh, here we are. Come up and we'll talk about it, and I'll work out something with Ground Patrol. If I can get you twenty-four hours' freedom of Earth, do you think you could get your business taken care of and get safely back out where you belong?"

"I sure could. 'Specially if you help with the business."

"We'll see who I know."

CHAPTER FOURTEEN

Ian Spencer looked at his morning mail in disbelief. *Two* letters from Investments, Inc. That was ominous. It wasn't time yet for them to send even one. He put the letters aside and programmed his dispenser for breakfast. This was his last day with the Patrol, but that wouldn't prevent I.I. from finding him. Even staying with the Patrol—a possibility he considered very briefly and discarded as pointless and unappealing in the extreme—wouldn't stop I.I. from taking him apart if they decided to.

They shouldn't decide to, yet. He had plenty of time before any repayment was due on the money he had borrowed to build the equipment to defeat the Skyrider. But I.I. didn't write letters just to be sociable. "You could open one and find out what they want," he told himself. But he knew what they wanted. "Shut up, I'm having breakfast," he said aloud to his silent room.

Tucking the unopened letters neatly under his newsfax printout, he consumed an enormous breakfast with the uncomplicated greed of a child. Afterward he drank three steaming cups of coffee and read every major article in the printout before he finally put it aside and looked at the letters again.

It was almost time for him to report for duty. He scowled at the letters, but the boyish innocence of his face made the expression look more petulant than threatening. After hours spent in front of mirrors trying to produce an expression that even on his face would look threatening, Spencer had given up and henceforth never again scowled in public. By happy accident he had learned that a cheerful smile was actually more effective in scowling situations, anyway. It unnerved people that displeasure made him smile. On making that discovery, he had spent sufficient time and energy training himself so that now rage actually made him chuckle, a fact which had a very satisfactorily unsettling effect on his enemies.

In private he still sometimes reverted to his old ways and scowled in sullen petulance at things he didn't like. He didn't like dunning letters from people to whom he owed money. He opened them, scowling so fiercely that he looked like a child denied an expected treat.

The letters were postmarked, so he knew in what order to read them. As usual they were couched in very formal legal terms which he translated automatically into standard English. The first said that "due to the changing political climate," which he understood to mean "because we may be able to get away with it," his payment date would probably be moved forward and he should be prepared to repay his loan in full, with interest, on short notice. The second one explained briefly that his repayment was overdue, that late charges had been added, and that if he did not pay at once and in full he would suffer consequences which were ominously left unspecified.

He knew exactly what consequences I.I. had in mind: he had suffered them before. Broken bones, however readily they could be mended by modern medical technology, were still painful and very much to be avoided when possible. But how the hell was he going to repay the fortune he had invested in his Patrol boat and in the computer hard- and software he had used to win his bet with the Skyrider, when he couldn't yet collect from her?

Damn his impulsive generosity. He shouldn't have given her a month to pay up. He should have known that his investors wouldn't stick to the month they had promised him. With the President ill and nobody really in charge of the Corporation till she recovered or was replaced, agreements that would otherwise be legally binding on both parties were now binding only on the weaker party.

Unfortunately, Spencer was the obviously weaker party in this one. I.I. had all the power: they could break him, literally, into small pieces. He could break a few of their hirelings, but not the lot. However many he managed to break, they would hire more. Sooner or later, no matter how artfully he dodged and fought, Spencer would be the one who got broken. Permanently broken, if he made them angry enough.

He would have to go after the head man. Not just the hirelings, and not even the top executives, but the shadow man whose power secretly ran the entire investment agency. Spencer knew who that man was; he had done considerable research into the matter before he had borrowed the money. The man thought his connections with the agency were obscured in secrecy and deliberate legal tangles; but Spencer knew his way around legal thickets, and secrecy was usually susceptible to bribes, threats, or simple computer expertise. Spencer had used all three, judiciously, and had learned what he wanted to know. The man whose motivating force he had found behind Investments, Inc. was powerful, but he was neither omnipotent nor immortal. Spencer might be able to get at him.

It was that possibility which had decided Spencer when he was choosing investment agencies. That and the fact that it amused him to risk I.I.'s money in the asteroid belt, where their head man would least want to lose it. But Spencer hadn't expected to lose it, and he hadn't expected to be forced to go after the head man, either. The necessity was annoying, at best. He had been looking forward to having a holiday when he left the Patrol.

Still, this could be an interesting challenge. Stephen B. Newcomb would not be an easy man to intimidate, but it could probably be done. Spencer was unaware that his ineffective scowl had turned into a wide, boyish, and very deadly grin.

CHAPTER FIFTEEN

It was the silks that did it. Everything else was loaded well before Melacha's twenty-four hours were up, but the silks were delayed in arrival. Haioshi tried to talk her into leaving without them, but she laughed at him. "No, you were right," she said. "They are worth waiting for."

"They were worth waiting for, before the Patrol gave you a time limit," said Haioshi. "They aren't worth getting killed over." He stared at her in sudden dismay. "I suppose now you regard it as a challenge."

She shrugged. "I'm not lifting without a full cargo."

"I have plenty of other luxury items you could use to fill your hold."

She grinned at him. "I want silks. Don't be an old man, Haioshi. There's plenty of time yet."

But there wasn't plenty of time, and they both knew it. By the time the silks arrived and were loaded, there was no time at all. Melacha could hear the Gypsies singing. Since Django died, all the ghosts of the asteroid belt, but especially the Gypsies among them, had sung to her of every danger, every bold or stealthy approach of Death in any guise. They sang to warn her, to support her, to comfort her, to guide her. And sometimes it seemed to her that they sang to welcome her. . . .

She didn't give *Defiance* time to warm up: she just lunged up through the atmosphere on engines that screamed in protest but did what they were told. Any further delay might have brought the Patrol to Haioshi's dock. She avoided that, but she didn't avoid the Patrol.

Often enough during her career as a smuggler, the Skyrider had been obliged to do battle alone against the Patrol in numbers ranging from one to a dozen. She had never before faced six squadrons, a total of thirty-six Patrol boats, all by herself.

They were waiting for her in the thin outer fringes of Earth's atmosphere, well clear of major shipping lines but still well within Earth's legal boundaries. Thirty-six red-and-black Patrol boats glittered like metal insects in the unfiltered sunlight, waiting for her.

The instant she saw them she altered her course, skipping sideways like a startled dragonfly; but the whisping fringe of atmosphere and the terrible pull of Earth's gravity both clutched at her, blunting the swift precision of her maneuver. Both were forces with which she was largely unfamiliar, at least at such close range. The Patrol knew that. It wasn't only knowledge of the law that made them await her just there, within Earth's legal boundaries. Knowledge of the Skyrider was probably a more powerful influence: the knowledge that in her natural habitat, in deep space, the Skyrider just might outfight and outfly even thirty-six Patrol boats. But not here. Not within reach of that killing monster rock called Earth.

The Comm Link signaled, but she didn't turn it on. If they wanted to give her instructions, she would only disregard them anyway; and if they wanted to gloat they would just have to do it quietly among themselves. She wasn't interested.

They had matched her first maneuver neatly, keeping their full force in a vast umbrella formation between her and the wild dark void she sought. She was effectively trapped between them and Earth. None had yet fired on her, but they would if she tried to punch her way through them. They would soon, anyway, if she didn't surrender. They were keeping it a flat-plane confrontation, the way Earthers liked it. The only space she could move in was that below her, occupied by the thick moist howling winds that would tear the wings off *Defiance* if she tried most of the familiar maneuvers that might have saved her life in space.

In sudden rage she kicked in the thrusters and plunged down into the gummy atmosphere, feeling it bounce and buffet her *Defiance*, tossing her like a chip of wood on a stormy sea. If she could withstand that . . . If she could pull up hard . . . now! . . . against Earth's deadly gravity . . . If she could catch the sweet invisible parabolic course line that would thrust her up and out again, ahead of the Patrol and running . . .

As skillfully as she dived and turned and fled, the Patrol was always ahead of her. There were too many of them, and this was their home ground. She was the alien here. For once she was the one whose instincts were inappropriate, untrustworthy. This time she was the one who was out of place. In the Belt, the Patrol often lost to her because they thought flat. Here, she was losing because she didn't really know how to think flat.

One of them fired. Maybe it was a warning shot, meant to miss, but it signaled the end of playtime. She flipped *Defiance* end for end and came up firing. Two of them were dead before they knew which way she was facing. *Thirty-four to go. . . .*

Only her fierce and stubborn pride kept her from giving up right then. Obviously she had finally killed herself with overconfidence, and all that was left was the formality of

determining exactly where and when she would lie down.
But she would not admit that, even to herself. She killed
another one, and dived back into the deadly thick atmosphere below to dodge the lasers that came at her from
every other direction.

She didn't dodge them all. One scarred *Defiance*'s bright
nose paint; one bounced off the starboard shield, sheeting
flame that dazzled and lingered in the roiling winds. Several others missed her entirely. One punched a hole right
through the port shield and the port side of *Defiance*. It
missed the port side of the Skyrider. Several pieces of
shrapnel didn't miss.

The song of the Gypsies drowned the sound of escaping
air howling through the tiny wound in the cockpit bulkhead. The Skyrider leaned on the controls, pushing *Defiance*
deeper into the raging winds of Earth while she caught up
a bottle of sealant, upended it, and sprayed sticky gray
foam thick over the hole in the bulkhead. The acrid fumes
brought tears to her eyes, but the sealant hardened on
contact and the whistle of escaping air was cut off.

The Gypsies were still singing. She was plunging dangerously near the planet, already cutting across busy shipping lines. Burning chunks of shrapnel had buried themselves
in her left thigh and arm. Not all had been hot enough to
cauterize the wounds they made; she could feel the sticky
warm blood dripping down onto her leg from her arm, but
she didn't have time to look, much less time to do anything about it.

The planet reached for *Defiance*. Winds yanked at her
wings and bucked under her with the fierce exuberance of
a predator sure of its prey. The deadly blue-and-white
expanse of Earth blotted out the world: all Melacha could
see in the viewport or screens was Patrol boats on one side
and Earth on the other. Earth was bigger than anything. It
was too big to exist. It might be too big for her to escape.

A glance in the rear screen showed the Patrol boats

following, some coming right after her and some spreading out above her so that wherever she came up, if she managed to come up, they would be waiting. They weren't firing now; perhaps they felt there was no need. Perhaps they thought Earth would do their killing for them.

"Not yet," she said under her breath. "Not yet, damn you." She tugged *Defiance*'s nose delicately up, jockeying against the winds, getting her engines aimed down into that powerful gravity well so their thrust might push her out of it. The Patrol boats were leading her, expecting her to try to skip across the atmosphere like a flat stone on water. If she could pull up almost vertical, she would be slow, and she might come up behind them. They would be slower still at turning around. She hoped.

A wave of dizziness turned the universe to slow motion for a timeless instant. Stars sparked before her eyes, and the song of the Gypsies sounded like the rush of wind in her ears. Gravity pressed her hard against the controls and she clung to them, willing herself to full consciousness, willing *Defiance* to climb, meter by meter like an animal clawing its way up out of a pit. . . . When she could see again, they were still pulling slowly, slowly, up and away from Earth.

The Patrol boats were still before and behind her. The left side of her flight suit felt damply stiff with congealing blood. The only reason the pain wasn't incapacitating was that she was in shock. Even if she fought her way up out of the atmosphere, there was nowhere to go: the Patrol would stop her. There were too many of them. Her effort to come up behind them would succeed only partially, and partially wasn't enough. Some would be ahead of her, and waste time getting turned to fight her again. At least half would still be behind her or hovering near enough to fire the moment they were sure she could otherwise pull out of the Earth trap.

She blinked. She was still in the shipping lanes, and a

massive passenger carrier was coming up fast in the screens. At first she couldn't tell which way it was headed, or even for sure whether its path would intersect with hers.

It would. The carrier was clumsy and couldn't maneuver worth a damn. Neither, in her present condition, could the Skyrider. The laser that had cut a hole in the port side of *Defiance* had by some miracle missed all the controls, but Melacha was losing blood fast: she felt as if she were moving in an atmosphere as thick as honey, and her mind was almost as slow as her reflexes.

Three Patrol boats fired on her at once, trying to knock her out of the carrier's path. They missed. The carrier lumbered helplessly toward her. She could kill the thrusters and miss it . . . and miss her chance to climb out of Earth's gravity well. She could jockey sideways, possibly missing the carrier, and possibly losing the thrust she needed to get clear of Earth. She could risk everything on a desperate effort to coax just enough more speed out of *Defiance*, just a little more. . . .

The engines howled. The carrier thundered toward her. She leaned forward, hugging the controls, bullying and pleading with *Defiance*, insanely adding carefully misdirected jockey thrusters to the effort, fighting wind and gravity and inertia and Death.

Another Patrol boat fired on her. If they hit her now, whether they killed her or not they would endanger the carrier, unless they could disintegrate *Defiance* entirely. Somebody must have realized that, and perhaps even guessed what she was doing: they didn't fire again.

There was nothing the carrier could do. It was in orbit, and by the laws of orbital dynamics if it slowed, its orbital diameter would increase, putting it even more certainly on a collision course with *Defiance*. It wasn't equipped to do much jockeying, even if its pilot knew which way to go. Not knowing for sure what the Skyrider was doing, he probably wouldn't have taken the chance if he could have.

Hers was the more maneuverable ship, so it was her responsibility to get out of the carrier's way. If she didn't, the carrier would be badly damaged, and passengers killed or injured. The Skyrider would be dead.

Defiance groaned with effort. The roar of the engines had become a vast sound, drowning out the universe. Multiple gravities in the cockpit pressed the Skyrider crushingly against the controls, but she was hardly aware of creaking bones and protesting muscles. She was aware only of the decreasing distance between *Defiance* and the monster carrier.

She wasn't sure, until the wind generated by the carrier buffeted *Defiance* in passing, that they had made it. There was no time to celebrate. The Patrol was waiting. When they saw her safely clear of the carrier, they knew she was also successfully breaking away from Earth, and they came after with renewed determination. She wasn't going to escape them this time.

She wondered dully why she fought it so hard. She was clear of the carrier, and had reached escape velocity: she could divert power for the gravity generator again, and make it compensate for the gravities generated by her flight. But she didn't. *Defiance* was picking up speed. There wasn't really any way she could escape the Patrol, but she could damn well punch a hole through their nearer ranks. They would kill her, but not without an effort.

Fighting dizziness, gravity, and pain that tore at every bone and joint in her body, she moved just enough to line up the lasers on the nearest Patrol boat. He was maneuvering to fire on her. She shot first. Another, from some other direction, fired on her and his laser sheeted across her aft shield, but she ignored it. She couldn't do anything about that one. There was another one in front of her about which she could do something. With weary, tedious care, she lined him up on her laser screen.

She blinked, and he disappeared. Just like that. She hadn't fired. He just disappeared.

For a long, painful moment she stared stupidly at the laser screen. Then she lifted her head, fighting gravity, to peer out the viewport. Nothing. No Patrol boats. She looked at the other screens.

They were there, in the screen that showed a view to starboard, and they were retreating, heading away from her and from Earth. Miraculously, ridiculously, she had won!

With the last of her strength she diverted power to the gravity generator, cut power to the engines, and queried the navigation computer. She was on a secure course toward Mars. It wasn't where she wanted to go, but it was away from Earth. She hadn't wits or energy just then to lay in a different course. All that mattered now was that she was free of Earth. And free of the Patrol. For whatever reason. Later she could look a miracle in its mouth. Right now she only wanted to close her eyes and rest.

CHAPTER SIXTEEN

She leaned back for a moment, but she didn't close her eyes; she knew that if she did she might never open them again. Relaxing wasn't a very good idea, either. Darkness was closing in on her. She was free of Earth's atmosphere now, but the winds still howled in her ears. And the Gypsies still sang. She had been wrong about them. They weren't welcoming her. They weren't exactly warning her, either, this time. There was an irresistible urgency to their song. She must do something. . . .

Impossible to think. Why had the Patrol retreated? They had been winning, but they couldn't have known how nearly they had already won. Why had they run without taking time first to finish her off? It didn't matter in the least, but the question nagged. She couldn't rest. Whatever it was the Gypsies wanted of her had nothing to do with the Patrol, and she knew she should attend to it . . . whatever it was. . . . Why had the Patrol run just then? The Link controls weren't far from her right hand, but it seemed to take an eternity and all her energy to reach them.

A woman's voice, strident with urgency, burst into the silent *Defiance* cockpit. ". . . Cargo liner *Marigold* bound for Mars. We have been attacked and our cargo plundered by pirates. Our drive has been disabled. . . ."

The voice faded into nonsense, in the way of voices heard at the edge of sleep—or of unconsciousness. Melacha jerked back to awareness in time to hear a Patrolman respond to the *Marigold*'s distressed report. Squadrons had been dispatched to search for the pirates, but had found nothing so far. Other Patrol boats were heading for rendezvous with the *Marigold* to see what could be done about her disabled drive. The Patrolmen wanted a more detailed report of what exactly the pirates had done.

Melacha shook her head: she must be hearing things. She was in pain, in shock, weak from loss of blood. They couldn't be talking about space pirates. She was having auditory hallucinations. It was the only reasonable explanation.

Leaving the Link on, she climbed to her feet and stood wavering on trembling legs while darkness threatened and receded again. There ought to have been a first aid kit in the cockpit, within reach of the pilot's seat, but she had used it some time ago and had not got around to replacing it. That was stupid. A smuggler should never space out without a first aid kit in reach.

"He was tall and dark," said a woman's voice. "The one they called the Pirate Prince. He wore a black-and-silver costume, like a jumpsuit sort of thing, with a cloak. His eyes were so *blue*. . . ."

The galley opened onto the cockpit, and there was a first aid kit in there. Melacha took one shuffling step and nearly fell as her injured leg collapsed under her. Fortunately she had her good hand on a sturdy freefall handhold, and managed to keep herself erect. If she had fallen, she might not have got up again.

"They only took Company cargo. No private shipments. Nothing belonging to colonists. The Pirate Prince said . . .''

She had to put her weight on that leg again. She just hadn't the strength to hop. Biting her lip, she swung the leg forward, locked the knee, and cautiously leaned her weight onto it. It held. She was going to make it.

A harsh male voice said too loudly, "No sign of any ships out here, sir. We got the report too late: he got away again. . . .''

She was leaving a trail of blood from the puddle under the pilot's seat right across the cockpit to the galley. The whole left side of her flight suit was wet and sticky with it. She was a small woman; she couldn't afford to lose so much blood. Blackness swirled across her mind. She stumbled, banging her injured arm against the galley hatch cover, and the shock of pain sent red shooting stars through the darkness, briefly clearing her mind. The first aid kit was almost in reach. . . .

''. . . Sly son of a bitch, this so-called Pirate Prince, but by God . . .''

The kit contained, among other things, the drug known familiarly in the asteroid belt as jockey juice. It was used to combat shock and to keep a person functional in an emergency. The instructions said absolutely never to use it with painkillers or in cases of severe loss of blood. Melacha didn't read the instructions; she had read them before and found them to be too limiting. She gave herself the injection and followed it with a moderate dose of a strong painkiller before she reached for the tools to stop the bleeding and patch herself together well enough to make it to a hospital or sick bay somewhere.

The Patrol and the *Marigold* had stopped chatting with each other about pirate princes by the time she returned to the cockpit. She moved with the creaky, exaggerated care of a very old woman. But she was alive, and fully conscious, and she wasn't bleeding anymore.

The Comm Link cracked static at her and she worked the controls, trying to find the Patrol again. Nobody was talking. On impulse she tried to hail the *Marigold*, but either she was out of range or the *Marigold*'s communications officer didn't like the sound of her voice. She had wanted to learn more about that Pirate Prince. . . . Could they really have been talking about a space pirate?

The idea was astrophysically absurd, at best. The course complexities involved, the orbital dynamics when they applied, most of all the sheer vast emptiness of space. . . . Melacha frowned at the silent Comm Link unit. Space piracy was improbable. Conceivable, but *she* had never thought of it. And if anyone were going to do anything as crazy impossible as that, she thought, it would have to be me. Nobody else is either dumb enough to try it or smart enough to pull it off.

Still, it seemed someone had done it. Someone who stole only Company cargo and left private shipments alone. Someone who called himself, rather theatrically, the Pirate Prince. Someone with as little sense and as much skill as the Skyrider. . . .

Whatever else he had done, he had saved her life. With no feeling of prescience at all, she hoped he wouldn't have cause to regret his inadvertent generosity.

CHAPTER SEVENTEEN

Most of JanMikal's crew were boys, barely post-adolescent, and very excited to be members of a pirate's crew. It was due to their enthusiastic hounding of Diadem's government officials that JanMikal had been granted a sleek racing scavenger shuttle, which some history buff had promptly dubbed *Corsair*. Nobody really knew why. JanMikal's boys liked the name, so it stuck.

They also liked the name Pirate Prince when Dr. Hale used it in an unguarded moment, so that stuck too. JanMikal felt moderately embarrassed about it, but at the same time he was aware that a reputation could be of more value to him than weapons. A name like the Pirate Prince, silly as it was, should be a good label under which people could file tales of his exploits, which he hoped would be magnified in the retelling.

He did need weapons, too. In fact, it was that need which originally brought him together with the boys who became his crew. After his encounter with the Patrol, when his plan to turn to piracy was still a vague idea that he meant to pursue alone, he had begun to look into the possibility of fabricating some kind of weapons on Diadem. Nobody wanted to talk about it until he met a group of rowdy young men at the swimming pool who were trying to build a sort of jetski out of a bicycle, a hang glider, and the motor from a life boat.

The jetski was a success. So was their inspired effort to turn industrial lasers into ships' weapons. And when JanMikal suggested the need for a handgun as well, they shouted and muttered and banged things around in their workshop, queried their computer, soldered and hammered and drilled and fiddled, and finally turned out the neatest little hand-held laser JanMikal could have imagined. They made him a hip holster for it, and he was surprised at the sense of relief he felt when he buckled it on, as though he hadn't been fully dressed without it.

The boys had calmly begun duplicating their efforts, making handguns and holsters for themselves as well. Startled and a little worried, JanMikal asked what they were doing. "You said you want to be a pirate, didn't you?" they said. "Well, a pirate has to have a crew." They were like good-natured puppies with a new toy. JanMikal knew they didn't really understand what they were proposing to do, but they wouldn't listen when he tried to warn them.

And the truth was that he really had needed a crew. They were right about that. He just hadn't known whether they would still want the job when they saw what it entailed, because he had no intention of being a kindly, harmless pirate. He wouldn't have much success that way. Besides, he had been talking with the families of *Jewel*'s crew. And he had heard about Newkansas, where hundreds had died because Earth wouldn't admit they existed. He was angry. The people of Diadem didn't want to make a fuss about it, but JanMikal wanted to. He intended to.

The boys had all been very quiet after their first raid. JanMikal hadn't been sure what to expect. He wouldn't

have been particularly surprised if they had quit and sur-
rendered their shiny new handguns to the enemy the first
time he had to kill somebody, but he knew that in the long
run they would succeed with a lot less killing if he was
utterly ruthless their first few times out, so he had killed
without hesitation. Quite possibly the boys never even
noticed that his weapon, covering the enemy crew, was
also positioned to defend himself from his own crew if
need be.

Their booty that first time had been whole crates of
paper, soaps, and beef in various forms—dried, freeze-
dried, tinned, and frozen. He couldn't have planned a better
first haul if he had been granted the pick of Earth's cargo
liners: those were all products rare and very highly prized
on Diadem, things difficult or impossible to produce on a
space colony of Diadem's size.

Diademan citizens were pleased with the cargo and
horrified by the boys' subdued description of how they had
got it. A number of people said they didn't want to use
products that had been obtained at the cost of three strangers' lives. The boys rallied at that, losing some of their
own awed horror at the killings as they tried to justify
JanMikal's behavior to people who wanted his piracy
stopped.

JanMikal didn't talk about it much with anyone except
Linda March, who tried hard to understand and tended to
stare at her former patient with a strange, half-frightened
look in her eyes. They still shared quarters at that time,
because March was still helping JanMikal adjust to Diademan
society, but not long after that first raid she found it
necessary to move back out to the torus to be nearer a new
patient who needed her more.

She wasn't deserting JanMikal, and she still spent much
of her free time with him. But she hadn't been able to
sleep comfortably so near him anymore. The bomb was
definitely armed now, the spring more tightly coiled, the

predator's jaws dripping with the blood of its recent victims. The fact that JanMikal actually looked more relaxed now and less dangerous than ever before had only increased her uneasiness.

After their second raid JanMikal's crew had recovered their boyish good spirits. There was one, the dark and brooding boy named Larton who had been unofficial leader of the group before they met JanMikal, who didn't join in their rowdy, good-natured play anymore, and who tended to watch JanMikal with cold, impersonal judgment that put JanMikal very much on his guard; but all the rest of the boys subsided into a very jolly but efficient and increasingly deadly crew absolutely loyal to their Pirate Prince.

They were growing up. Not that killing or breaking the law are particularly adult or even maturing activities; they are not. But these boys had never before allowed any serious purpose into their lives. The Pirate Prince had caught their imaginations, and what had initially been just a larger-scale adventure than they could manage on their own was now becoming a genuine cause, and one they cared very much about. They wanted to help supply Diadem, and they wanted to openly defy the government that denied Diadem's existence and made piracy the only viable means of supply. Stealing only government goods seemed a very appropriate form of defiance *and* supply.

The boys weren't aware of any particular change in themselves, but their Diademan friends and relatives noticed. Some were pleased with the boys' increased maturity, but all were disturbed by their lack of reverence for human life. This was a situation not covered by *The Way of Life According to Bill*, which made it all the more unsettling. It was a situation that had simply never occurred on Diadem before: the complex and subtle system of checks and balances intrinsic to a society in which everyone has a right to do whatever he wants to do had prevented it. The first generation, Bill's generation, had had its difficulties, but nothing like this; and succeeding generations had become more stable under Bill's *Way* till a situation like this was almost unthinkable . . . until JanMikal came to them from Outside.

Some of them wanted to send him back Outside. They called a Special Meeting to discuss it, and even held it in an empty low gravity warehouse in the Hub so JanMikal could attend in comfort. The low gravity was fairly comfortable for him, but the meeting wasn't. He didn't quite know what to expect, but he knew that his future was on trial and that he really had no defense at all if they wanted him to leave.

An alarming number of people showed up for the meeting. Most were strangers to JanMikal, though he did recognize a few of the boys' parents, old Davitz who had loaned him the tug to salvage the Lunar drone, and Robert Matlock who had refused him a job on the farms, as well as Linda March, Simon Hale, and Hale's secretary Celia Graham.

JanMikal was intentionally late to the meeting. He wanted to give them a little time to settle in before he showed up; it was a way of denying his anxiety. He intended to make no concessions to either their fear or his own. To that end he wore the dramatic cloaked jumpsuit costume he and the boys had designed for the Pirate Prince. The costume was as hokey as the name; he hoped the combination would help make him seem larger than life, more dangerous than an ordinary man—if not by creating an exotic, frightening image, then by creating an insane one. He thought it looked silly, but as Bill said in *The Way*, "Nothing that is useful should be discarded merely because it is also foolish." Wearing the costume to the meeting was an act of deliberate defiance, more useful than he knew: Diademans were accustomed to bizarre costumes. It made him seem more like an eccentric Diademan, less like an alien in their midst.

Everyone in the warehouse turned to look at him when he came in. The room was large and very brightly lighted, furnished only with rows of folding chairs that squeaked as their occupants craned their necks to see him over each other's heads. They were arranged in a rough half-circle, with aisles at intervals down which prospective speakers could walk to the podium at the focal point.

JanMikal hesitated at the door, wondering whether he should quietly take a back seat or go on forward and make some sort of speech. He couldn't think of anything to say, so he took a seat.

For a long moment nobody spoke. Nobody even moved. They were still staring at him. He became uncomfortably aware of the weapon at his hip; the costume was okay, but he should have left the weapon at home. And he didn't know what to do with his hands. He tried folding them in his lap, felt silly and awkward, put them on this thighs, and finally crossed his arms, aware it was a defensive posture but unable to keep from assuming it. He wondered, a trifle wildly, what other people did with their hands, but hadn't the courage to look around to find out. The silence was deadly. He stared fixedly at the podium, unaware of the arrogance of his expression, and listened to the blood in his ears.

When they finally looked away from him and started talking again, his relief was so great that he didn't hear anything that was said for a good five minutes or more. Consciousness returned slowly, so that the next few impassioned speeches made very little sense to him. Apparently they made sense to the rest of the crowd, since they occasioned heated responses from various quarters till the room was echoing with overlapping arguments.

A woman near JanMikal was shouting at a man four rows away from her, "He's my grandson, and by all that's balanced, I do know what's best for him, and it's not to be in a pirate's crew!'' JanMikal couldn't hear the man's response, because someone on his other side shouted, ''Yes, but they're not going to get *Jewel*'s crew back, are they!'' Across the room a man bellowed, ''Don't forget Newkansas. If they'd had a pirate—''

It wasn't clear to whom that last man was speaking, but there was a momentary lull in which nearly everyone heard what he said, and several people responded. The ones JanMikal sorted out were a woman who said Diadem wasn't Newkansas and a young girl who said that if they had to use outlaws for anything they ought to recruit them as needed and send them back Outside when the job was done, to which a man near her responded that Diademans were all outlaws anyway since Earth didn't recognize their existence, and the girl's companion said not very loudly that maybe the outlaw you didn't know would be an even worse threat than the one you did know. Someone else said that at least the one you didn't know wouldn't corrupt your children, and the argument threatened to degenerate into a discussion of child-rearing.

Davitz rose abruptly and walked forward to take the deserted podium. The confused babble of voices subsided; he was well-known and respected, and they all looked at him expectantly, waiting to see which side he was on. He ran a hand through his thick silver hair, leaving it wildly disarrayed, and smiled at them almost apologetically. ''I know JanMikal—the Pirate Prince—looks dangerous to us,'' he said, and waited patiently for the hoots and jeers to subside. ''Okay, I know JanMikal *is* dangerous to us.'' He held up a hand for silence and, amazingly, got it. ''But do you all have so little faith in Bill's *Way*?'' That elicited a confused murmur and then a slightly chastened silence as he continued: ''We need the cargo the Pirate Prince is bringing us.''

A grizzled worker said just audibly, ''But it's stolen.''

Davitz gave him a fatherly look. "Everything that has come to us from Outside for a number of years now has been stolen." His craggy face looked friendly and sympathetic. He put both hands on the podium and leaned forward, a kindly grandfather confiding in his family. "As long as Earth refuses to recognize us, the only way we can get anything from Outside is to steal."

A beautifully cared-for young man in a sari stood up and stared directly across the room at JanMikal. "But we don't kill when we steal." His voice was clear and sweet and deadly. He looked at Davitz, produced a startlingly innocent smile, and sat down.

"That is true," said Davitz. "We also do not steal much anymore, since *Jewel* was taken. JanMikal is still willing to do it, despite the danger. And I believe that *The Way* will protect us—and our children—from the disruptive influence of any Outsider."

A woman, the one who had said her grandson shouldn't be in a pirate's crew, stood up to say, "But they are changing, Davitz. They're good boys, but they're *changing*, working with him."

Davitz waited till she sat down again, slowly surveyed the whole half-circle of anxious, hostile faces, and quoted from *The Way*: " 'Change is the only constant.' "

Someone made a rude sound and then quoted right back at him, " 'Change for its own sake may be inadvisable.' "

Davitz nodded. "That is right," he said agreeably. "It *may be* inadvisable. Then again, it may not. Do you ever rearrange the furniture in your home?" He smiled faintly and looked around. "But of course this is a more serious matter than moving furniture. And it is not change for its own sake. Any change, good or bad, in any of us as a result of JanMikal's work is a side effect of something we want and need very badly: a source of supply." He looked slowly around the half-circle again, acknowledging a few faces with a nod or a smile, then looked at the room as a whole and quoted again: " 'An open mind is advisable, because change is mandatory.' "

Nobody responded to that. After a long moment Davitz turned to look at JanMikal. "I think it is your turn, boy," he said softly.

JanMikal wanted to refuse. Davitz was doing well enough without him. Better, probably, than he could do. There were so many of them. . . .

He rose, conscious again of the gun at his hip and the hokey drama of his costume. The silver-lined cape swirled as he stepped into the aisle and moved toward the podium. His expression wasn't arrogant now, but it was still threatening. He looked more than ever like a sullen, frightened—and therefore dangerous—boy.

But the costume caught people's attention, as it was meant to do: and a line from *The Way*, unexpectedly remembered, dissolved JanMikal's ferocious scowl. It was the first thing he said when he reached the podium and Davitz had retired to a nearby chair.

" 'The Divine Fool wears a lot of hats.' " His voice was clear and strong, and the room was suddenly as still and silent as when he had first entered it. The last thing anyone had expected was to hear him quoting *The Way*—and one of the more obscure passages, at that. They stared, waiting. He smiled sheepishly and it transformed his face: now he was everybody's little brother, caught with his hand in the cookie jar. "I know I'm not the Divine Fool, of course. I hardly even have the courage to try to be." They waited, still startled and wary, not wanting to like him but beginning to anyway.

Flicking his cape almost nervously, he turned slowly, surveying the whole room. His eyes were wide and very blue. "You know, I wasn't sure whether I should wear this silly costume here." He tossed the cape back and leaned on the podium, watching them. "When I decided to wear it, I told myself it was in an effort to be fair; I wanted you to see me at my worst.'' To his surprise they remained gratifyingly attentive, and it seemed to him that some of them were looking a little less hostile. He smiled again, tentatively. ''The truth is, I think, that I wore it to give myself courage. I'm not half as brave as the Pirate Prince is.''

''But you are the Pirate Prince!'' It was a boy's voice, startled into speaking and embarrassed to hear his own voice. After a brief hesitation he added defiantly, ''Well, you are.''

JanMikal found him in the crowd and nodded at him seriously. ''Yes, I am. I am a pirate, and a warrior, and a killer of men.'' There were a few audibly indrawn breaths at that, but he didn't give them time to speak. ''I am also,'' he said, a little more loudly to be sure he was heard over the murmurs of shock and protest. They subsided, and he repeated: ''I am also,'' and tried to look at as many individuals as he could, as sincerely as he could. ''I am also an ordinary man. Friend to a few people here.'' He drew a breath. ''I am also a freefall mutant. I am also a damn good pilot. A fairly good navigator. A rotten cook.'' A wry grin pulled at his lips. ''Also a not-very-good housekeeper and a poor poker player. For a while I was a teacher, and I think I was a good one—'' Here he had to raise his voice again, and did it without blinking. ''I think somewhere, Outside, in the past I can't remember, I am a father.'' He had trouble with that word, but got it out. ''I'm a lot of things, just as everybody here is a lot of things, a lot of people. Nobody is all good or all bad, and most of the things we do are not all good or all bad. 'The Divine Fool wears a lot of hats.' '' He had to raise his voice again. ''If I seem a little rough around the edges to some of you, maybe that's because I'm not the Divine Fool.'' They quieted, and he lowered his voice again. ''I'm doing my best.''

"By killing?" That was Linda March, and she asked it as gently as she could, but it was a harsh question.

It was also a question he knew he had to answer. His whole future might ride on it. He looked at her without expression and said slowly, "I am also from Outside."

"That doesn't answer the question," said Robert Matlock.

"No. Not entirely. It is a part of the answer, though." He hesitated. "If I were Diademan, if I had been raised on Bill's *Way*, I don't suppose I could kill, at least not the way I have done as the Pirate Prince; not for profit." There were nods and shouts of agreement. He waited till they subsided. "I wasn't raised on Bill's *Way*. I don't know where or how I was raised, or who I was before I came to you, but whoever I was, I probably hadn't even heard of *The Way*. That doesn't mean I wasn't the best person I knew how to be. I hope I was. But I know I wasn't Diademan."

"You still aren't," someone said belligerently.

"No, I'm not." He didn't even look for the speaker. "But now I have studied *The Way*, and I am doing my Outsider's best to incorporate it into my life." He hesitated again, watching them. "*I want* to help supply Diadem, to repay what I owe and to help a colony and a people I have come to respect. *I want* to help Diadem avoid the situation Newkansas faced, and I think the way to do that is to keep some kind of supply lines open. *I want* to raise a fuss with Earth government—get revenge, maybe—for the imprisonment of *Jewel*'s crew. And *I want* to do what I do best—*I want* to fly—*I want*—"

He had let his voice get a little louder with each *I want*: now, abruptly, he fell silent, looking at his audience. They looked back at him, involuntarily carried along on the strength of his wants, trying to break the spell and find ways to express their objections.

He did it for them. "I know the Diademan philosophy is not just a matter of somebody declaring his wants and getting them satisfied. We don't always get what we want. Nobody does. At least, not on the casual surface level of just wanting and getting: sometimes we have to decide between mutually exclusive wants." He looked them over while they waited. "As Diademans born and bred, you all want peace, an absence of violence, more than you want the supplies you could get by going out and committing violence. I understand that. I respect it. But I came from Outside, and I have different wants."

He paused again, and Davitz said in a slow, puzzled voice, "Are you trying . . . Do you want to be the Divine Fool?"

JanMikal looked at him. "I know I can't be. That's really the nature of the Divine Fool—I doubt that any of us here has a realistic hope of it. But I repeat, I am doing my best." He looked at Linda March. "How do you know the Divine Fool wouldn't kill for profit? Do you know that? Did Bill say it?"

"He didn't have to," said March.

"This is ridiculous," said Hale. "Your arguments are irrational at best."

" 'Irrational behavior is always a matter of perspective,' " said JanMikal.

Hale was already shaking his head before he realized that, too, had been a quote from *The Way*. He said almost petulantly, "You're twisting *The Way* to suit your needs."

JanMikal nodded. "Quite possibly. That is a natural tendency people have: we twist things to suit our needs. But . . . don't you think the Divine Fool, in the flesh, would seem irrational to us?"

For a moment no one spoke. Then Celia Graham said stubbornly, "I don't want to use products got at the cost of people's lives."

JanMikal looked at her. "You're living in a 'product' made at the cost of people's lives. Do you know how many people died in the construction of Diadem?"

"That's different."

"Maybe. I think it could be successfully argued either way." He looked down at the podium for a moment, then looked back up at the people and said slowly, "We're not going to resolve the killing easily. If you let me stay, I'll continue my work, which will very probably mean more killing. If that possibility outweighs all other considerations for you, there's nothing I can say to change your minds." He thought about it, sighed, and began again, quietly at first. "You will need supplies. Not just in emergencies like the one at Newkansas, but for your daily lives. There is no legal way to get them. The illegal ways that don't involve the possibility of violence have failed. I can get supplies for you. Will you let me?"

It took six more hours of fierce argument, but they finally—grudgingly—decided in favor of the Pirate Prince.

CHAPTER EIGHTEEN

The Pirate Prince leaned negligently against a box of cargo, his long frame apparently relaxed and his expression deceptively sleepy: but his eyes were wary and his hand never strayed far from the weapon spring-holstered at his hip. To the men and women whose ship he had waylaid he seemed exactly what the growing legend had led them to expect: arrogant, distant, deadly.

His own people moved silently at their tasks, shifting cargo from the waylaid liner to their own sleek *Corsair* with swift efficiency, taking no apparent notice of the lean dark Prince who was their master. They were dressed as he was; in plain black jumpsuits with gleaming metal fittings, lacking only the swirling silver-lined cape the Prince wore; and tall black space boots with soft soles and ankle-holstered knives. Their faces were younger than his, and less arrogant, but no less threatening to the men and women he held hostage.

As ever, the pirates took only Company cargo and left all individual shipments as well as goods marked for Mars or for freeholdings in the Belt. There was little talk among

them, and no hesitation over policy, even when they came
to Mars-marked shipments of obviously greater value than
the Company cargo they took. It was all over in a matter
of minutes. People had learned not to resist the Pirate
Prince once their ships were in his hands. It was no use.
He could not be beaten. He would match violence with
violence at any level and emerge victorious, but if his
conquest went unchallenged, his hostages were invariably
released unharmed.

Company policy, of course, encouraged resistance. Since
the reorganizations following the Brief War between Earth
and the colonies, there were few Company employees left
who were willing to die for a matter of policy. The crew of
the plundered ship waited in submissive silence as the last
load was carried out of the cargo hold and the Pirate Prince
moved to follow his crew back to his own ship, closely
attended by two black-and-silver-clad bodyguards.

He paused at the cargo hatch to study his hostages a
moment before he smiled. It was a sardonic smile, cold
and calculating and as deadly as the weapon near which
his hand still hovered in readiness. His bodyguards de-
fended him with drawn weapons, but he had not, since
boarding this ship, drawn his own. That was fortunate.
When the Pirate Prince drew his weapon, people died.

"You have been patient." His voice was low and surprisingly pleasant. His accent was a mystery over which
bitter arguments daily ensued throughout the Solar System.
"I am sorry to have to disable your ship; she's a good ship
and you've done me no harm. But I don't want to fight
another battle over this cargo. It's mine, now." He said it
just like that, as if another battle were a pesky inconvenience he wanted to avoid just to save time. "So I can't
leave you means to chase me." He smiled again. "But
I've left you the Comm Link. Call the Patrol if you like;
I'll be gone." He turned calmly and walked away. His

bodyguards backed out after him, their weapons ready and their faces predatory. No one challenged them.

Back inside *Corsair*, JanMikal the Pirate Prince could at last relax in gravity set more nearly to his liking. Boarding conquered ships kept at full Earth gravity was a more painful task every time he undertook it. His crew knew it. In their affection for him, they always worked at impressive speed to get cargoes off-loaded onto *Corsair*, to shorten his ordeal. But they couldn't argue against his boarding the ships at all. They knew as well as he did that much of their success as pirates depended on the mystery surrounding the dark and dangerous Pirate Prince.

Seeing him more comfortable now, his bodyguards burst into explosive laughter and holstered their weapons. " 'Call the Patrol if you like; I'll be gone,' " crowed one, a short fair boy with the scraggly hint of a new beard showing. "That was rich, JanMikal. The way you said it! You begin to *sound* like a prince."

JanMikal grinned ruefully. "It's the gravity," he said. "Pain makes me arrogant."

The other bodyguard was almost as tall as JanMikal, but darker, with a face nearly feminine in its beauty. He grinned briefly at Jan Mikal and said, "Everything makes you arrogant, it seems."

The Prince glared. "Watch your tongue, Hobart, or I'll make you walk the plank."

Hobart made a sound deep in his throat. "Not unless we scavenge a plank from Earth."

JanMikal shook his head. "Not scavenge. Pirate. We're not scavengers anymore." While they talked, they had been closing the hatch and helping to secure the cargo for breakaway; now JanMikal turned from the work and walked with his careful, painful grace toward the cockpit to command their flight.

His crew was skilled and well trained. When he reached the cockpit everything was in readiness for breakaway, awaiting his order. The navigator had plotted their course, the helmsman had laid it in, and the Comm Link officer was intercepting Patrol reports in order to steer them clear of Patrol activity. They all looked up when JanMikal entered and watched with sympathy that in no way diminished their respect as he seated himself carefully in what they insisted on calling the command chair, which they had personally redesigned to ease his discomfort under acceleration when the gravity generators couldn't adequately compensate.

"Let's go home," said the Pirate Prince.

The Comm Link officer, a skinny boy with long dark hair and spaniel eyes, said without looking up from his instruments, "Patrol between us and home. Maybe better try Luna."

JanMikal gave the order to the helmsman, who fed it to the computer. "If there were more of us, we wouldn't always have to run from the Patrol," said the helmsman. He was a sturdy redhead unaccustomed to running from anyone.

JanMikal smiled. "You think they'd run from an over-crowded pirate ship?"

"I meant more ships." The helmsman glanced up at JanMikal and grinned. "And you know it."

"I know it," said JanMikal. "Because we've been over it so often before. Who's going to join us?"

"You could try other colonies."

"Maybe I will, but not today." JanMikal gave the helmsman a curious look. "You think they'd run from more ships?"

"Armed ships," said the helmsman.

"Armed ships that fired on them, maybe," said the Comm Link officer. "They're not going to be scared off by sheer numbers."

"So we'll fire on them," said the helmsman, shrugging.

"And kill them?" asked the Comm Link officer.

"If we had to," said the helmsman.

Hobart, having emerged from the direction of the cargo hold in the middle of this conversation, said with considerable satisfaction, "Well, I hope we don't have to today; the cargo we just took is worth too much to risk in a firefight."

JanMikal gave him a wry look. "Especially one we'd be bound to lose." He looked at the Comm Link officer. "How're we doing, Abi?"

"They're looking the wrong way," Abi said scornfully. He briefly detailed the overheard actions of the Patrol, his thin face smug. "They always look the wrong way."

"That's because they know we can't come from Luna," said the helmsman.

"Ah, but we do come from Luna," said JanMikal. "Don't get too smug, Abi, or you either, Jade." The warning look he gave both the Comm Link officer and the helmsman was tempered by the hint of a smile. "The Patrol isn't as stupid as it looks. They'll figure out we've got an auxiliary base on Luna if we don't find some other course to avoid them soon."

"If we had more ships," began Jade.

"That's enough about more ships for now," said JanMikal. "Let's concentrate on getting home in the one we've got."

"That gravity wears you out," said Hobart.

JanMikal shrugged. "We've been over that, too."

"I know, you have to board. But we could make them turn down their gravity."

"And let them know that the Pirate Prince has a major exploitable weakness?" JanMikal shook his head. "Bad plan."

"Then we should run in freefall," said Hobart.

"If we divert enough power to the gravity generator to run in freefall, we won't be running very fast, will we?" asked JanMikal.

Jade, delighted to discover in himself an area of superiority over Hobart, snorted in exaggerated disgust. "You'd make a pretty poor helmsman, Hobey, if you don't know that much."

"And you'd make a pretty poor bodyguard for our Pirate Prince here," said Hobart, "which is why you're helmsman and I'm bodyguard and cargo hauler."

"I'd make a perfectly good bodyguard," Jade said with unexpected fierceness. "It's just that I'm a better helmsman."

"You, a bodyguard?" This time it was Hobart who snorted. "That I'd like to see. You couldn't—"

"Boys," said JanMikal.

Abi, who hadn't taken part in this bickering, said in a primly self-satisfied voice, "We can't run for home yet. We'll probably have to go ahead and land on Luna and wait till the search is called off."

"The captain's supposed to decide what we're going to do," Jade said sullenly.

JanMikal sighed audibly. All three boys were silent for a long moment. Then almost simultaneously they all said, "Sorry, sir."

JanMikal looked at them. "Just don't any of you ever act like this in front of hostages, that's all I ask. You'd ruin my reputation."

Three bloodthirsty pirates, much chastened, said again in near-unison, "Sorry, sir."

"Course for Lunar landing, sir?" Jade asked in such a subdued and respectful voice that JanMikal could barely hear it.

"Yes, please," said the Pirate Prince.

CHAPTER NINETEEN

Stephen B. Newcomb left his staff meeting at a dignified trot, looking as self-satisfied as he felt. He was a plump middle-aged man with a face that could look both villainous and cherubic at once, a mixed impression that was aided on the side of villainy by a meticulously trimmed moustache and goatee in a dark-sand color more liberally sprinkled with gray than his receding hair, which was well-greased and combed fiercely straight back away from his mottled forehead.

He wore a brocade jacket and pants in rich shades of peacock blue and green threaded with gold, and a lavishly ruffled yellow silk shirt just enough too small for him that pink, hairy strips of protruding stomach were exposed and concealed again between strained buttons as he moved. His feet, shod in brocade zori to match his suit, made tiny slapping sounds as he walked, despite the thickness of the government-issue carpet in the corridor outside the meeting room. The two Ground Patrolmen stationed one on either side of the meeting room's wide oak doors watched him expressionlessly as he passed.

The young man waiting in the corridor for Newcomb was dressed as elegantly as Newcomb, in a brocade suit of muted purple and lavender with a deep purple shirt, heavily ruffled, and high-topped suede boots in the same deep purple. He wore no facial hair, and in fact looked too young to grow any, an impression that was emphasized rather than mitigated by his almost lugubrious expression.

As Newcomb approached him, the young man stepped forward and bowed deeply with no change of expression. "Mr. Newcomb?" His voice was quiet, well modulated, businesslike. "I'm Ian Spencer. We spoke on the Comm Link earlier today, if you remember?"

Newcomb scowled importantly. "Something about some investment corporation, wasn't it?" He made an imperious gesture. "Come along, come along. As I told you on the Link, I've no time for these minor business matters now; my government needs me." This last was said not just seriously, but smugly.

"Yes, sir," Spencer said. "I'm aware of that, sir." He fell into step beside the older man, his expression still ridiculously sober. "But this matter—I think you'll agree, sir—is of the utmost importance to you personally, and quite urgent."

"Yes, yes, you said that before. That's why I agreed to meet with you." Newcomb pulled an antique pocket watch from its place of concealment in his jacket, caused it to spring open, scowled at the resultant digital display, and tucked it fastidiously away. "I can give you five minutes. I have the use of a small back office on this floor. Come along." Without a glance at Spencer he increased his pace, leading the younger man around two corners and down an uncarpeted back corridor to a pale wooden door marked with Newcomb's name in small iridescent blue letters. His palm print unlocked it and he led the way inside.

Rather to Spencer's surprise, Newcomb made no apologies for the size of the office, which was small, nor for the condition of the furnishings, which were aged but not antique and were extremely battered. The large Comm Link screen was the only furnishing of any real interest to Spencer. Newcomb gestured toward a chair with a torn cushion and Spencer obediently sat in it while Newcomb fussily arranged himself behind the desk. "Now, what is it?" He spoke as one might to a troublesome child.

"Investments, Incorporated," said Spencer. "I think you're familiar with it?"

Newcomb studied him with a thin-lipped, evil interest. "I may have heard of it."

"I.I. invested in a project of mine." Spencer leaned comfortably back in his chair and crossed his legs. "Now they want to move the payment date forward. In fact, I've already had to deal with two of their so-called collectors, who seemed to believe the payment date had already been moved forward. I tried to explain that it wasn't going to be, but they wouldn't listen. I'm afraid they're not feeling well now."

Newcomb was making impatient gestures while continuing his disapproving study of Spencer. As soon as Spencer fell silent, Newcomb said crossly, "Yes? Yes? What has that to do with me?"

"I don't want the payment date moved forward."

Newcomb folded his hands over the ruffles on his protuberant belly. "Young man, I'm afraid I fail to see quite why you are bringing your personal problems to my attention. I am a very busy man—"

"Perhaps not anymore." Spencer made no move at all except to smile. It was a nice, open, boyish smile. For some reason it made Newcomb distinctly uneasy.

"This interview is concluded." He pressed the alarm that would call Ground Patrol to remove his visitor, forcibly if necessary, from his little borrowed office.

"I don't think so." Spencer still didn't move, but his smile widened.

"I warn you, young man, I've called Ground Patrol; they'll be here in a moment. It would be better for all concerned if you were to leave now, of your own volition."

"Punch up I.I. on your Comm Link, why don't you?" Spencer leaned forward, folded his hands around one knee, and smiled confidently at Newcomb. "There's no sense waiting for Ground Patrol; they aren't coming."

Newcomb waited silently for Ground Patrol to arrive. When a considerable time had passed without any arrivals, he shifted uncomfortably, cleared his throat, and scowled at Spencer, who had been waiting patiently and smiling throughout. "What have you done to the alarm system?"

"Nothing, really. I'm carrying a damper." Spencer lifted one hand to reveal a tiny cylindrical object fastened to one finger. "It won't affect the Comm Link, if you want to call them on that. But I really do think you ought to punch up I.I. first."

Newcomb called Ground Patrol, watching Spencer, who merely smiled. When Ground Patrol answered, Newcomb frowned at Spencer, made an excuse to Ground Patrol for misdialing, apologized, and disconnected. Then, still frowning at Spencer, he punched up I.I. The picture that appeared on the screen was not the smiling face of I.I.'s receptionist: it was a complete listing of I.I.'s top executives, including Newcomb. There followed a selective listing of I.I.'s investments, including only those that would be damaging to Newcomb's reputation and, consequently, to his political aspirations. He stared at it, mesmerized, his eyes wide.

"That's what anyone will get who calls I.I.," said Spencer. "I haven't got the sound worked out yet, but later there'll be a voice-over to read those lists for any blind or illiterate callers."

"This is illegal. You can't do this to me." Newcomb

turned to stare at Spencer, his eyes narrowing. "I'll have you shot. I'll have you in jail so fast your eyes will spin. I'll—"

"Maybe," Spencer said. "Or, if the wrong people call I.I. and read those lists before you get I.I. to back off and forget I even borrowed from them, which is the only way I'll take that offline, maybe *you'll* be shot. Or in jail. Several of I.I.'s listed activities are not exactly what you might call legal, if I'm not mistaken."

"My men will find you," said Newcomb. "I won't be bullied. I'll have you taken apart bone by bone. Nobody threatens Stephen B. Newcomb."

Spencer shrugged. "Stalemate, then, for now." He rose, still grinning amiably, and walked to the office door. When he had it open he hesitated, looking back at Newcomb. "I'd advise you to think about it, Newcomb. I've survived your bone-breakers before. Can you survive *that*?" He indicated the Comm Link screen. "Remember, I can get it offline in minutes, anytime, anywhere, as soon as I hear—favorably, of course—from I.I." He turned to leave, hesitated again, and turned back. "You'll want your own experts to check out my work, of course. I feel I should warn you that it's protected. They won't be able to match my programming, and if they try to remove my jam, the display you'll get will be a lot more damaging than that one." He shrugged again. "But it's your funeral, and all the same to me; either way, I'll be off the hook."

Newcomb's Comm Link signaled for his attention. Spencer closed the door quietly behind him as he left.

CHAPTER TWENTY

Melacha's rock seemed more like home the next time she saw it. She had stopped at Home Base only long enough for the med-techs to patch her together; she wanted to get her cargo off-loaded and safely stashed so she could get back to Home Base and reload with new purchases before her time ran out and she had to turn the account over to Ian Spencer. She had used too much time in transit, and had wasted days on the side trip to Newkansas.

The reward for that, however, was waiting at the second dock on her rock: another *Defiance,* identical in all important respects with the original. When she had the original *Defiance* securely docked she took time to go over to the other dock to investigate the new one. Everything seemed to be in order. She didn't want to waste much time over it. A quick computer check showed all systems in excellent condition. The Newkansans had been very grateful; hundreds had died before she got there, but thousands more would have died if she hadn't gone. They had even duplicated *Defiance*'s enlarged fuel capacity, improved conversion engines, and concealed smuggling hold. The only real

difference between the two ships seemed to be that the
new one still smelled new.

Satisfied, she went back into her rock and resolutely
began off-loading *Defiance*'s cargo. Her left arm wasn't
entirely functional yet, and her left leg ached: that would
slow the work badly. Fortunately this load included a great
many perishable luxuries, which she could take with her
back to Home Base and get someone else to off-load as
part of the deal when she sold them.

She wondered absently about the Pirate Prince while she
worked. What an absurd name—Pirate Prince—but he
must be doing something right, if the Patrol felt obliged to
pull all those Patrol boats off her to go after him. She was
very grateful to him for that, whoever he was.

He might well be that young tug pilot whose eyes
looked so much like Jamin's. What was his name?
—JanMikal, that was it. JanMikal had hinted at some
mysterious means of supplying his colony. Diadem was
one of the old Stanford torus colonies, Haioshi had told
her. Haioshi had also told her in some detail of the arrest
of Diadem's salvage crew and the confiscation of their
ship *Jewel*. How he happened to know so much about it,
she hadn't asked. But his story had completed a picture
that JanMikal had only partially drawn, and she knew after
talking with Haioshi that Diadem hadn't many options for
supply. Piracy might look very good to them.

She thought about JanMikal and remembered the blue of
his eyes, so very like Jamin's, and the recklessness of his
smile. What was it that woman on the *Marigold* had said
of the Pirate Prince? He was tall and dark, and "His eyes
were so *blue*." That sounded like JanMikal. She hadn't
seen how tall he was, but he had seemed long and lean,
with dark hair like Jamin's. . . .

Perhaps the only reason she had liked him or even
particularly remembered him was that he reminded her so

much of Jamin. Still, she hoped that if he was the Pirate Prince, those swarming Patrol boats hadn't found him. Somehow she didn't think they would have. Surely the Patrol couldn't catch a man with a smile like that.

Of course not. And they always say please when they want something. Grinning at her own foolishness, she stacked the last crate of cargo in her crowded storeroom and returned to her shuttle for the run back to Home Base.

The Skyrider hugged a teddy bear under her chin while she soberly examined the toy store's extensive collection of baby dolls, prodded a ruffled garment here and a fat cheek there, pinched plump plastic toes, and gently smoothed acrylic curls back from hard china foreheads. A rag doll caught her eye. It had yellow yarn hair and button eyes, improbably long legs, and mitten hands. She picked it up, dubiously eyeing the Colonial Fleet insignia on the breast of its calico Martian dress.

"Your cousin's children will like that one," said the storekeeper. "It's a very popular model since the war."

Startled, the Skyrider looked up from the dolls; she had forgotten for a moment that she wasn't alone in the store. "Oh. Yeah. Thanks." She looked at the doll in her hand, remembered the bear hugged cozily in the other arm, and hastily stuffed both of them under one arm with a guilty show of indifference. "Martian kids are pretty young for their age, yeah? It's hard to tell what they'll want. You think the older boys might like one of these model shuttles?" She reached for a box without looking to see which shuttle was inside.

"They'd probably prefer a Colonial model," said the storekeeper. "Have you seen the one we have of the *Defiance*? That's the Skyrider's shuttle. Kids love it." He took down a box, looked at the Skyrider's picture on its top, looked at the Skyrider, and his eyes widened in surprise. "I, that is, are you . . . ?"

She shrugged, more interested in the box he held than in his awe and confusion over actually meeting the Skyrider. "That's really a model *Defiance*? —Hey, it looks pretty good. It's even got her oversized engine nacelles. I'll take one of those. How many toys does that make, altogether?"

The storekeeper moved back to the counter, still staring at the Skyrider. His manner was suddenly much more tolerant and less impatient than it had been since she entered the store. "Let's see, I think, yes, five toys here, plus those two under your arm if you've decided . . . ?"

She remembered the bear and the doll and shoved them onto the counter next to the other toys. "Sure. And the model *Defiance*."

He nodded, barely able to count the toys in his excitement. He had never met a real live hero before. "That's, let me see, eight toys. How many children did you say your cousin has?"

Wry amusement pulled at the corners of her mouth. "I'm not just sure. Maybe we ought to make it an even dozen, just to be on the safe side. How about a couple of those board games back there, I don't care which ones, something good for a wide age range since I don't know how old they are. And maybe a couple more dolls; I didn't get much for girls."

"We have a new doll, just in," he said. "I haven't even got them onto the shelves yet. Would you like to see it?" He reached under the counter as he spoke, and pulled out a box that was leaking packing material. "It's supposed to look like that Pirate Prince everyone's talking about." He pulled one out of the box and held it out for her inspection.

It was a big old-fashioned soft doll with its face painted on in pastels. "This doesn't look like anyone," she said. "Is this what he really wears?"

"That's what I meant about looking like him, not the face," said the storekeeper. "Of course I don't know what he actually does wear, but they say he wears black like this, with silver trim and fittings, and the doll comes with detachable cloak—see, it's lined with silver—and the little laser comes free from the holster, it's a perfect miniature complete with batteries, and the holster will come off too, of course, though the rest of the clothes are as you can see stitched on, in fact they're actually part of the structure of the doll—''

"I'll take it, that will be fine," said the Skyrider. Her voice was flat and bored, but she eyed the doll with obvious interest. "You'll wrap them all for me? Except this little navigation computer; that's separate. I guess I'll wrap it myself."

"Is that for your friend's son?" the storekeeper asked. "The boy whose father—" He caught the Skyrider's glance and his voice trailed off uncertainly. "Oh, sorry. I thought, that is . . .''

"It's for Collis," said the Skyrider. "The boy whose father died saving my life." Her voice was toneless.

"I'm really very sorry," said the storekeeper. "I didn't mean, um, well . . ." He looked at the Pirate doll again, in search of a safer topic. "Listen, what do *you* think of this Pirate Prince person? I mean, it's really strange, isn't it, how he only takes Company goods and only waylays Company liners? They say he speaks with a Belter accent."

"I heard it was Martian."

"Well, yeah," said the storekeeper, busy boxing her purchases. "And one guy on the newsfax said it was Earther, so I guess you can't tell, but what do you think? I mean, a *pirate*. That's really something, yeah?"

Something flickered in the dark of her eyes. "Some people never grow up." She was studying the doll again.

He looked up from his packaging, vulnerable, humbly ready to accept insult. He was older than the Skyrider by at least ten years, but because she was a hero and an

outlaw, he related to her as if the age difference went the
other way. "I guess maybe it is childish to admire an
outlaw."

Unexpectedly, she laughed. "I'd be a fine one to say
that!" When he looked still more confused and potentially
crushed, she said almost impatiently, "Look, I didn't
mean to laugh at you, but I'm not exactly your average
Patrol material myself, you know."

He looked back at the toys on the counter and silently
continued wrapping them, looking puzzled and obstinate.

"I meant the Pirate Prince never grew up." Her tone
was conversational, her expression mildly bored. "I only
said it because of the nickname—Pirate Prince—and that
may not even be his fault. I mean, I never asked to be
called the Skyrider, and I guess it's just luck that that's not
equally cute and offensive."

"You think the Pirate Prince is offensive? The name?"

She looked at him seriously for a moment, shrugged,
and looked at the toys under his hands.

"But what about the Prince himself?" he asked. "What
he does? What do you think of that?"

She grinned ruefully. "You a Company spy, or what?"

He finished his toy-wrapping and prepared to box the
whole collection for shipment to Mars. Casual conversation with a hero wasn't easy. He wished now that he had
never mentioned the Pirate Prince. He'd only done it to
cover the much worse bungle of having mentioned that
pilot who died in the war, whose son was living with the
Skyrider's cousin on Mars. He'd heard she was in love
with him.

It was difficult to imagine the Skyrider in love with
anyone. Her face was deceptively sweet and gentle, but
those eyes were deadly. "No, I'm no spy," he said humbly,
knowing she knew he wasn't a spy but not sure why she
had asked. And suddenly, between answering that question

and taking the next breath, he'd had enough of being humble. So what if she *was* the Skyrider? So what if she was world-famous and, besides, could knock him down with one hand tied behind her back (and gossip said she'd do it, too, at the smallest provocation)? Her friend the pilot wasn't the only one who'd died in the Brief War. Other people had to live with grief, too, and they didn't get pointlessly rude to strangers on that account. "I just mentioned the Pirate Prince because I admire him. I don't know why he's doing what he's doing, but I'm *glad* he's doing it. The Company deserves it. And he never steals from colonists."

"He steals from those who have to buy goods from the Company, and pay outrageous prices because he's created a scarcity," said the Skyrider.

He had half expected her to hit him instead of answering. Relief made him unsteady. Not that he was that much afraid of her. . . . But of course he *was* that much afraid of her. It was only that he also had some self-respect. "They can order direct from Earth," he said.

"Some of them can. But it's not a solution."

He knew it wasn't; they had to pay shipping when they ordered from Earth, or had to band together to order whole shipments so they would only have to pay for the run. "I don't care. I still admire him."

She smiled; a bewilderingly sweet smile, friendly and wholly unexpected. "Good for you. So do I, but don't tell anyone."

"Oh, I wouldn't," he began, and then realized it was a joke. She didn't care what he told anyone. Unless, he thought with unaccustomed cattiness, he pulled the store's security tapes and let everyone see her cuddling that teddy bear, and told them how carefully she had selected a dozen toys for her cousin's children. That didn't quite fit her macho image. But he wouldn't tell anyone that, either, and he wouldn't pull the tapes for public display. Rude or not, she *was* a hero. Like the Pirate Prince. A hero of the people.

He didn't realize he had said that aloud till she made an indelicate sound that could only be called a snort. "A hero of the people, is he?" It was amazing to him that a face so essentially sweet could look so derisive. "You know what he probably is, really?" she asked. "He's probably some vicious, greedy little rockhead who decided he wanted a quick-and-easy way to make his fortune, and the only reason he steals only from the Company is to keep public opinion from forcing the Patrol to give top priority to catching him."

"You think they don't give it top priority now?"

"Sure, they probably do," she said negligently. "But they're not very damn good at their work. If he didn't have public opinion on his side, some of the Belter civilians might help the Patrol, and then where would he be?"

"You really think that's why? I mean, that he lets colonists' shipments go just to keep from getting caught? That he's nothing more than a common criminal?"

She shrugged. "What else could he be?"

He studied her, wondering whether she would laugh if he told her what he thought the Pirate Prince really was. He hadn't yet shared his pet theory with anyone, and the Skyrider was a hell of a place to start. But he had her toys packaged now, and had already run her credit card through the computer. He didn't have anything to lose. "You know what I think? I think he's from some outer rock that got legislated out of existence, and piracy is the only way they can get their supplies."

"It's a thought." She actually took his idea seriously. "It would explain a lot." She gave him the address for the package of toys and looked thoughtfully at the little computer she had held aside to wrap and send herself. Looking at it, her expression softened, and when she looked at the storekeeper again much of the habitual ferocity was gone from her eyes. "He is a romantic figure, isn't he?" she said. "You can't help wondering. And . . . the Pirate Prince. It's hokey, but it's hell of effective. I mean, it just doesn't sound like a rockhead, somehow."

"It sounds exciting."

She nodded thoughtfully. "Yeah. Exciting." She put the computer under her arm and turned to leave. "Thanks for all your help. My cousin's kids will be grateful." She grinned, and for just a moment she looked like a little girl. "I'll bet they like the Pirate Prince doll most."

"More even than your *Defiance*?" He hadn't meant to say that, and waited a little nervously for her response. But she only nodded, still grinning.

"I'm afraid so. I'm old suit by now. He's the daredevil renegade hero these days. And more power to him. It's a dirty job, but somebody's got to do it." She grinned recklessly, waved one hand in a half-salute, and closed the door softly behind her.

He stood alone in his shop and wondered why he felt so much at a loss, and so strangely sad.

Melacha had imagined that Ian Spencer would be waiting, possibly tapping his fingers with impatience, to collect his winnings in person, but he was nowhere to be found on Home Base.

She had sold her perishables and stashed the money, using credit to reload *Defiance* with supplies to outfit both her new rock and her new shuttle: afterward she had bought gifts to be sent to everybody she could think of, charged the most expensive meal she could find on Home Base, and bought herself a new handgun. She couldn't think of any more ways to spend credit, so it was without any real regret at all that she went to the Finance Department, expecting to find Spencer there before her.

She went ahead and transferred the account in his absence; a debt was a debt. Then she spent a little time looking for him, but it didn't matter that she didn't find him. The transfer was on record now throughout the World, Incorporated. He was rich wherever he was. Being an Earther, he might never return to Home Base at all.

She had more important things to think about. Feeling unexpectedly cross, and resolutely telling herself she wasn't, she headed for the flight deck.

CHAPTER TWENTY-ONE

It was a simple lift-off from Home Base, an exercise Melacha had performed so many times in the past that she could almost do it with her eyes closed. This time it nearly killed her. Not because it was in any way more difficult or more hazardous than usual, but because she wasn't paying any attention at all: at the moment of lift-off she saw Jamin come onto the flight deck from the ready room, and when she should have been attending to her controls she was staring at him, paralyzed, with her heart in her throat.

Of course it wasn't Jamin. Afterward she blamed the toy store clerk, or perhaps the Pirate Prince, for putting thoughts of Jamin back in her mind when she had so successfully repressed them recently. The conversation about the Pirate Prince had reminded her of JanMikal's unspecified plans, which she was perhaps illogically convinced were piracy, making him the Pirate Prince. From there it was all too small a step to remembering how like Jamin's his eyes and his easy laughter were.

Then a tall, lean man with dark hair and arrogant posture stepped onto the flight deck. In the same heart-stopping instant that she thought she recognized him, she knew already that it was a mistake: he wasn't really even like Jamin. But that momentary distraction had come at a very bad time. It might have killed a lesser pilot in the same situation. Most lesser pilots wouldn't have got into the same situation, though, because part of the problem was that she had begun lift-off with the shuttle equivalent of a hot-rodding teenager's squealing tires.

Flight Control yelled something at her over the Comm Link when she lost control. *Defiance* plunged toward the endpanel wall in a breathless sideways slide across air. A nearby shuttle, waiting for lift-off clearance, panicked and lifted without clearance to get away from her, thus putting itself in the only otherwise clear path she had out of her skid.

Cursing fluently, she forced *Defiance* into a full spin and simultaneous dive and, with apparent disregard for all the laws of physics as well as for shuttle stress tolerances, took the spin off by bouncing her off the panel beneath the panicking shuttle and straight from there into the same exit path she would have taken if the other shuttle hadn't lifted. The whole maneuver looked utterly impossible, and probably would have been for nearly any other pilot. The Skyrider made it possible.

When she had time to listen to the Comm Link again, Flight Control was cursing her as uninhibitedly as she had cursed the other pilot. She flipped on the visual, grinned at the white face that stared at her out of the screen, and said quite calmly, "Sorry about that, Granger."

"Sorry—!" His face contorted as he tried to think of a suitably cutting response, but the other pilot interrupted before he managed one.

"My fault," said Ian Spencer's voice. He flipped on his visual and the Skyrider's screen obligingly split to accommodate both images: Granger's face, twisted with rage, frustration, and the aftermath of shock; and Spencer's disarming boyish grin. They made an interesting study in contrasts. Spencer, ignoring Granger completely, echoed the Skyrider: "Sorry about that, Skyrider. I guess I panicked."

"I guess you did," said the Skyrider. She was now safely outside the force screen that protected the flight deck from the vacuum of space. From there it was easy to look back at the glittering deck with Spencer's shuttle just settling back onto a panel, and grin. "S'pose you thought I'd run right into you."

He said, still grinning, "It did seem like a distinct possibility there for a minute. What happened?"

Deliberately misunderstanding the question, she shrugged. "I went under you." Then, to avoid any further inquiries from him, she said quickly, "Where've you been, anyway? I expected to find you impatiently waiting in the Finance Department."

Granger cleared his throat. "Since no damage occurred," he said, "there'll be no legal action taken, Skyrider. But I've warned you before about hot-rodding your lift-offs."

"I know you have." She grinned at him.

He tried to look stern. His face wasn't made for it. "Then you can take another warning as read, and get out of here—or at least get off my Comm Link frequency. I have work to do."

They got off his frequency. "I had to make a run to Earth," said Spencer, "among other things. You mean you already signed over your account?"

"Your account, now." She stressed the pronoun. "A debt's a debt. Sorry you missed your chance to gloat, but you're a rich man now, anyway. Got any plans for your ill-gotten gains?" He was more attractive than any man had a right to be. And that daft, innocent grin didn't fool her. She wondered what he was hiding.

"I meant to pay a debt, too," he said, "but it seems to've got itself cancelled, so now I don't know. Maybe I'll just go on a spending spree like you did. I could use a rock of my own, for instance.''

''But you're an Earther.''

That grin again. ''Even Earthers have to live somewhere.''

''I suppose you do, but why a rock? Why not another chunk of Earth if you don't want to live on the one you've got?''

Something darkened his eyes. They seemed to go flat and opaque like burnished metal and for the first time she noticed what an unusual color they were: not blue, and not gray either. They looked almost silver, with startlingly vivid flecks of amber around the pupil, like jeweled mirrors. ''I may be an Earther, but that doesn't mean I have to like living on Earth.'' He blinked, and the shining hostility went out of his eyes, leaving them a more ordinary gray, still jeweled with amber. ''Did you have time to get everything you need before you turned over the account? I imagine you had a lot of needs.'' He grinned again with genuine humor and it almost turned his eyes blue. They were remarkable eyes.

She matched his grin. ''I did. It's funny how many things you turn out to need when you get started buying. But I think I got everything.''

''I thought you would. Did you buy your shuttle a new weapons system?''

''No need; the one I have works fine against anybody but you.''

For just an instant his grin froze and his eyes were silver again, watching her with a wary intensity that startled her. It was a look so fleeting most people wouldn't have noticed it. The Skyrider wasn't most people. Fully aware of that, he produced a convincing laugh and said, ''Good luck, Skyrider. And thanks for paying up without a hassle.''

''No problem.'' She frowned, watching him. ''You wanta try that bet again? Now? Double or nothing?''

''You can't double an unlimited account: and I can't

double my chunk of Earth. Thanks anyway, Skyrider."
His eyes were silver mirrors, his smile all boyish innocence. "Besides, I'm not half sure I could handle it. Giving you a chance to kill me once was a gamble. Twice would be suicide."

"Why? Because there's nothing wrong with my weapons system this time?"

His smile didn't falter. "Because I'm not confident enough of my flying. There was nothing wrong with your weapons system last time, was there? When I mentioned it, I thought I was just teasing."

"I wonder." He was a consummate actor, but she wasn't convinced by wide-eyed innocence. Perhaps because he *was* so good at it. She grinned at him, just as disingenuously as he was grinning at her. "Nothing I could find at the time, but I'll keep looking."

CHAPTER TWENTY-TWO

In the end, the Pirate Prince didn't have to find other colonists willing to join his pirate pack; they found him. Some of them had tried making raids on their own, after they'd heard of him, but they had neither JanMikal's skill and warrior training nor the strength of the Pirate Prince legend that had already built up around him. They lost their battles and were lucky to escape the Patrol.

Most of them hadn't even tried on their own. They knew a good thing when they saw it, and their colony worlds were badly in need of the kind of supplies JanMikal was bringing home to Diadem. But by now Earth had begun to send a Patrol escort with all ships carrying government cargo, and even the Pirate Prince would have difficulty overcoming them with only one pirate ship. The prospective pirates weren't as particular as JanMikal about stealing only from the government, but they saw Earth's new policy as a fine opportunity to convince the Pirate Prince he needed them. Together, a pack of some half-dozen pirate ships could take on the most heavily escorted cargo liner, and they should be able to take enough plunder to provide for all three colony worlds represented.

JanMikal accepted all of them, provisionally. Together they performed several raids with good success; and while some of the new men were hard to handle, tending toward a ruthless violence with which his Diademan crew could not feel comfortable, the Pirate Prince managed somehow to keep them all in line. The only defector was a Diademan: Larton, the dark brooding boy who had been leader of the boy-pack before they met JanMikal, and who had never really been comfortable in a lesser role. He nearly got himself killed in a knife fight with one of the men from Skye over, of all things, where their plunder should be stacked prior to being divided among them. The Pirate Prince was obliged to save Larton's life, which in the logic of sullen boys turned out to be something for which Larton could never forgive JanMikal. He took the next opportunity to return, disillusioned, to a peaceful life on Diadem. He might have been further disillusioned to realize how very little the Pirate Prince or any of the other pirates missed him. Meantime JanMikal was able to use his triumph in the knifing incident to good advantage in strengthening his own position as leader of these unruly men from Skye and Newkansas, so some good came of it.

The remaining Diademan boys did their best to fit in with the new pirates. They were fascinated with these wild, desperate, bewildering men from Outside who seemed to live and breathe the wonderful adventure called outlawry. The Diademan boys had thought that they, together with JanMikal, were inventing outlawry when they invented the Pirate Prince, and had thought themselves dashingly fierce and dangerous. Now they saw that theirs had been the ferocity of newborn kittens, about as dangerous as carrots.

The boys had grappled long and hard with their philosophy just to play at their outlaw drama: now they became almost hopelessly entangled in adjustments to ramifications they had never even imagined. Within their own closed world, the belief that if everyone does exactly what he wants to do all will be well had worked. It created its own counterbalances among people raised in the practice. It forced the entire society to live a somewhat selfish but automatic and very effective empathy that was unfamiliar to many Outsiders and wholly alien to these hard, cynical outlaws, who regarded the Diademan empathy as a sort of wide-eyed innocence just waiting to be exploited.

JanMikal saw what was happening, but there was little he could do to help his boys. He had his own problems with the new men. As long as nobody's life was at stake it was usually safest to let matters run their course, though the wear and tear was inevitably hard on the Diademans. They *would* trust the others, and expect behavior reasonable by their own standards, no matter how often their expectations went unmet. They weren't stupid boys, but they were very slow to learn this negative lesson. It was counter to everything in their philosophy, everything they thought they knew about people. They had never before dealt with anyone wholly devoid of empathy or even of basic considerateness. Even JanMikal had *some* empathy, and he was the only Outsider they had met before.

The new pirates, if they had ever had any tendencies toward unselfishness in any form, had long since ruthlessly purged it from their systems. Newkansas and Skye were ordinary colonies with ordinary citizens, some good and some bad. It just happened that those interested in piracy were what most people on Diadem would call bad. They were adventurers, more interested in the hunt itself than in its outcome. Most of them had lived hard lives one way and another, and had learned as a basic necessity to think only of themselves except in combat situations, where they thought of their companions because that, too, was one of the rules of survival.

They had hard and fast friendships among them, but they were friendships of a sort no one from Diadem would even recognize, much less understand. They were friendships as rough as the men who made them, involving very little trust and nothing at all that a Diademan would recognize as love. Altogether they were quite an education for the Diademan boys, most of whom learned what they learned the hard way, and some of them—like Larton—very nearly at the cost of their lives.

It bewildered them that JanMikal did not always leap immediately to their defense. He let them get hurt and humiliated with terrible frequency, interfering only when their lives were at stake; in many ways they began to see him as more like the new pirates than like themselves. If he didn't take part in the new pirates' cruel mockery, neither did he prevent it. He let the new men play dangerous tricks on the boys who had all but invented the Pirate Prince for him. He let the new men have all the most dashing, dangerous jobs, relegating the boys to flying their own ship and carrying cargo. He even spent more of his free time with the new men than he did with the Diademans. He laughed at their jokes and drank their liquor and joined in their poker and Planets games and even smoked their noxious cigars.

The Diademans were too young, too ignorant, and in this situation too insecure to understand that JanMikal had to spend more time with the new men precisely because they were less trustworthy and harder to control than the Diademans: because, in short, he liked them less. They saw only that he had deserted and seemingly all but forgotten those who had given him his start. As a result, they became increasingly withdrawn and sullen, thus inadvertently adding to JanMikal's problems.

* * *

The cargo liner *Mariposa* lumbered away from a near-Earth warehouse station, closely followed by six Patrol boats like ducklings swarming after their mother. Once clear of the station the ducklings closed in around their mother in chattering excitement: but they weren't ducklings, they weren't excited, and the chattering consisted entirely of brisk military exchanges on the Comm Link.

They were an ideal target for the pirate pack. That many Patrol boats guarding one liner indicated a very rich cargo, and the astrophysics of their location relative to the pirates' couldn't have been better.

Another liner, *Polestar,* left the station just after *Mariposa* and blundered heavily off toward the asteroid belt, but she was unaccompanied by Patrol and the pirates ignored her. They didn't notice when *Polestar* put on an unexpected burst of speed that sent her quickly beyond their reach. She wouldn't have anything aboard that the pirates would want; if she had, she would have been escorted.

When the six ill-matched pirate ships overtook the *Mariposa*, the Patrol fought for her as fiercely as they fought for any of the ships they escorted, but the Pirate Prince had planned his attack well. The Patrol wasn't outnumbered, but they were at a disadvantage, having come from the station's up-sun side with the glaring light in their eyes. The pirates took advantage of that by swinging around to come at the Patrol straight out of the sun in a perfect ambush: two of the Patrol died before they even knew they were under attack.

The remaining four put up a creditable fight, but they were outnumbered and outmaneuvered and never really had a chance. They gallantly crowded in between the pirates and *Mariposa*, trying to shield her massive bulk with their own frail boats while they herded her toward relative safety, or at least away from the source of danger.

JanMikal ordered the Newkansas pirates after them, right in under *Mariposa*'s broad black belly. He intended to position the Skye shuttles and *Corsair* so that the last four Patrol boats would be as effectively encircled as six pirate shuttles could encircle them while still keeping *Mariposa* in the line of fire. But the Newkansas shuttles didn't wait. They crowded the Patrol boats, blasted one, and bullied the other three away from *Mariposa* to where the Skye shuttles could get at them.

Neither the Newkansas pirates nor the Skye pirates were even looking when *Mariposa* swung her ponderous bulk in an elegant arc to position herself for escape. Left alone a few moments longer, she could have dived back to the safety of the station too quickly for them to follow.

JanMikal had wanted to take her without firing on her; he had tried throughout his brief pirate career to do as little damage as possible to the cargo liners he plundered. That was part of the reputation he was building: if they didn't defy him they could escape unharmed except for the loss of government cargo. To make that effective, he had to make sure that if they did defy him, the results would be disastrous for them. His response had to be sudden and ruthless. Above all he must make sure that none ever did escape him. And that meant a good chance of damaged cargo and loss of life on the target ship. But it enforced the idea that once the Pirate Prince had waylaid a liner, its best bet was to sit still and wait for him to release it.

Because his unruly pack had disobeyed his orders, he had to fire on *Mariposa* without hesitation. It was only luck that gave him an angle on her such that he could take out her engines with minimal damage to crew and cargo compartments. There was no time for the luxury of selected targets.

"Space *damn* them," he said.

"We didn't hurt anyone," said Jade at *Corsair*'s helm.

"No thanks to those bastards from Newkansas and Skye," said JanMikal. Then, realizing his crew were staring at him in sullen confusion, which seemed to be their most common expression of late, he grimaced and glanced again at the screen that displayed *Mariposa* for him. "Prepare for boarding," he said, impassive now. "She has two docks. Which shuttle takes this load?"

"*Blue Lady*, sir," said Abi, his Comm Link officer. "From Skye. Shall I signal her?"

"The worst of a bad lot." JanMikal scowled at *Mariposa*. "Yes, all right. You know the routine." He hoped he looked and sounded more confident than he felt: his control of this pirate pack was shakier with the unkempt outlaws on *Blue Lady* than with any of the others. In his present mood he wasn't sure he could maintain the calm, cool arrogance required to handle any of them, but it might have been a little easier with one of the other ships.

As it turned out, his embattled control would have snapped no matter which crew boarded with him: *Mariposa* was carrying only private shipments for colonists, and no government goods at all. Her captain was delighted to inform them that her sister ship *Polestar*, which the pirates had blissfully ignored when she left the station unescorted at the same time as *Mariposa* left with her Patrol escort, had been carrying a full consignment of government goods.

They were standing in the cargo hold when they heard this news. The Pirate Prince with his bodyguards Hobart and Irving stood next to *Mariposa*'s Captain Jastrow on one side of the hatch with the cargo handlers from *Corsair*. The men from Skye lounged on the opposite side of the hatch, looking and acting like members of an Earther motorcycle gang. Two particularly scruffy individuals from their number were roughly examining the cargo, confirming what they had already observed: that none of it was what the Prince would call fair game.

Blue Lady's Captain Nguyen and the rest of her cargo handlers stood nearer the Prince and Captain Jastrow. Unlike the pirates from *Corsair*, *Blue Lady*'s men had refused to adopt the black-and-silver pirate costume designed to match the Prince's. They wore battered spacer outfits in leather and synthetics, as grubby and tattered as the men themselves. Several, including the captain, wore a ridiculous number of knives and handguns strapped to various portions of their anatomy; and several, including the captain, had their handguns drawn and ready.

"We'll take this stuff, then," said Captain Nguyen. "It's as good as government shipments any day. Maybe better."

Captain Jastrow looked stunned. "But—"

The Pirate Prince straightened his shoulders and met the challenging stare of the captain from *Blue Lady*. "Captain Nguyen . . ."

Nguyen's weapon, which had been aimed negligently at a point somewhere to the right of the Prince's feet, was suddenly centered on his chest. "Yes?"

The Prince's face remained impassive. "We do have a policy of taking only government goods," he said. "These things have been paid for already, by individuals. Colonists."

"Their own damn fault," said Nguyen. "They should've shipped in an unescorted ship. Then we'd've knowed."

"That is a point," said the Prince.

"Damned hard fight, getting this ship," said Nguyen.

"That's true, too," said the Prince.

"You'll help off-load onto *Blue Lady*, then?"

"My men will," said the Prince. "I'll stay here and keep Captain Jastrow company till the goods are loaded and you've cleared the dock; his men won't make trouble while I'm with him."

Nguyen nodded. "Good thinking." He studied the Prince for a moment. "Wasn't sure you'd see your way clear."

The Prince shrugged. "They shouldn't have tricked us. I don't like being tricked."

The Diademans stared for a moment in sullen confusion,

but at a signal from Nguyen the cargo handlers dutifully followed the Skye men into the corridors of cargo and began the job of off-loading it while Hobart, Irving, and the Pirate Prince stood guard with Captain Jastrow of *Mariposa* and the two of his men who had accompanied him to the hold.

No one said anything. No one did anything, except off-load cargo. Hobart had his weapon in his hand, but he didn't use it. The Pirate Prince had somehow managed to get in his way at the start of Nguyen's near-mutiny, and since then there didn't seem to be a comfortable opportunity. It wasn't even clear whether a mutiny had actually occurred. This didn't seem to be a good time to ask.

CHAPTER TWENTY-THREE

"Sorry for the inconvenience, Captain Jastrow," said the Pirate Prince. "You have been patient, and we're grateful for that. Sorry we had to disable your ship; you shouldn't have tried to run, you know." His voice was mild, almost bored. Captain Jastrow simply stared, as did the Prince's bodyguards; they hadn't known what to expect when Captain Nguyen finished off-loading his selections from *Mariposa*'s cargo, but this—the Pirate Prince's standard exit speech, delivered with his standard polite indifference—was the last thing they would have guessed he would do.

He continued as if this were an absolutely normal raid: "We'll leave you the Comm Link so you can call the Patrol for rescue." He sketched a regal little bow, as graceful as if movement didn't pain him. "Good day, sir." Glancing at his bodyguards, he turned and walked away. Hobart and Irving looked at him, looked at each other, and looked a warning at Captain Jastrow while they backed out after the Prince, their weapons ready and their expressions dangerous.

When they got back inside *Corsair* they found JanMikal already in his command chair issuing orders to disengage from *Mariposa*. "Are you going to let them get away with that?" asked Irving.

JanMikal glanced at him and back at his control screens. "Abi," he said, "get me the other captains on Link. Jade, be warned: if it comes to a battle, I'll take control from here."

"But sir," said Jade.

"It's nothing to do with you. You're a good helmsman. I'm better. Have you got them, Abi?"

"Ready, sir. Broadcast when ready."

JanMikal straightened in his chair and glared at the Comm Link screen. "Now hear this. This is the Pirate Prince speaking from *Corsair*. We have just disengaged from the Terran cargo liner *Mariposa*. She was carrying only Colonial cargo. It is our policy never to plunder Colonial cargo. Captain Nguyen off-loaded that cargo against my known wishes, and I want it returned. To that end I intend to give chase and capture Nguyen's *Blue Lady* if he will not surrender. You have one chance, Captain Nguyen, to surrender peaceably, or I'll take you by force. Which is it to be?"

Blue Lady had fled at the first sound of the Prince's voice. Her answer to him now was to flip end-for-end, throw one hasty laser shot at him, flip again, and keep running.

The Prince took the controls and hurled *Corsair* after her, but he never stopped glaring at the Comm Link screen, which was split four ways to show the two Newkansas pirate captains and the two Skye captains who hadn't mutinied. Captain Nguyen had blanked his screen before he ran.

Duane Higgins, captain of the *Born Loser* from Skye, scowled as viciously as the Pirate Prince and looked a good deal more dangerous doing it, since his face was older and uglier to begin with and was bisected by an old, angry knife scar that pulled his right eyebrow and the right corner of his mouth down and showed purple across his otherwise pale cheek. "Colonial goods are as good as any," he said.

"We don't take Colonial goods," said the Prince. He was close on the tail of *Blue Lady*, and the other pirates were following him in an undecided cluster.

"Why the hell not?" asked Captain Jones of the *Shark* from Newkansas.

"Because I say we don't," said the Prince. "That's all the reason you need." He closed in on *Blue Lady* and threw a laser bolt across her forward shield. "Nguyen, surrender or you're dead."

"The hell he is!" Higgins brought his fleet little *Born Loser* around in a dive on *Corsair* that caught the Prince by surprise and knocked *Corsair* off course without doing any other damage except to JanMikal's pride.

"Space take him," he muttered, pulling *Corsair* up. "And thank all the gods for the cleverness of inventive boys." He had lasers where no ship had ever had lasers before. And they were good ones. His shields were powerful. His ship was fleet. And he was the best pilot in the pack. Whether that would be enough, he didn't know, but he intended to make them a very good fight. As a first step, he threw a shot sideways at the now retreating *Born Loser* and simultaneously lined up *Blue Lady* in his forward screens, hesitated, and finally directed the shot a little off the mark. "Nguyen, I'm giving you a chance. I really don't want to destroy that cargo; it isn't ours."

"It is now," said Nguyen.

"Not if the Prince says it isn't," the captain of the *Shark* said unexpectedly. "You guys, we wouldn't even be here if it weren't for him. I don't know why he wants to make these idiot rules of his, but by gods we'd better follow them if we want to keep on. We can't keep this pack together without him.''

"I can," said Nguyen.

"The hell you can," said Higgins. "I'll take that load off you quicker than you can blink, and *I'll* be the Pirate Prince."

"We're going to return that cargo," said the Prince. "If it survives."

"Oh, it'll survive," said Nguyen. "The question is, will *you?*" He flipped *Blue Lady* and fired where he thought *Corsair* would be, but in the same instant *Corsair* danced lightly sideways and fired another warning shot at *Born Loser*.

"Hot damn," said the second Newkansas pirate, a little old man called Gramps who flew a rattletrap but very well armed shuttle named *Marilyn*. He never talked to anybody, and obviously saw no reason to start now. He just cackled with pleasure and began to fire indiscriminately on all the pirate ships.

There followed some very fancy flying by all of them, and a few successful laser strikes but no real damage to anyone. All three of the ships from Skye and Gramps from Newkansas turned against the Pirate Prince; but Captain Jones of the *Shark*, also from Newkansas, took the Prince's side. In a way, so did Gramps, since he was firing at everyone. JanMikal wondered a little hysterically if they would have to kill Gramps to get him to stop, but he wasn't going to worry about it till he had the Skye ships under control again.

He had to hole *Blue Lady* to do it, and burn out all *Born Loser*'s shields, but he did get them under control. He was the best pilot, and he proved it. They probably imagined he had also proved he was the toughest, or the meanest, or generally the fiercest of them all, but he wasn't thinking about that. He was just thinking how to keep a bunch of

unruly losers from ruining a good thing once they'd got it
going so well.

There was minor hysteria over the Comm Link from
Blue Lady till they got the hole patched with sealant and
the one injured crewmember patched with spray-on stick-
ing plaster and curses. The other ships rode in a tight circle
around *Blue Lady* while her crew checked for further
damage afterward. Gramps had finally stopped firing when
everyone else did. He was still cackling now and then, and
none of the other ships went near him. JanMikal thought
sourly that if he got himself killed, Gramps would probably be the one to take over the pack. He was the only one
crazy enough to make a go of it.

Higgins in *Born Loser* was lecturing his crew, on the
open Link, on the wonderfulness of the Pirate Prince and
how they couldn't possibly keep up this pirate scam without him. Nguyen still had his screen blanked, but the
babble of sound from *Blue Lady* was such that Abi had to
turn the Link sound down. Gramps emitted an occasional
cackle from *Marilyn*, Jones on the *Shark* cursed quietly for
no apparent reason, and Captain Au on *Bar Sinister* merely
stared imperturbably at the Link screen as he had been
doing throughout the battle and before it.

"When you're ready," said the Pirate Prince, "we'll
take that cargo back to *Mariposa* where it belongs."

Nguyen turned on his Link screen the better to yell at it.
"You goddamned maniac, we can't go back there for
chrissake no matter whether we should've taken the bloody
cargo or not. You got rocks for brains? The Patrol will be
there, it's a wonder they aren't *here*, my God, man—"

"He's right," said Captain Au. "I am tracking the Patrol. They have converged on *Mariposa* and will shortly
come after us. If we do not move they will find us of a
certainty."

"Where the hell can we go, holed by our own goddamned leader and one of my crew bleeding for chrissake I want to know anyway?'' said Nguyen.

"Serves you bloody well right," said Higgins. "You got us into this mess. We ought to leave you out here."

Nguyen sneered at him. "While you go where for chrissake you goddamned rockhead?"

Gramps cackled cheerfully.

"I must admit a certain wariness about the advisability to return to *Mariposa* at this point in time," said Captain Au. "While true that we perhaps should have taken no cargo from her, I do not wish to die or to be captured in the attempt to return same cargo now."

"Besides, we do need the damn stuff, no matter whose it was before," said Higgins. "Winnie shouldn't've took it, but we got it now, what say, eh?"

"They're right, I think," said Jones.

At least they were asking him nicely now. JanMikal looked at Abi, who confirmed the reported Patrol movements. "All right," said JanMikal. "We'll retreat to the Lunar base and wait them out."

"And divvy up the goods?" asked Higgins.

"And divide the goods," said JanMikal. "I don't see what else we can do about them at this point."

Gramps cackled maniacally and blanked his Link screen. The rest of them looked startled at his outburst and one by one took their leave of the Pirate Prince, blanked their screens, and positioned their ships for the run to Luna. It had taken JanMikal some effort to teach them to fly the pack in formation, but they did it well now. By the time the Patrol searched that sector they were long gone.

CHAPTER TWENTY-FOUR

It didn't take long at all for news of the pirate raid on *Mariposa* to spread through the colonies. The pirate pack had hardly reached their Lunar base to divide up their spoils before the colonists for whom the shipments had been intended were informed of their losses and had begun to spread the news with varying degrees of shock and outrage. The Pirate Prince, erstwhile "hero of the people," was suddenly high in the running for Villain of the Year.

Melacha hadn't heard from Board Advisor Brown, so she didn't know how the Board Advisor was doing in her effort to find *Jewel*'s crew or to find out what could be done about Earth's rigid salvage laws. Aside from *Jewel*, Diadem's problems hadn't seemed urgent as long as the Pirate Prince and his pack were supplying the needy colonies. That was assuming, of course, that the Pirate Prince was JanMikal and not a common thief, but Melacha had been assuming that.

Now, whether he was JanMikal or not, it seemed urgent to do something about him. With Earth's politics in such

upheaval it wasn't at all clear that Melacha still had any
official standing as Ombudsman, so she might not be able
to do Diadem much good, though she was willing to try:
but she could do JanMikal some good if he was the Pirate
Prince. She could provide him with obviously needed
instruction as to what cargo was fair game for his pirate
pack and what cargo wasn't.

On the way to Diadem in search of the Pirate Prince,
she put in a call to Haioshi to see if he had come up with
any information about Spencer. That much too good-looking
gentleman's reaction to her remark about her weapons
system had been altogether too suspicious to overlook. She
couldn't imagine how he could have sabotaged her system
in such a way that neither she nor her computer could find
any evidence of it, but that didn't mean he couldn't have
done it. It might only mean she had insufficient data to
work with.

If insufficient data was the problem, Haioshi wasn't able
to supply it. "If I'm right," he said, "your Ian Spencer is
the man who pulled a scam in NYork six years ago
that nobody ever did figure out. An inheritance. Some
Manhattan property that had been in the Maston family for
generations. . . . I suppose you've heard of the Mastons?
Shipping and storage? Unpleasant people on the whole,
but old money and plenty of it. Well, when the old man
died, everyone assumed the entire estate would go to his
son, and the bulk of it did. But this piece of Manhattan he
left to a junior CommNet clerk nobody had ever heard
of."

"Ian Spencer?"

"The same. Everyone knew there was something funny
about it, and the lawyers tied up the property as long as
they could, but they couldn't prove anything and finally
had to turn it over. And that's the only information in the
CommNet on any Ian Spencer at all. I'm still tracking
him, though. If it's the same Ian Spencer . . . I suppose

you'll agree there was something wrong with his bet with you? He's not a better pilot than you, is he?"

"If I ever thought he might be, I found out for sure today that he's not. But I still can't see how he could have cheated on the bet. It isn't as if I'd been in somebody else's shuttle. I know *Defiance*. And I checked all her systems, during the run and afterward. There was nothing wrong."

"There was something wrong, or Spencer wouldn't have won."

She grinned at him. "I'd like to believe that. But maybe he just had a lucky day."

The Link screen flopped Haioshi's face sideways as the computer pulled power for a brief evasive maneuver from a wild rock. When the screen cleared, Haioshi's expression was serious and thoughtful. "I suppose you could say he just had a lucky day when old Maston died, too, but I doubt it. There's something very wrong here. Could he have interfered somehow with your computer or your weapons system?"

"I don't see how. There was no sign of it." She looked thoughtful for a moment, considering Spencer's response to her remark about the weapons system. "I have wondered. But anyone doing that would leave traces. I'd have found them."

Haioshi played absently with a perfume-stiffened ringlet over his ear. "I haven't had as much time for this as I'd like, but I'll keep on it. I have a feeling there's something about him that I'm forgetting or overlooking." He wrapped the ringlet around his finger and released it. "Something damned obvious. But what could it be?"

"I don't know. I can't imagine."

Haioshi sighed. "Well. Meantime, had you heard that Nuke 'em B. Newcomb seems to be pulling out of the presidential running?" He reached offscreen to do something she couldn't see; presumably some bit of business on another computer board, or one of the many other things he was always doing all at once. "I don't know exactly what's going on, because the Board of Directors is blockading all news. It's a mess down here. The President's health is failing. I suppose she may be dead already. Nobody knows. And nobody knows who might take her place, if Newcomb backs out."

"Why would he? What happened?"

He shook his head. "Nobody knows. Or if they do, they're not telling. I can tell you this much, though. I suppose you've heard of Investments, Incorporated? Well, I happened to ring them up a few days ago, and I got a very interesting response: a list of I.I.'s top executives."

"Yeah? So?"

"Most of them were no surprise. But I suppose you wouldn't like to guess who headed the list?"

"Guessing games are not my favorite, Haioshi."

"Nuke 'em B. Newcomb." He looked smug.

"That *is* interesting. Wow. Top exec of I.I. —They have lots of money tied up in the colonies. That can't be good for Newcomb's image, can it."

"Not exactly."

She thought about it. "Would that be enough to make him pull out? I mean that somehow it got online his Link? It's not even sure anybody saw it besides you, yeah? I mean did you check? Did it stay online?"

"It's off now. I suppose I should have instructed my computer to keep track, but I didn't think of it in time. It simply didn't occur to me how important it could be. He hadn't started ducking politics then."

"You think that's why he's started now?"

"I suppose it might be. What I'm more curious about is how it happened. Somebody got through his safeguards, obviously; that wasn't meant to be public information. And then to get it online his Link. . . .That's a very sophisticated trick. And for what purpose?"

"To get him out of the race?"

"Except there's no race. Nobody opposed him. And there's been no visible effort to get anyone to replace him."

"You said it's not sure yet that he's pulling out. Maybe whoever did it is waiting till it's sure he's out before producing the substitute."

"Why? I suppose that's possible, but I don't quite see a reason to do it that way. And they'd better not wait too long, if that is what's going on. I don't know what the Board is doing, but I don't think they do either, so that's no embarrassment. Things are getting crazier down here by the minute. The whole government is falling apart. Right now the colonies—or anybody else who could afford it—could probably buy out the Corporation, that's how bad it is."

"Buy the World, Incorporated? With what?"

He restrained a smile. "Money in one form or another is the usual currency for a transaction of that nature."

"There's not that much money in the colonies. There's not that much money anywhere. Not to buy the whole World, Incorporated."

"Obviously you're not a merchant, in spite of your recent purchases. I suppose there might be enough money to buy a very small corporation somewhere, but I doubt it. That's why we have credit. Nobody pays cash for anything anymore."

She grinned. "I see what you mean. And you know, it is a fascinating idea. It might be real interesting to own the World." The computer compensated for Link shift and his face suddenly became clearer. She frowned at it. "But no: once you owned it, you'd have to figure out how to run it. It'd be like getting elected God."

"I suppose, in a way." The thought was clearly not unappealing to him. "But you get a President and Board of Directors for the dirty work."

"Not me." She shook her head. "No, it's interesting as a concept, but not for me. Maybe you should do it. How 'bout that? Gustov Haioshi, owner of the World? It has a certain ring to it, don't you think?"

He smiled. "No. I'm happy running my own little empire. Which I suppose I'd better get back to doing, much as I enjoy chatting with you. I'll keep tracking your Spencer . . ."

"—He's not *my* Spencer."

"—And let you know if I come up with anything. I haven't found the *Jewel* crew yet, by the way, but I did find *Jewel* herself. She's impounded as evidence."

"Evidence of what, for space sake?"

He shrugged ineffably. "Falsified registration, of course. All her papers are Diademan. Since according to the Corporation there is no Diadem . . . well, you see."

"That's ridiculous!"

"On the contrary, it's faultlessly logical. And now I really must get back to work."

Melacha had never before docked at one of the antique man-built stations. There was no synch system, but the docking module was off the Hub, and the station's one rpm rotation was nullified there by a "de-spin system" between the module and the Hub, so docking was relatively simple. She had only the station's orbital velocity to worry about—that, and whether the ancient docking facilities would accept the modern mechanisms on the *Defiance*.

She talked by Comm Link to several people on Diadem, none of whom knew for sure whether the docking mechanisms would match adequately. The last one, a Dr. Simon Hale, seemed to be the colony's official liaison with the outside world, and even he wasn't certain.

"Hell with it," said the Skyrider. "I'm willing to take a chance on it if you are."

Hale hesitated. "It's not really my field. The engineers

described it to you. If from their description you think it will work, and you want to try . . .''

"I think it'll fit," she said. "And if it doesn't, I think I can back off without harm to the station. Damned if I want to sit out here dodging this monster mirror anymore." She wasn't really dodging it; it wasn't even near her. But it did fill a considerable portion of the nearby environment, and she had taken an irrational dislike to it the moment she saw it.

Hale didn't know how to respond to that. She sounded hostile toward an object he had always accepted as a necessary part of the world. He had never seen the mirror except in pictures, since he had never been outside Diadem in his life. He was aware of it, of course; it was a disc over half a mile in diameter that reflected sunlight down onto slanted panels and into chevron shields that screened out cosmic rays. It was, in effect, the sun of Diadem, and every schoolchild on Diadem was taught all about it in considerable detail in the required Environmental Studies. Since then, Hale had never particularly thought of it again.

The Skyrider took his silence for acceptance of her plan, and brought *Defiance* smoothly in for a perfect docking. The mechanisms matched adequately and held easily. Dr. Hale was waiting to greet her when she came through the airlock into Diadem. Asked whether he had ever heard of the Pirate Prince, however, he frowned abstractedly and wondered whether it was a work of fiction.

"No, it's a man," said Melacha. "A pirate. He's been stealing government property for some time now, raiding Company cargo haulers out from Earth. But he just took a load of Colonial goods, and I decided it was time to look him up and straighten him out a little. You really haven't heard of him? Don't you guys get newsfax or anything?''

Hale, anxiously aware of the remote but real possibility of missing incoming calls about *Jewel* or her crew, was leading Melacha to a communications center in the Hub as

they spoke. "Took a load of Colonial goods?" he asked
absently. "Who did? I'm sorry to rush you, I haven't even
asked you why you're here, you see we're having a crisis
of sorts, at least I suppose it might not seem a very great
crisis to an Outsider, but to us it is, we've lost an entire
salvage ship and her crew and I don't want to miss any
calls."

"*Lost* a ship? Oh, you mean *Jewel*? The ship Earth
confiscated?"

"That's right." They were in extremely low gravity,
and Hale was not at his best in low gravity. It was difficult
to maintain one's dignity when uncertain of one's balance.
"Where did you hear of her?"

"From a Diademan pilot I met a while ago. Fellow
named JanMikal. That's who I thought might be the Pirate
Prince, which is why I'm here."

"Oh, Dr. March's patient." Hale nodded knowledge-
ably, looked startled, and turned awkwardly to face Melacha.
"Oh, did you say the Pirate Prince? I'm sorry, I'm afraid
I'm rather distracted. . . . JanMikal is the Pirate Prince,
yes. We had quite a meeting about it because a lot of our
people don't approve of his methods. He kills people, you
know. But we do need the goods, and there didn't seem to
be any other way of getting them. Yes, of course. I'd
forgotten, there's been so much else to think about. You
see, I thought I was getting through to the Bureau of
Regional Resources, but . . ." He shrugged. "It fell
through. I'm still hoping for a callback from them, but
perhaps I only believe they might call because I want to
believe it." At her puzzled look, he remembered he was
talking to an Outsider, and added diffidently, "Wishful
thinking, I suppose you'd say."

"You were talking to them about *Jewel*?"

"Yes, of course. They won't tell us where she is, or
where they've put her crew, or how to get them back. It's
most distressing."

"*Jewel* is impounded for evidence," said Melacha. "I haven't found her crew yet, but I'm working on it."

Hale turned so suddenly he lost his balance and didn't even notice how undignified he looked as a result. "*You* are working on it? Why? I mean . . ."

"Well, I am a mercenary. I thought there might be something in it for me, if I could get them back for you. Usually I arrange payment in advance for that kind of job, but I happened to be Earthside just after I heard about *Jewel*, so I, well, started work on it."

Hale regained his composure and led her through another corridor and into the communications center before he spoke again. "You seem to have been more successful than I. I couldn't even get Earth to admit they had *Jewel*, much less admit she was impounded for evidence. Evidence of what? Salvaging?"

"No, falsified registration. Because her papers are Diademan and Earth doesn't recognize Diadem."

"Oh, of course." Hale went directly to a communications console and seated himself with evident relief. There were several nearby chairs, and Melacha pulled one up to the console and sat on it. Hale didn't even notice; he was busy scanning the CommNet screen in front of him. "No calls." He studied the screen a moment longer, sighed, and turned to Melacha. "Well. How did you get them to admit they had *Jewel*?"

"I didn't, really. A friend of mine did. Listen, let me use your Link; I'll see if we're getting anywhere about the crew."

Hale, having long since lost the pride that only a few months ago would have made him offended by her offer, humbly moved aside to let her at the keyboard. His eyes widened as she calmly called on a Board Advisor, punched in her identity code, and was put through without any fuss.

Board Advisor Brown's amiable face filled the screen. "You're getting impatient in your old age, Skyrider," she said. "I haven't had time to do much. I think I have your crew located, but whether I'm right, and if so, whether I can do anything about getting them or their ship released . . . I don't know. Where are you?"

"On Diadem. Looking for the Pirate Prince. By the way, did I ask you if you'd ever heard of a guy named Ian Spencer?"

"You asked. I told you I hadn't. Let me talk to someone in authority there, Skyrider. It'll save time if I'm in direct communication. You've already done enough to justify your pay, whatever it is, if we get these Diademans freed, haven't you? What *are* they paying you? You never said."

"Um," said Melacha.

Brown nodded, smiling. "That's what I thought. You'll work it out, I'm sure. Now who's there I can talk to?"

Melacha introduced her to Hale and sat back, pondering what exactly a station like Diadem would have that she could ask in return for her work on behalf of their lost salvage crew. They must have something she wanted. It wouldn't do her reputation any good to do a job like that for free.

CHAPTER TWENTY-FIVE

The division of their stolen property went more smoothly than the Pirate Prince had dared hope. All six of the pirate ships had landed on Luna after the raid on *Mariposa*, and four of them were fully loaded from that and previous raids. It was their custom to divide up the spoils during every Lunar landing, and this was the first raid in a series that had forced them into such a landing. Four ship-loads divided among the six of them would almost justify separating and carrying their portions home. After their recent altercation, JanMikal thought they could all use a little home leave.

While he was overseeing the division of spoils he debated making an announcement to that effect. They were all working so well together under his command that it made him nervous. Home leave sounded extremely attractive, even to a man with no true home to go to. Even the captains who had ordered their ships to fire on his were scrupulously obedient to him now. It wasn't like these men to be quite so humble.

The *Mariposa* encounter had snapped his control over

them, and this ostentatious deference that had resulted from their space battle afterward would be temporary at best unless he could find a way to reinforce his position. Since they respected nothing but strength and violence, that would not be an easy task for him in Luna's gravity. They knew he could beat them in space, but that might not be enough to hold them.

He sighed, watching the men shift crates and boxes in the odd, almost slow-motion movements gravity-dwellers used in one-sixth their normal gravity. Their base here was an abandoned mining colony with a dome large enough to accommodate all six of their mismatched ships, so they needn't wear space suits while working. There were nearly three dozen pirates, counting the Diademans. Three dozen ragged antisocial misfits performing a delicate slow-motion ballet with crates of stolen goods: it was a ludicrous image. He might have smiled, if he hadn't at that moment caught sight of one of the Colonial crates being shifted from one ship to another.

That was the problem on which the future of the pirate pack might depend. Up till now, cargo ships carrying only Colonial cargo had gone unescorted, so the pirates knew not to bother raiding them. But now the government must have figured out that since only escorted ships were waylaid, and only government cargo was stolen, they could confuse the issue by escorting all ships or even by letting some with government cargo go unescorted, as they had with *Polestar*. That way the pirates couldn't tell so readily which would be profitable to plunder.

That was assuming, of course, that the pirates would leave an escorted Colonial load once they learned what the cargo was. Perhaps, by taking the Colonial cargo from *Mariposa*, the pirates had already responded to the problem in a way that would alter the government's strategy. But in what way? Would they go back to the original policy? Would they begin to escort *all* ships regardless of

cargo? They could hardly cease to escort any. There would
almost certainly continue to be some escorts; and that
meant the pirates had to agree on a policy. Were they to
continue their original policy, taking only government goods
and letting Colonial goods go? Or would the pirates from
Newkansas and Skye mutiny again if he tried to make
them leave another *Mariposa*?

There must be a method of determining which ships to
raid, and a way for JanMikal to enforce his decision as to
which cargoes to keep. But he didn't see how. Already the
Newkansans were clustering with the men from Skye, heat-
edly arguing all over again their decision on the *Mariposa*,
and general opinion seemed to be that the pirates had
honorably won the cargo no matter what its original destination. JanMikal had fought them for taking it, and he had
won the fight, but they were keeping the cargo anyway.
That wouldn't serve as much of a lesson to them.

Government cargo tended to be richer than Colonial
shipments. Could he use that to lead them the way he
wanted them to go? He could point out that taking Colonial cargo filled their holds with less valuable goods so
they didn't have room for more valuable ones when they
found them. But cargo ships on courses they could readily
intercept really weren't all that common; the chance that
they would ever have to let one go because they were
already loaded was small.

In freefall he might have tried to bully them into obey-
ing him: they had followed him this far primarily because
they respected him for managing to seem even rougher and
more unruly than they. In isolated incidents he had outwit-
ted and overpowered a couple of their fiercest bullies, and
that had kept the others in line. But this time there would
be too many against him. Even in freefall he wouldn't be
able to win against all of them; it was just an impulse born
of the bravado of frustration.

He needed them. His men had been right about that.

Once the government started escorting cargo liners, one pirate ship could not reasonably hope to meet with much success, alone. He needed the other five to help him overcome the liners' escorts.

But they didn't really need him. They needed a leader. Any leader would do. If they could agree on one of their own number to take his place, they could get along just fine without him. And if he gave them time to think of that, he would be in trouble.

" 'Ey, Prince!"

Mildly startled, JanMikal looked up from his absent-minded contemplation of a row of metal drums his men had been moving onto *Corsair*, and found himself confronted by one of the roughest of the pirates from Skye. "Yes?" He kept his expression bland, studying the man's pale, pitted face with no evident interest at all. Breem, that was the fellow's name. Navigator under Captain Higgins of *Born Loser*. Higgins had mutinied. With his crew's approval? Breem was almost as ugly as Higgins and on more than one occasion had proved himself to be as vicious, but what did that mean? They were all vicious.

Breem smiled, an expression that caused folds of doughy white flesh to bunch up till his eyes were almost hidden. The effect was not pleasant. "So what," he said, "you go tell us what ships to take?"

JanMikal didn't notice that Breem was speaking the pidgin of the asteroid belt; he simply responded in kind: "Shoots, brud. Why, you no like?"

Breem's hideous smile was transformed instantly into a puzzled frown. " 'Ey, but. Whatsamattayou, go leave Colonial da kine, eh, you?"

"Whatsamattah *me*?" JanMikal didn't bother to straighten from leaning negligently against a shipping crate, but that didn't diminish the threat inherent in his scowl. "Whatsamattah *you*, whatsamatta. Cannot handle. Stupid, eh, you. You know what. Get the Patrol chasing us, okay, fine, not? The Colonial Fleet, but.'' He shook his head. ''Maybe fine, maybe not so fine, yeah? And for why? No need, eh? Colonial da kine not even too much good, des ka?''

Breem shrugged. ''Not too bad. So what? The Colonial Fleet one big deal?''

Behind JanMikal, someone said, ''You ought to know, Breem.'' JanMikal turned to find Captain Higgins studying him with considerable interest. ''So, Prince,'' he said. ''I thought you was from Diadem.''

JanMikal frowned. ''Yeah? So?''

''So how come you're talking that damned pidgin with Breem like you was raised out there?''

''Out where? What pidgin?'' JanMikal paused, thinking about it. ''Oh. I didn't notice. I guess we weren't speaking Standard English, were we?''

''Not quite.'' The scar that bisected Higgins's face made his expressions almost unreadable. ''So you know all about the Colonial Fleet, do you? You spend some time in it, like Breem here?''

JanMikal had seen no reason to tell these people his history, and he felt no inclination to begin telling them now. He smiled enigmatically and shrugged his shoulders. ''Maybe. Anyway I know enough about them to know I don't want them after us.''

The other captains were converging on their little group, some with their crews and some without. The Pirate Prince was going to have to lay down the law now, if ever. And he still had no idea how to go about it.

''I am hearing some parts of this,'' said Captain Au of *Bar Sinister*. His brown face was round and earnest and deceptively innocent. ''This is your reason for wishing to abandon Colonial goods? This unwillingness to offend the Colonial Fleet?''

JanMikal looked at him, trying to read some expression into his black marble eyes. "You could put it like that."

"You are thinking they will come after us? In their entirety?" asked Au.

"I'm thinking it's a chance we don't need to take."

Au nodded. "This reasoning is not without logic."

"To hell with logic," said Nguyen, standing to one side of the group with his crewmembers gathered close around him for support. "Cargo's cargo."

Jones of the *Shark* stood opposite Nguyen, also with his crew around him. He grinned and said not quite under his breath, "And war's war."

JanMikal waved that aside. "I'm not worried we're going to start a war. As easily as the Fleet could wipe us out, you'd hardly call a war. What I'm worried about is getting the Fleet's attention. As long as we take only Company cargo they'll leave us alone, but if we start on Colonial goods they will come after us, sooner or later, and they're hell of better at that than the Patrol is. If the Fleet comes after us, they'll catch us. And they can stop us. Why take the chance?"

"We cannot take they?" asked Au.

JanMikal shrugged. "Maybe. I doubt it. Point is, why bother? There's plenty Company goods out there for the taking, and it's not as if we had anything to prove."

"Prove the Fleet can't stop us," said Higgins.

"I don't need to prove that, even if I could," said JanMikal. "Why would you?"

"Buggahs tink day somebodies, des ka?" said Breem.

"Maybe they are," said JanMikal. "So what?"

"My reasoning for becoming this pirate," said Au, "was almost only for supplying Skye. . . ." He hesitated, frowning earnestly, and added conscientiously, "At a price, of course. Nothing I am doing for only the dubious glory thereof. So. For supplying Skye, it is necessary to encounter this Colonial Fleet, yes I will taking that risk. But if not necessary, why be doing it?''

"I ain't scared of no damn Colonial Fleet," said Higgins.

"Did someone suggest that you were?" asked JanMikal.

Higgins scowled at them all and said stubbornly, "I ain't scared of them, that's all."

"Okay," said JanMikal. "Maybe none of us are. Maybe some of us are. So what? Doesn't matter. The point isn't are we scared, it's are we smart enough to run the smallest risk we can?"

"Meaning you are wanting us henceforward to have left Colonial goods where we found them?" asked Au.

JanMikal nodded. "We take only Company goods."

"But how will we be knowing till already we are having the ship in our clutches," said Au, "if the Company is escorting Colonial goods unlike before?"

"Next time we find ourselves with a shipful of Colonial goods," said JanMikal, "we'll leave 'em. There's no damn sense in loading ourselves down with that stuff. There's enough Company loads out there."

There was a brief silence. They all knew he hadn't answered Au's question, and a couple of them were considering whether to challenge him on it. He looked at them steadily till they decided against it. At such moments they tended to forget the disadvantage he was under, trying to assert himself with them in gravity; even one-sixth Earth-normal gravity was a trial for him, but that only served to make him look even more dangerous than usual. They all agreed, reluctantly and not all very convincingly, to leave Colonial cargo alone in future. All he could do was wait to see how well their agreement held up in practice.

CHAPTER TWENTY-SIX

The test came sooner than JanMikal expected. The pirates had agreed to separate and carry their loads home when they left Luna, but they saved power in their Lunar base by opening the dome only once, for the pack to lift off as a unit. They were still in lift-off formation when they spotted a Company cargo hauler headed for one of the newer bases on the other side of Luna.

She was unescorted, and clearly marked with the bright red blazon of the Interplanatery Postal Service, which meant that most of her cargo would be privately owned by colonists. She shouldn't have been a target. All three ships from Skye were in attack mode before the Pirate Prince could stop them.

"Hot damn," said Higgins. "And I hate going home half empty. The gods are smiling."

"Just look at her," said Nguyen. "All fat and sassy and unprotected. Coming, Prince?"

"Even though I am agreeing with you in principle only," said Au, "I am agreeing also with Higgins that the gods have smiling. This ship is in the manner of a gift, yes? It cannot be that you are expecting us to be ignoring her?''

"She'll be loaded with Colonial cargo," said JanMikal. "She's a postal ship. You can see that. If she carries any Company cargo at all it won't be worth as much as the energy you'll expend to catch her."

"Cargo's cargo," said Nguyen. He had patched his ship at Luna and had perhaps already forgotten who holed it, and why; he wasn't an altogether intelligent man.

"He's right," Jade said unexpectedly from *Corsair's* helm. "Colonial goods are as good as any. And I don't like going home half-empty, either. I want to take 'em."

"Me, too," said Abi. "You don't know. A postal ship, I mean. There might be anything."

JanMikal had half-expected the Diademans to mutiny eventually. A lifetime of doing what they wanted when they wanted without any restrictions except the knowledge that they would have to accept responsibility for the consequences of their actions, and that everyone around them was exercising the same self-will, had not prepared them for a world in which people expected to fight for what they wanted. It didn't surprise him, but it didn't please him, either. He said sharply, "Didn't either of you see any part of the wars? Don't you know what the Colonial Fleet can do?''

"We have a right to do what we want to do," said Abi.

"And accept the consequences," said JanMikal. "In this case that includes getting blown up by the Colonial Fleet if you steal Colonial goods."

"So you say," said Jade. "I say we could take them. After all, we have six ships."

"You think so?" That was Nguyen's voice over the Comm Link that Abi had neglected to turn off.

"You mean you guys wouldn't fight with us, if the Fleet came after us?" asked Jade.

Nguyen's answer was a laugh as the three Skye ships

moved in on the postal ship. After a fractional hesitation, the Newkansas ships joined them. "To hell with policy," said Jones. "Listen, Prince, I'm with you for the most part, but this ship's getting out of range and the damn thing's bulging with goodies. Let's argue politics later, what say?"

Jade moved *Corsair* forward in a lurching motion made doubly awkward by JanMikal's wrestling of the controls from him and cutting off the power. "I'll run the ship from here," said JanMikal.

"The hell you will," said Jade, rising from his seat.

Hobart had watched all this in silence; but now he stepped forward with an inarticulate growl. Jade hesitated, looking at him. JanMikal didn't even glance up; he was moving *Corsair* forward in an effort to position her between the pirate pack and the postal ship. Hobart frowned at him. "I don't want," he said, and hesitated, and looked at Jade. "I don't like this."

"Damn it, Hobey, they're going to take the postal ship anyway," said Jade. "Let's get in on it, or we won't get any of the cargo."

"JanMikal doesn't think we should."

"Is JanMikal God?" asked Abi.

"I can remember when you just about thought he was," said Hobart.

"Oh, hell," said Abi.

"I want that ship," said Jade. He hadn't sat down again, but he wasn't moving toward JanMikal, either.

"Look, we just went through this same thing with the *Mariposa*," said Hobart. "You guys supported JanMikal then. How come you won't support him now?"

"Look what we got for our trouble, last time." Jade flailed his arms, boylike, to indicate the uselessness of their past efforts. "We risked our lives fighting the whole damn pirate pack, and ended up with the Colonial goods in our cargo hold all the same. If it's so crucial that we don't take Colonial goods, what are we doing with a holdful of them now?''

"It isn't a holdful." Hobart looked uncertain. "I mean it's just a little, and we couldn't very well give it back, could we?''

"Okay, maybe that postal ship's just got a little cargo," said Abi. "And the pack's gonna take it anyway. I want our share.''

"They're not going to take it." JanMikal didn't glance up from his instruments. "If I have to kill all of them and all of you, they're not going to take it." None of them had noticed him drawing his weapon, but it was in his hand, and they were all in easy range of it. They stared at him uneasily. Jade sat abruptly back at his console and Hobart backed up till he ran into Jade's chair.

"You wouldn't," said Abi.

"Try me." JanMikal's voice was the implacable voice of the Pirate Prince, and his eyes were cold. "I've had about all I'll take from the lot of you. We don't take Colonial goods.''

Gramps cackled unexpectedly over the Comm Link, making them all start nervously. "She's armed, by God,'' he said, and at just that moment the postal ship fired on him as he swooped in under the three Skye ships to attack her.

It was a direct hit. His ship *Marilyn* hadn't been shielded. When the laser bolt struck her, she exploded in a blinding ball of fire and shrapnel that cut off the sound of his maniacal laughter and left them all staring at an empty place where his ship had been.

"By all that's balanced," said Hobart, his voice subdued. "By God." And before JanMikal could react in the drag of gravity, Hobart had propelled himself off Jade's chair in a dive that took him right into JanMikal's arms. "Grab the gun," he said, holding JanMikal's gun arm up in the air where Abi could get at it. "Abi, grab the gun.''

He was stronger than JanMikal, and his inexperience at fighting was more than balanced by JanMikal's discomfort in gravity. Abi grabbed the gun.

"Got it," he said, aiming it somewhat wildly at JanMikal.

Hobart released JanMikal. "Put it away," he said. "JanMikal, I don't want to hurt you. But we're going after that postal ship."

Abi held JanMikal's gun in both hands and leveled it at JanMikal's head. "I want to go after that ship. I liked Gramps."

"So did I," said JanMikal.

"Put the gun away," said Hobart.

"I have control," said Jade. "We're going in."

"At least put up the shields, would you?" said JanMikal.

Jade looked startled and put up the shields. "Oh," he said. "Oh. Um. Thanks."

JanMikal didn't say anything. There wasn't really anything to say.

CHAPTER TWENTY-SEVEN

Melacha had been about to take off for Newkansas in hope of finding the Pirate Prince there when she had run into a retired member of his crew named Larton who told her about the Lunar base where the pirates concealed themselves to divide their stolen merchandise. Larton was happy to betray JanMikal; he was caught in the bitter throes of some childish resentment toward his erstwhile captain which Melacha neither fully understood nor cared to. The important part was that he was willing to give her the coordinates of the base, and in exchange all she had to do was to fail to disabuse him of the notion that he was thereby turning the whole Colonial Fleet against the pirates. She justified that by telling herself she was more of a hazard to them than the Fleet would be.

After her conversation via Comm Link with Board Advisor Brown, who was apparently getting little further in her inquiries than Melacha herself had done, she was feeling cross and obscurely helpless; planning a single-handed attack on the entire pirate pack was just what she needed.

She set out after them in a spirit of vengeance which she imagined to be simple good cheer.

By the time she neared Luna, she'd had time to think about it. She didn't really want to take on the whole pack, single-handed or otherwise; if she could convince them to return to their original policy of stealing only Company goods, they would be doing a fine job that she didn't want to discourage. The thought of trying to convince them was depressing. When she thought of the one time she had seen JanMikal, and heard him laugh, she nearly turned back. Larton was right; the Colonial Fleet would come after them if they stole Colonial goods. It was really a job for the Fleet anyway. Nobody had promised the Skyrider any reward for interfering. It was none of her business. She had nothing to gain by confronting the pirates, and no desire at all to confront JanMikal.

She had actually started programming a flight path back to the asteroid belt when she came upon the battle between the pirate pack and a single Interplanetary Postal Service ship. Cursing, she aborted the program of retreat and hurled *Defiance* into the fray on the side of the underdog.

If they had been after any other kind of ship she could have turned her back on it . . . at least, anything short of a hospital ship or a school shuttle, and the pirates would have no reason to attack a ship of that nature. But a postal ship, obviously on its way to Luna, was absolutely not fair game for Colonial pirates. All it could have on board was Colonial goods. Maybe a few government items—several of the active Lunar bases were government installations, and all of them were governed from Earth. But most of the people on Luna, to whom the postal ship would be making deliveries, were colonists.

"Damn it, you don't steal from colonists," she said aloud. The Comm Link was off, and her voice echoed strangely in the empty cockpit. Flipping on the Link, she switched to the government frequency and identified herself to the postal ship, which was armed and probably nervous enough to shoot first and ask questions later. "Hang loose," she told it. "I'll see if I can get these idiots off your back."

One of the ships from Newkansas caught *Defiance* in an unexpected burst of laser fire. Her shields held, and the Skyrider swung her ship neatly around to blast the Newkansas ship before she could fire again. Her shields held, too. Switching to the Comm Link frequency she had been told the pirates used, Melacha said very quietly, "Back off, you bastards. Postal ships are not fair game."

The Newkansas ship was already angling to fire on her again. A quick glance aft showed the postal ship acquiescent for the moment, but it would be manned by Earthers; she wasn't going to plan on their cooperation, even at their own rescue. That meant she had to be ready to evade their fire as well as the pirates', so she kept an eye on them while she studied the pirates' attack pattern. JanMikal's ship *Corsair* seemed to be hanging back, but the three from Skye were right in there with the Newkansan, trying to get an angle on the *Defiance*.

The Skyrider threw a warning shot across their noses and punched up the visual on the Link so she could scowl at them. "Leave the postal ship alone, rockheads," she said. "You want the whole damn Colonial Fleet after you? JanMikal?" The three pirate faces that suddenly appeared on her Link screen startled her with their ugliness. None of them was JanMikal. "Who's in charge of this rockpatch?" she demanded. "Is one of you the Pirate Prince?"

Three hideous grins were their only answer. None of those three made any move toward her, but the fourth ship, the one from Newkansas that had fired on her first, was just about in position to fire again, and her pilot hadn't activated the visual on his Link. Nor had JanMikal, if he was indeed in the ship that was still holding back.

One swift, graceful roll of her ship gave the Skyrider a

good shot at the Newkansan. She threw it away in another warning display, reluctant to destroy any of these ships if she could avoid it. "That was a warning," she said. "This is the Skyrider. I don't want to kill you, but I will if I have to. Colonial goods are not fair game. JanMikal, damn you, where the hell are you?"

The three Skye captains moved almost simultaneously, switching off their visuals and throwing their ships into a neat pattern that, combined with the ship from Newkansas, almost trapped her against the belly of the postal ship. She was through the only opening they left before they were aware they had left it, but that put the postal ship at their mercy. Once clear of them, she flipped *Defiance* and fired for effect, trying to distract them from the postal ship. "JanMikal, if you're in that Diademan ship, damn you, answer me! What in space are you doing, leading these rockheads in a raid on a postal ship? JanMikal!"

Two of the Skye ships had followed her, but one of them and the Newkansas ship were concentrating on the postal ship, which returned their fire without any apparent effort to dodge. Flipping her Link back to the government frequency, she asked the postal ship why it wasn't running. If anyone answered, she didn't hear it; the Skye ships nearly cornered her and one got in a lucky shot that burned out her starboard shield. Enraged, she killed them without thinking.

The pirates' frequency on the Link buzzed for attention and she flipped it on. "You'll be sorry about that, little lady," said a silky male voice. "You shouldn't've killed Higgins, you know. That wasn't nice."

The two ships that had been concentrating on the postal ship turned back to the *Defiance*, one of them swinging in a neat curve all the way around the postal ship and exposing itself to fire from the Earthers, who didn't take advantage of the opportunity thus offered. Melacha didn't have

time to turn back to the government frequency to curse
them for it, but she thought about it.

"Aw, hell, Winnie," said one of the pirates. "Higgins
was no good anyway."

"Is that meaning you have no wish to avenge him
only?" asked another. "Perhaps because you are coming
from Newkansas where men have no sense of pride?"

The one from Newkansas responded unprintably. Melacha
watched and waited, wondering if they would be idiot
enough to kill themselves without her help. But just then
Corsair leapt suddenly forward and fired on the *Defiance*,
so unexpectedly that if her aim had been any good the
Defiance might well have been put out of action.

The movement distracted the other pirates from their
internal argument, and suddenly Melacha was fighting all
four of them. They were doing their best to herd her away
from the postal ship, and three of them were very good at
it. Only *Corsair* was clumsy, and even she got in a lucky
shot occasionally.

"Damn you, JanMikal!" Melacha hurled the *Defiance*
through a narrow slot between two pirate ships and came
up under the postal ship, riding inertia backward with her
nose pointed toward the pirates. The postal ship jockeyed
sideways for inscrutable Earther reasons, keeping *Defiance*
tucked neatly under her belly. "Thanks, guys," Melacha
muttered under her breath. "I don't know what your game
is, but that's handy. JanMikal, what's going on here?
What the hell *is* this? What are you doing, damn you?"

The Newkansas ship got an angle on the *Defiance*. Both
ships fired at once. Melacha's aim was better. *Defiance*
rocked heavily sideways under the shock of a striking laser
bolt, but the Newkansas ship exploded. Melacha didn't
have time to enjoy her victory; her instruments were failing and *Corsair* as well as the two remaining ships from
Skye were closing in on her.

Dodging clumsily away from the postal ship, Melacha

put her Comm Link on the government frequency again
and demanded why they weren't firing on the pirates. This
time at least they answered her: "Laser malfunction. Sorry.
They got in a couple of good shots, you know. We have a
lot of instrument failure here. . . ."

"Join the club," she said bitterly, and switched back to
the pirate frequency. "JanMikal, do you really intend to
die for a bunch of Colonial mail? Because I will kill you if
I have to."

One of the Skye ships sprang at her, lasers glaring, at
exactly the same instant that JanMikal finally opened the
Comm Link between *Defiance* and *Corsair*. The visual
came on too, but she didn't have time to look at it; the
Skye ship's lasers rocked *Defiance* and her answering fire
was clumsy, crippling him but not killing him. She hadn't
time to make sure he was crippled enough to stay out of
the battle: *Defiance* was holed.

"Skyrider, I'm sorry."

She glanced at the Link screen and in the heat of the
moment responded without thinking: "Jamin, damn you,
sorry won't save us." Grabbing a bottle of sealant, she
sprayed the hole in the cockpit bulkhead and, halfway
through the job, heard what she had said. Fortunately she
kept the sealant aimed at the hole while she turned back to
the Link screen to stare at him. "Jamin?" He had Jamin's
eyes. He had Jamin's voice. What was it Simon Hale had
said about him? Something about reconstructive surgery
because he'd been in an accident. . . .

But if he were Jamin, wouldn't he *say* so?

But . . . He had Jamin's eyes. He had Jamin's voice.
And he was staring at her out of that strange not-Jamin
face and *he was Jamin!*

"Jamin?"

He'd been in an accident or something. What was it
Hale had said? A pilot they'd salvaged unintentionally. If
he'd been that badly injured . . . What if he just didn't

remember? Was that possible? What if he had amnesia? It would explain why he didn't identify himself, why he didn't come back to Collis, why he didn't know much about Diadem but didn't say he came from somewhere else. . . . And why he was staring at her with startled, almost frightened confusion darkening those incredible ice-blue arrogant eyes. . . .

"Jamin. Damn you, Jamin. *Remember!*"

Corsair was coming in for the kill. There was nothing the Skyrider could do about it. *Defiance* moved only sluggishly at her command, and while she might be able to get in a quick shot before *Corsair* did, she couldn't take the chance of killing Jamin now that she had found him. Shouting his name in rage and despair, she bullied the *Defiance* into an awkward evasive maneuver she knew wouldn't save her, and braced herself for the final laser bolt.

CHAPTER TWENTY-EIGHT

Pain made him as dully obedient as a sick child. His head hurt. She told him to remember and he remembered. . . .

The laughter of a blue-eyed boy . . . The whine of shuttle engines stressed almost past bearing in a series of battle maneuvers against the gathered Earth Fighter Fleet . . . The wry twist of a woman's smile, and the dark of her fierce eyes, and the shattering insistence of her voice calling his name . . . The reek of burnt electronics, the glare of a laser bolt sheeting across the failing shields of his shuttle when he hurled her into the space between *Defiance* and the attacking Earth Fighters . . . Then only chaos and blinding pain that swallowed the universe. . . .

Jamin blinked hard and put both hands on the console before him, to steady him. The Skyrider's face stared at him out of a Comm Link screen, the wry grin missing, but her implacable eyes as steady and demanding as he remembered them. He blinked again. His head hurt. He must have banged it against something when the Earth Fighters . . .

A movement behind him caught his attention. There

were people on board his shuttle. No, not his shuttle. . . . He shook his head dizzily, staring. Boys. Or, rather, young men. Crewing this ship. They were . . . They had been . . . But another wave of pain, shockingly intense, blinded him. He couldn't see or think or even move. He stood still, head hanging, clinging to the edge of the console like a winded runner, and let the pain wash over him. . . .

Lasers whined through his personal dark silence. The ship's engines screamed as her helmsman brought her around in a big, clumsy, swooping dive that would surely overshoot its mark and almost knocked Jamin from his feet. Rage gave him the strength to stay upright. "Rock bastard," he muttered, "you'll tear her apart with moves like that." No ship should have to endure such brutally amateur piloting. Gasping for breath against the pain in his head and the agony of acceleration-induced gravity, he forced his eyes open, and found himself staring again at the Skyrider's Comm Link image.

She wasn't looking at him; she needed all her attention for her controls and her curses. *Defiance* must be badly damaged; smoke filled her cockpit and he could see warning lights blinking across half the panels visible on the Link screen. The Skyrider looked harried and oddly frail. There had always been an unexpected element of vulnerability about her, completely at odds with her public personality and for the most part concealed by it. Now it was as if her tough facade had been worn by time and hardships till it was frayed at the edges and so threadbare that he could see a glimpse through it of the no less strong but undeniably gentler and more vulnerable private woman beneath. She looked, for the first time since he had known her, capable of tears. The impression, obscurely, frightened him. And that made him angry.

"What the hell is going on here?" His voice cracked, and he cleared his throat.

She glanced up at him. For an instant those implacable eyes studied him, and he could not read the confusion of shadows in them. A frown pulled at her brows. The hint of her old reckless smile curved the corners of her mouth. She said, softly, "Jamin?" A klaxon blared in her cockpit and she reached around to throw switches and key something into her computer. "I won't fire on your ship, Jamin." She was looking at her instrument panel. "And I can't outrun you." Looking up suddenly, she startled him with the intensity of her gaze. "*Defiance* is *dying*, damn you! Cease fire before you kill me!"

He stared. *Cease fire?* Was his ship firing on hers? But why? That didn't make any sense. He turned to look at the youthful crew of this ship: three boys, distantly remembered as from a half-forgotten dream, all clustered around the helmsman's console, seemingly unaware of Jamin. As he watched, they all three tensed over the helm and one of them whispered, "You've got her. Easy . . . easy . . . *Now!*" The one seated at the helm pressed a button. Lasers whined. Interior lights faded as power was drawn from life support into weaponry. The Comm Link screen before Jamin flopped sideways, catching his attention, and he turned back to it in time to see the Skyrider knocked from her seat on board *Defiance* before the Link went blank and then, deprived of the Skyrider's signal, switched automatically to the scanner frequency to show *Defiance* tumbling away from his own ship, chased by another ship he hadn't seen before.

It was the last of the pirates, rushing in to make sure of *Corsair's* kill. But there was no need: the Skyrider would never let *Defiance* tumble out of control like that if she were capable of controlling it. *Defiance* must be dead; and with her, quite possibly, the Skyrider. And still that other ship was lining up to fire on her, with Jamin's ship jockeying in to follow.

There were controls in the captain's seat. He remembered that, an isolated fact out of a kaleidoscopic past he could not understand. His handgun was on the Comm Link console where Abi had left it. It felt odd in his hand, not the familiar stun gun he was used to but smaller and lighter and, he thought, more deadly. It would do. Holding it ready, he hurled himself into the captain's chair. The scanner screen there was smaller, but it showed the same scene: *Defiance* tumbling helplessly before the sleek on-coming pirate ship, both of them growing in the screen as *Corsair* neared them.

The crew of *Corsair* was tensing to fire again. The other ship was clearly angling for a shot. He had no control over the other ship, and if he took control of *Corsair* now the helmsman might still twitch that deadly finger held poised over the firing button. If the Skyrider still lived, even a glancing laser strike might kill her; *Defiance* obviously had no shields left.

He waited, unaware that he was holding his breath.

Defiance stopped tumbling. Her engines flared, fighting inertia. The other ship—*Blue Lady*, he remembered vaguely, from a colony called Skye—fired her jockey thrusters, balancing for one clear shot. The boys in charge of Jamin's ship were doing the same. Jamin held his weapon steadily on them, in case they remembered his presence, and poised one hand against the ship's controls in the arm of his chair. His timing had to be perfect. He had to be alert, to be ready at exactly the moment he was needed . . . and chaotic visions of past and present and possible future disoriented him, increasing the terrible pain in his head. . . .

Small boys laughing and shouting in a very low-grav swimming pool . . . *Where?* . . . Collis smiling at him . . . Fields in neat rows under an oddly curving sky . . . Linda soothing him when he woke from nightmares . . . Collis laughing, talking, playing . . . lasers flaring. . . .

He blinked, forcing his eyes to focus on the scanner screen. Any second now . . .

An enormous curving chamber, big enough to contain buildings and whole farms, like an inside-out planet, too big to feel comfortable to a man who had spent his entire life inside asteroids and space ships. . . .

Collis in the Skyrider's arms, and the sheepish way she looked over his shoulder at Jamin, defenseless against a small boy's love. . . .

Blue Lady had her angle. So had *Corsair*. Both were focused on *Defiance*. If *Corsair*'s crew would fire fractionally sooner than *Blue Lady* . . . and if Jamin could react in time . . .

Collis always hurtled into his arms like a little whirlwind, small arms hugging, eyes laughing, telling all his latest accomplishments and demanding to know how long his papa would be home between runs this time. . . . "Oh, *Collis*!" Jamin whispered, and tightened his fingers on the controls. *Now!*

Defiance had thrown a laser bolt at *Blue Lady*, but the shot went wild. *Blue Lady* was ready to fire, but Jamin had been forced to wait till *Corsair* fired before he snatched the controls and, in the same second that her helmsman pulled the firing button, threw her around so her laser caught *Blue Lady* instead of *Defiance*. The maneuver worked; *Corsair*'s laser bolt caught *Blue Lady* head-on, burning out all her shields and right on through till she exploded in a silent ball of flame and shrapnel. But *Blue Lady* had fired first, and her aim was all too good.

Defiance had no shields left to protect her. She took the laser hit in the aft section, which exploded almost as dramatically as *Blue Lady* did only seconds later. And Jamin couldn't even take time to watch; his crew were fully aware of him now. The only thing that stopped them attacking him personally was the unfamiliar little weapon in his hand. Each of them wore a similar weapon, but none reached for it or even seemed to remember it.

He very nearly killed them all in that moment. It would

have taken only one small movement of one finger, a flick of the wrist. . . . She had survived so many impossible missions, shuttle crashes, terrorist tactics, and apparently even a war, only to die at the hands of these ignorant boys playing pirates. . . . But it was the Skyrider herself who had once told him, "There's no good way to die."

"You killed Winnie," said the red-headed boy. The helmsman. James? No: Jade. And the thin one beside him was the Comm Link officer. Abi. The bigger one, tall and dark and staring, was Hobart. Jamin couldn't remember what his job was.

It didn't matter. He looked at them all for a long moment before he said, "Winnie?"

Hobart frowned. "Nguyen. The captain of *Blue Lady*. What's the matter with you? JanMikal?"

"My name is Jamin." His voice was flat, impersonal, almost uninterested. "And you have just killed my best friend."

"Who?" asked Abi, while Jade said simultaneously, "Come on, JanMikal. Prince? Quit fooling around. Why are you aiming that laser at us?"

Jamin's expression didn't change. It was as hard and cold and arrogant as any of them had ever seen it. His eyes were blank and wide and oddly frightening. There were blue smudges under them, like bruises. He didn't blink. "Death is the usual penalty for mutiny, I believe."

"Aw, space, Prince!" Abi's voice wavered and fell silent. He shifted uncomfortably and shook his long, dark hair out of his wide spaniel eyes. "Look, we just wanted . . ." His voice cracked. "You can't . . ."

Jade was staring at Jamin, his face so pale it was almost translucent, making the bright red curls of his hair look oddly synthetic where they fell across his forehead. "Hey, it wasn't exactly mutiny." He said it gently, tentatively, as one might speak to a wild animal or a dangerously disturbed human. "We have a right to do what we want, and you were the only one who didn't want that postal ship. We had a right to take over *Corsair*." The sentence ended on a rising note, turning it almost into a plea.

"Are there more of you aboard this ship?" Jamin's expression still hadn't changed, and his wild eyes still didn't blink.

"Of course there are." Abi broke off with a startled squeak when Hobart kicked him.

"No," said Hobart. "Just the three of us." He gave Abi a hard look. "You remember; the others were aboard *Bar Sinister*, this run."

Jamin's finger tightened against his weapon's firing button and a narrow, barely visible beam of light sprang from it to burn a pinpoint hole in the bulkhead just beyond Hobart. Escaping atmosphere whined thinly in the otherwise silent cockpit. "Don't lie to me." His tone was conversational and disconcertingly mild. "I won't hesitate to kill you, you know. How many are there?"

"Three more," Abi squeaked. He turned his frightened dark eyes to Hobart. "Don't lie to him anymore, for gods' sake. He's gone m—" He cut himself off and stared wildly at Jamin. "I mean . . ."

"You think I'm insane," Jamin said equably. "That's fine. Maybe I am. And maybe, if you do exactly what I tell you, I won't kill you."

"Can we sealant that hole?" asked Jade.

"No. Stay where you are." When Jade had settled anxiously back into his chair, Jamin asked them very politely to tell him what they knew about him, which they did, stumbling over each other's words in their eagerness to please him and to justify themselves. It kept them busy while he looked at the scanners again, searching for possible other pirate ships, and for *Defiance*. The postal ship moved silently away unchallenged. *Defiance* was still there, a tangled mass of wreckage, dead and silent.

When the boys reached the end of their story he was

looking only at them, his weapon held ready, his expression devoid of any emotion at all. "Okay. You know me as JanMikal. The Pirate Prince. That's fine. Call me that, if you like. I don't remember half of what you've just told me, but I'll take your word for it." That lack of memory was confusing. In other circumstances it would have been frightening. He didn't take their word for anything, really. But just now it didn't really seem to matter. His free hand went absently to his face, exploring the shape of it, gently prodding at flesh and bones as though he could by feel alone determine not only his new appearance but also whether the rest of their story was true. "What I do remember," he said in the same flat, lifeless voice, "is who I was before Diadem. I was a Colonial Warrior. A killer." His gaze flicked briefly to the scanner screens. "That ship out there, the one you helped to destroy . . . *Defiance* . . . that was my wingmate's ship."

All three of them turned as one to look at the scanner screen nearest them. *Defiance* floated serenely toward them, a crumpled ball of carbon-scarred metal trailing shards of plasteel, surrounded by a glittering halo of debris.

"Your wingmate," said Abi.

Hobart made a sound deep in his throat. "That could mean anything. People aren't always even friends with their wingmates."

"I was," said Jamin. "I gave my life to save hers."

All three of them turned, again almost as one, to stare at him. "*Hers?*" said Jade.

"That was a *woman?*" said Abi, his voice squeaking. It was he who had turned off the Link and so prevented them from hearing her voice.

"She tried to stop us," said Hobart. "We had a right . . ."

Jamin cut him off with a look. "And I have a right to kill you, if I want to, haven't I?"

"Oh, but," said Abi.

Hobart met Jamin's gaze without flinching. "You have that right. Will you exercise it?"

"I don't know."

"I didn't know that was a woman," said Jade. His voice sounded small and frightened. "I've killed a woman."

Jamin looked at him. "You consider that more reprehensible than killing a man?"

"Well, yes, of course, I mean, a *woman*!"

Jamin produced a very bleak smile. "Lucky for you she can't hear you."

"Oh, but I can," said the Skyrider.

CHAPTER TWENTY-NINE

Defiance was too badly damaged to fly, and *Corsair* was not built for tug work, so the pirates were obliged to transfer Melacha from the wreck of her shuttle before they could rush her back to Diadem for medical treatment. Even though the boys lost all interest in their mutiny and became scrupulously obedient to Jamin, it wasn't an easy task. After that one wry comment Melacha lapsed into alternate silence and incoherence and was very little help to them at all. They did eventually get her to admit to having got into a spacesuit in preparation for the transfer, and that helped.

All that was left of the pirate pack was *Corsair* and a badly crippled *Bar Sinister* with Captain Au in charge. But Au, like *Corsair*'s crew, was suddenly and completely obedient to the Pirate Prince again, and managed to be of considerable help in the transfer. He seemed not at all ruffled by the fact that the Pirate Prince now referred to himself as Jamin and had little memory of ever having met Au before.

Melacha herself was of no help in the move and even

tried at one point to start a fight with her spacesuited rescuers, but she was too weak and confused to do any real harm and the outburst was actually welcome in a way, since prior to it they had begun to wonder whether they were risking their lives to rescue a dead woman. The abortive fistfight did establish, rather neatly, that she was alive.

As soon as they got her safely aboard *Corsair* they cut loose the wreckage of *Defiance*. Jamin watched briefly as she tumbled awkwardly away against the star-studded black velvet backdrop of space before he turned to help Hobart and Irving, his erstwhile bodyguards, remove Melacha's spacesuit.

She lay still under their ministrations, making an occasional feeble effort to assist them as needed, but mostly just staring with blank disinterest at whatever happened to be in front of her. When they peeled off the body of her suit and found it red inside with blood, Hobart made a sound in his throat; but it wasn't until they pulled her arms out of the sleeves and found one of them badly broken that he paused, staring, and asked aloud, "How in the world did she put this suit on in her condition?"

Her lips twitched in the ghost of her old reckless grin. "With extreme difficulty." Her voice was a thin reedy whisper, barely audible in the echoing cargo hold where they had stopped to unsuit.

The broken arm was by no means her only injury. But she was alive, and somehow she stayed alive all the way to Diadem. Captain Au and his crew in their battered *Bar Sinister* trailed gamely along behind *Corsair* at the best speed they could manage, repeatedly urging Jamin not to wait for them. He waited anyway, because there was no way of knowing whether *Bar Sinister* could make the whole trip, and while *Corsair* couldn't tow her in if she failed, a search-and-rescue mission would have a lot better chance of finding her if *Corsair*'s computer knew exactly where and when she failed.

The journey seemed endless. They had put Melacha in crew quarters, and Jamin stayed with her the whole way. He held her hand and talked to her even when her eyes glazed and her hand went limp in his and Hobart said gently, "She can't hear you, Prince . . . Jamin."

"She can. She has to." He didn't look up from the pale, shadowed face with its dark halo of tumbled hair on the pillow around it and its cheeks smudged with smoke and blood and tears. "Skyrider, wait. Listen to me. You can't die, damn you. You can't. It's not right; I won't let you. I want . . . I want . . ." His voice broke and he scowled at her fiercely. "I want you to live, do you hear me? . . . And if that's not a good enough reason, think of Collis. If you die, he'll never forgive me. What could I tell him? Damn it, if you want to die, you'd damn well better think of an answer to that, first. You owe me that much."

She blinked. After a long moment she turned her eyes toward him and achieved another frail ghost of that old mischievous grin. "Owe you . . . more than that." She paused for a long moment while the grin faded and her eyes closed and he thought she had lost consciousness again. But she had only been gathering her strength. "Waiting . . . never one of my better tricks. . . . But I'll do it. . . ."

He didn't give the doctors at Diadem a chance to exercise their rights. Hobart and Irving carried Melacha onto the colony. Jamin carried his handgun.

"You know that wasn't really necessary, Jan—I mean Jamin," said Dr. March. "Your girlfriend would have got medical attention anyway. You didn't have to stand over the doctors with a gun."

"I wasn't sure." He accepted the cup of tea she offered him. "And she's not my girlfriend. Unless by that you mean friend-who-is-female."

March sat on the waiting room couch beside him and

put her own tea on the low table in front of them. "Oh, I thought—I mean, the way you . . . You seemed very concerned about her for someone who's just a friend."

He looked at her. "I didn't say 'just.' " His eyes were smudged with weariness and pain. "She's my wingmate. My best friend. We're . . . you might say—partners. I *care* about her. A lot." He made a wry face. "I guess that's obvious."

"But no romance?"

He shrugged. "No romance. Why? Does a close male-female relationship seem incomplete to you without romance? We are good in bed together, but we're just not life-mates, at least not that way. We're . . . best friends."

"It does seem unusual. But perhaps not, Outside. I think the sexual roles are less rigid there. They must be, to produce women like the President, and Board Advisor Brown, and your Skyrider."

He grinned suddenly. It transformed his face; he looked years younger and startlingly vulnerable. "If she heard you call her 'my' Skyrider she'd probably punch you."

"Why? It's only a way of speaking."

"For her, so are fistfights. She has a short temper. And a quick right jab." He fingered his jaw reflexively.

March stared. "You've had fistfights with her?"

"Sure. We don't always agree on everything."

"But—but surely, even a woman who has fistfights— Surely only with other women? Not with men?"

He looked puzzled. "Why not?"

She shook her head. "Outside must be very different from Diadem."

"I think it is," he said. "But, you know, I don't really remember Diadem very clearly."

She said quickly, "That's perfectly normal, JanMikal . . . I mean Jamin. It may come back to you later, or you may never recall it. But you do remember everything from before the accident?"

"Yes. It wasn't an accident, you know. It was an act of war." He hesitated. "Dr. March?"

"Yes, Jan— Jamin?"

"It was hearing the Skyrider say my name that did it, wasn't it? But JanMikal is similar to Jamin. I got to thinking . . . what if you'd named me something even closer? James, maybe. Would I have remembered when you called me it? Or would I have got so used to it that I *wouldn't* have remembered when the Skyrider called me Jamin?"

"It wasn't just hearing her say your name that did it, really; it must have been the extreme stress of the whole situation. You would have remembered anyway, sooner or later; the fact that you did remember proves that. The Skyrider's voice saying your name in that moment of intense stress just provided the catalyst. But you probably would have remembered right then, even if she had kept silent. You were in fear for her life."

"I still am."

The medical facilities on Diadem were almost antique by Outside standards, but they proved adequate to save Melacha's life. Jamin was waiting beside her when she woke, his unfamiliar face bruised by fatigue and his wholly familiar eyes dark with worry. For a long moment she studied him in silence, trying to match the planes and shadows of this new face with those of his face in her memory. There were few distinct similarities. The bone structure was perhaps not much changed, and yet . . . it was a face that might have belonged to a brother of Jamin, but not to Jamin. A stranger's face with Jamin's eyes. . . .

She smiled at him tentatively. "Hi, stranger."

His sudden responding grin was pure Jamin. "Skyrider. I wasn't sure you were really awake this time. How do you feel?"

"About a hundred years old. What happened?"

"You don't remember?"

She frowned, piecing together fragments of memory, and said slowly, "Those damn pirates . . . after a postal ship. . . ." Her eyes widened as memory returned. "Oh! *Defiance*!"

He looked miserable. "I'm sorry, Skyrider."

"She was totaled?"

He nodded. "We left her—what was left of her—behind."

"Too bad. There were goodies in the smuggling hold."

He stared. "That's it? Just goodies in the hold? But—I thought you'd be—I mean—*Defiance* was—"

She laughed at his expression. "It's okay, Jamin; I have another one just like her at home."

Davitz gave Jamin *Corsair* in thanks for resources "brought in from Outside and out from inside," a phrase with which he was obviously quite pleased. When Jamin objected, reminding Davitz that any good he had done for Diadem had been inadequate repayment for his own life, Davitz dismissed his objections with an impatient gesture. "Nonsense," he said. "Saving your life was what Dr. March wanted to do. And giving you *Corsair* is what I want to do. Surely you haven't entirely forgotten Bill's *Way* just because you've remembered the Way you followed before. Of course you do have a right to refuse my gift if you want to." He smiled suddenly and very sweetly. "But if you do, how will you get back to your Outside world?"

Jamin accepted *Corsair*.

Linda March and Jamin were with Melacha when Simon Hale and Celia Graham came to visit her. At sight of March, Graham displayed a great many of her perfect teeth in a predatory smile and immediately clasped hands with

Hale, who did not seem to notice the gesture. March noticed it, and her lips twitched in a private smile.

"Board Advisor Brown just called," said Hale. "*Jewel* and her crew are on their way home, and the B.R.R. has rescinded the worst of the salvage laws." He shifted absently to accommodate the arm Celia Graham was rather sinuously twining about him. "She wanted to know what payment you'd asked."

Melacha looked at him. "What did you tell her?"

He shifted uncomfortably. "Well, just that our doctors saved your life. . . ."

There was a glint of amusement in Melacha's eyes. "You think that's adequate?"

Hale tried to look severe. "I had certainly hoped you would think it was."

Melacha sighed in mock despair, and shrugged. "My own fault for not setting a price beforehand. I guess I'll have to make do."

"But," said Hale.

"You have more news?" asked March. There was humor in her eyes too, but she didn't smile; she just looked expectantly at Hale and waited.

He looked confused. "Oh. Um. The President's condition is critical and apparently the Board's favorite to replace her—who I gather had something to do with creating those salvage laws—is apparently involved in some political scandal that will prevent his being elected."

"Who was that?" asked Jamin.

The Skyrider grinned at him. "Would you believe Nuke 'em B. Newcomb?"

"You're joking!"

"Nope. Fortunately it seems he's been put out of the running. I've no idea who'll replace him."

"Neither has Board Advisor Brown," said Hale. "And she said that with things as they are she just hasn't enough influence to get you cleared of some Patrol charges—

something to do with interfering with Patrol boats on active duty and disturbing the peace?—so you're not to return to Earth until that's cleared up."

"That's okay, I never much liked Earth anyway."

"And she said your unlimited account has been cut off. I assumed you'd know what that was about?"

The Skyrider laughed aloud. "I do indeed," she said. "That was a bank account that a man named Ian Spencer recently won from me. Serves him right."

Jamin looked startled. "Ian Spencer the computer wizard? That Ian Spencer?"

She looked at him. "I don't know. Why?"

"Because he's a master confidence man and hustler. If there were computers involved—"

She shook her head. "He bet I couldn't kill him, and I couldn't."

Jamin frowned. "In a fair fight?"

"A firefight. *Defiance* against his Patrol boat. So you see it couldn't have been computer wizardry."

"Oh, no? What about your on-board computers?"

She shook her head. "I couldn't find anything wrong with them, or with the weapons system, and I did check."

"Of course you couldn't." Jamin shook his head. "I'm surprised at you, Skyrider."

"Why?"

"Spencer is an expert at computer intrusion, you rockhead. He probably got into yours. I'll bet he had ample opportunity to do it beforehand and clear it after, right?"

"But he couldn't have got on board *Defiance*," she said doubtfully.

"He didn't need to. He could do it from anywhere nearby. Space, he practically invented the GE Mark IV laser system."

"Oh." She thought about it. "Oh. Then he has all the internal access codes."

"That's right."

"He could program it to produce only visible light. Nothing lethal. And prevent that from showing on a systems check."

"That's right."

"Why, that baby-faced bloody bastard—"

"That's right."

After a long moment she laughed again. "Well, hell. Because of him I pulled more tangible assets than I know what to do with out of that account, and now that it's his they've closed it down before he had much chance to use it. I gained more than he did." She looked thoughtful. "All the same, if I ever get my hands on that—that—"

Celia Graham, who had been paying very little attention to this conversation, said suddenly to Dr. Hale, "Can't we tell them now, darling?"

Hale smiled at her fatuously and patted her rump. "If you want to, sweetheart."

Graham immediately produced another of her predatory smiles, directed almost exclusively and in obvious triumph at Linda March, and said, "Simon and I are getting married." She touched her flat stomach smugly. "I'm pregnant."

March's look of relief, hastily concealed behind a genuinely friendly smile, was perhaps fortunately not noticed by either of the happy couple, though Jamin saw it and concealed a grin. "I'm very happy for you both," said March. "With your genotypes I'm sure you'll produce absolutely perfect children."

Graham leaned comfortably into Hale's encircling arm. "That's what Simon says," she said happily. "We plan to have six. Mostly boys."

"Speaking of boys," said the Skyrider, "there's one who's been waiting a long time to see Jamin. I think it's about time we got started to him; it's a long way to Mars."

"But—are you well enough?" asked March. "I was just talking with your doctor—"

"Hell with doctors," said the Skyrider. "No offense, you guys, but all med-techs fuss too much. I can't be bothered. Collis is waiting for us."

They met Collis at Mars Station, where gravity quarters were maintained and had been recently enlarged to accommodate the increasing number of Colonial "Grounder" children who could not tolerate freefall. No one knew why the incidence of that affliction among Grounder children was increasing so dramatically in recent years. While scientists and doctors studied the problem, more and more families moved to places like Mars Station where there were freefall quarters for the mutant Fallers among them and gravity for the Grounder children. People like the Skyrider who had one gene for each trait—freefall and gravity tolerance—"floated" between the two environments at will and held their families together as best they could.

Most adult Grounders could live and work in freefall for long periods of time without harm, but few Fallers could endure gravity for long and none could survive prolonged exposure. Jamin could have landed on Mars to meet Collis, but due to the multiple gravities generated by the acceleration required to reach escape velocity he could never have left Mars again, and he could not have survived long on its surface. They called ahead to let Collis know they were coming, and Michael brought him out to Mars Station to meet them.

Mars Station was where they had left him when they went off at the beginning of the Brief War on the mission that had taken the Skyrider to Earth and Jamin very nearly to his death. Because he had so little memory of the time since then, and his memories of the Station were so clear and recent, Jamin felt in a way that it had been only days since he had left Collis; but at the same time he felt very sharply the pain of their long separation. And despite his eagerness to see his son again, he felt oddly ill-at-ease, as if he were about to meet a very important stranger. Some of that was due to the unfamiliar face he wore, which startled him every time he looked in a mirror. He was horribly conscious of it now. Collis had been warned, but what if that wasn't enough? What if Collis didn't recognize him, and didn't believe he was really Jamin? The boy was only seven years old. What if—

But then they were in the gravity corridors, and *what if* became *now*: Collis emerged from a doorway ahead of them and stood still, staring, his small body rigid with tension. Jamin and Melacha wordlessly slowed to a stop, watching Collis. For a long moment the three of them just looked at each other. Then Jamin said, on the end of a sigh, "Oh, *Collis*!" It was almost a whisper, barely audible and cracked with emotion, but it was Jamin's voice! Collis produced one blinding smile and hurtled into his father's arms. Melacha, grinning foolishly and swallowing hard, beat a hasty retreat, unnoticed.

She had expected to have to go all the way back to Home Base to catch up with Ian Spencer, but by what seemed to be a remarkable coincidence she tracked him down right there on Mars Station. In fact it wasn't coincidental at all, since he had started looking for her before she started looking for him.

The first thing he said when he saw her was, "How in space did you get them to cut it off?"

Melacha grinned amiably. "Cut what off? That old credit account? Hell, that wasn't hard. They were glad to."

His eyebrows lifted. He smiled dangerously. "So you *did* do it? I thought you'd deny it."

"Would you have believed me?"

"It was a damned dirty trick, you know. Or don't Belters believe in paying their debts?" His smile was very sweet and very deadly.

"Oh, come now. I paid, didn't I? Even though I'd been hustled. In fact, considering everything, you might just say I paid in kind." Her smile wasn't as sweet as his, but it was just as deadly.

"What the hell kind of Belter trick are you trying to pull? If you can't face the fact that I beat you fair and square—"

Her smile widened. "What, I owe you money?"

He had been in the Belt too long. It wasn't as though she hadn't already established her ability to rearrange his face to her satisfaction. But he didn't have time to think about that; he just started swinging.

They were in a public rec room, so Station Patrol broke it up before they could do each other much damage. But not before both were bloodied, thoroughly winded, and well aware which one was winning. Spencer wasn't smiling anymore. The Skyrider was, but it was an effort. Between gasps for breath she even managed a feeble laugh. "Thanks, I needed that."

He looked at her in surprise. "What, a fight?"

"Sure. Didn't you?"

"No."

She studied him. "Then why did you?"

He shrugged off the Station Patrolman who was still holding him. "Because you seemed to want to."

"You always do what other people want?" She shrugged off a Patrolman and glared at another who stood poised, ready to jump between her and Spencer if need be.

Spencer made a wry face and absently wiped blood from the corner of his mouth. "Not usually." He looked startled and jumped forward to support her when her knees buckled. "What the hell? Damn it, I *thought* that was too easy. You were hurt when we started!"

"No big deal." She tried to stand unsupported, and nearly toppled. "I'm all right."

The curve of his arm held her upright. "In many ways, you certainly are." He grinned, and this time the danger in it was of a very different sort.

She looked at him. "I could still break your face."

THE BEST IN SCIENCE FICTION

Buy them at your local bookstore or use this handy coupon:
Clip and mail this page with your order

TOR BOOKS—Reader Service Dept.
49 W. 24 Street, New York, N.Y. 10010

Please send me the book(s) I have checked above. I am enclosing
$_____ (please add $1.00 to cover postage and handling).
Send check or money order only—no cash or C.O.D.'s.

Mr./Mrs./Miss _____

Address _____

City _____ State/Zip _____

Please allow six weeks for delivery. Prices subject to change without notice.

Ben Bova

☐	53200-7	AS ON A DARKLING PLAIN		$2.95
	53201-5		Canada	$3.50
☐	53217-1	THE ASTRAL MIRROR		$2.95
	53218-X		Canada	$3.50
☐	53212-0	ESCAPE PLUS		$2.95
	53213-9		Canada	$3.50
☐	53221-X	GREMLINS GO HOME		$2.75
	53222-8	(with Gordon R. Dickson)	Canada	$3.25
☐	53215-5	ORION		$3.50
	53216-3		Canada	$3.95
☐	53210-4	OUT OF THE SUN		$2.95
	53211-2		Canada	$3.50
☐	53223-6	PRIVATEERS		$3.50
	53224-4		Canada	$4.50
☐	53208-2	TEST OF FIRE		$2.95
	53209-0		Canada	$3.50

Buy them at your local bookstore or use this handy coupon:
Clip and mail this page with your order

TOR BOOKS—Reader Service Dept.
49 W. 24th Street, 9th Floor, New York, NY 10010

Please send me the book(s) I have checked above. I am enclosing
$_____ (please add $1.00 to cover postage and handling).
Send check or money order only—no cash or C.O.D.'s.

Mr./Mrs./Miss _____

Address _____

City _____ State/Zip _____

Please allow six weeks for delivery. Prices subject to change without
notice.